For the love of money is the root of all evil; which while some coveted after, they have erred from the faith, and pierced themselves through with many sorrows.

1 Timothy, 6:10   The Holy Bible

DANNY
BRODERICK

When

MONEY

TALKS

Buford Tucker Listens

PUBLISHED BY djb ENTERPRISES, INC.

AND
Booksurge Publishing

Book design by Patrick Broderick and Sarah Thomison

Inquiries: danny@broderickbooks.com

ISBN 978-1-4392-0464-1

PRINTED IN THE UNITED STATES OF AMERICA

For my two boys, Jack and Patrick.

WHEN MONEY TALKS

Buford Tucker Listens

By

Danny Broderick

1

THE POLICE OFFICER WAS careful as he looked over the sharp cliff and down upon the scene of the crash. He slowly shook his head with dismay. He would never get used to this part of the job. How could he? Being the first to arrive in answer to a call concerning a serious accident was never a pleasant experience. The oscillating red emergency lights on his squad, together with the spot light, helped, slightly, to illuminate the area, but the topography of the site did not allow for direct lighting. He could, however, see the dim outline of the crumpled red mass that was once someone's dream come true, a brand new Mercedes SL 600. "What a waste," he thought; still shaking his head while he haltingly stepped sideways, attempting to negotiate the steep incline on the side of one of Hollywood's famous "hills." Today the trek was particularly hazardous due to the rain. Instead of the dry, powdery, sandy, red-brown earth, there was slippery, sloppy mud underfoot.

As he got closer, he saw steam from a severed heater hose rising up then quickly dissipating and becoming one with the thick, humid air and he heard the loud hiss as it escaped under pressure. He then detected the overpowering smell of gasoline. "No smoking zone," he mused silently. "Whew!" He also heard the wail of approaching sirens and was glad that soon he would be joined by other professionals that would help him sort out this mess. He covered his mouth and nose with his sleeve. When he was finally able to see inside the driver's side window of the wrecked car, he nearly lost his lunch. There was blood everywhere. Clearly a major artery had been severed. He looked away and spat but didn't wretch. He really never did get used to this. An LAPD helicopter appeared noisily overhead; its searchlight beam sliced through the raindrops and illuminated them as silver dots zipping past. The rain dripped of the cops face in the bright light, as he looked skyward waving one arm and pointing with the other. The noise was deafening and the wind from the blades annoying as hell, as it blew the small desert scrubs around wildly; but at least he could see a little better. Thank god for the rain… no dust.

"What do you need?" The voice came from above and was almost drowned out by the sound of the chopper. Another officer had arrived and was bellowing down his question.

He cupped both hands around his mouth and yelled through them like a bullhorn. "Tell the EMTs to hurry up" He glanced back at the car and its passenger and heaved a huge sigh. His chest expanded and contracted. "You might as well call the Coroner, too. And, radio the chopper to keep the light on for now, until we have ground lights, but tell him to get a little higher. Back up a little." He was motioning with his hands, pointing up. " And, baby-sit that witness till I get back up there, OK?"

"Gotcha." The other cop gave a thumbs-up and disappeared from view.

He turned back to the crumpled car. This time he was prepared for the blood. He looked in. Even drenched in blood, he could see how beautiful she was. The way she was laying across the steering wheel exposed her back. She was wearing a sweater and jeans. He could see the curve of her hips, the small of her back. The hip-hugging jeans ended low and the sweater was pushed up. He could see the area where the young girls put the tattoos. It was smooth supple skin, meticulously cared for, with a perfect tan. Her limited, very classy jewelry screamed money... lots of money. She wasn't breathing and what was left of her face had the gray, ashen sheen that he had seen all too many times in his relatively young life. They were going to have to cut her out of the mangled mess that was the car. "Those EMT guys had better really hurry," he muttered. He could not get to her. He wanted to, but the way the car had landed and the way it was crushed, made that impossible. He felt helpless. Less than a half hour ago she was probably smiling, maybe had the radio on, singing along with her favorite song, going somewhere... "How does something like this happen?" he wondered. "Why?"

Earlier that evening Anna Khan was scurrying around in a tizzy. She was not what you would call...organized. Much to the contrary, she was a mess. No...not really...not a mess. She wasn't what you would call a mess. Let's see, what was she?

She was beautiful, 5' 7'', 115 lbs., great ass! She had the kind of silky blonde hair that could not have come from a bottle, multi-shaded, real, together with the biggest and bluest eyes you ever saw. Her smile could melt most mortal men. But, she was always a bit discombobulated. It was part of her charm. Everyone she knew liked her. No one talked about her behind her back, not even the catty ones. The people that didn't like her... loved her. There were plenty that fell into that category. She made 45 look like 27–without the ditziness. Anyone would agree. She pretty much had everything a gal could want: great car, great house, great husband, great job. All these matched her great ass. Funny how that works, so often, all of the above go hand in hand.

It was raining... just what she needed. She didn't like the rain. Anna liked the sun. There was a meeting that evening at a restaurant in town, and she was running late, as usual. She didn't mean to be late, but always was. You could make book on that. This was a new client, so she was trying to hurry. While Anna rummaged around their sprawling, Hollywood Hills home searching for her keys, she could hear the rain slapping the windows. She wandered from room to spacious room of the professionally decorated home, looking under throw pillows, and between the cracks and crevasses of each piece of expensive furniture, cursing under her breath. "I have to get my shit together." She entered the huge, gourmet kitchen and looked at the hook on the wall marked KEYS. There she saw the familiar leather Mercedes' Benz key chain. Her shoulders dropped, and she exhaled in a "humph." She cocked her head. "I know I didn't put those there," she said out loud to no one. "I have never use that stupid hook." Her husband, Ned, had hung the gaudy, J.C. Penny's wall piece on the kitchen wall, specifically because Anna could never find her keys; and Anna never used it because it was Ned's idea to hang it there. It didn't matter to Anna that it was a good idea to have it, or, when used, she always found her keys. But, that was Anna, always trying to show how strong she was, rough, tough and hard to diaper. Really, she was the pussycat of pussycats.

"OK, do I have everything now?" she was talking to herself again, checking the list in her mind. She decided she did, waved goodbye to their Persian cat, Mustafa, who was sitting on the window ledge, and headed for the front door, still fussing over the keys. "Ned must have put those keys there," she thought. "I certainly didn't." She locked the huge oak door behind her and headed into the steady rain. She heard the distant ring of the telephone back in the house but decided to ignore it. "If it's important, they will leave a message or call back."

It wasn't just raining; it was downright cold. "I'm surprised it's raining instead of snowing! This isn't typical California weather. The Weather Channel predicted chilly, but this is ridiculous! Burrr!" Anna was correcting Mother Nature. She then stopped dead in her tracks. "Where is the car?" She looked around, frantic. Then she immediately calmed down. "There is a frigging gate at the end of the driveway," she muttered, "it can't be stolen." She looked at the garage. "Why would he put the car in the garage?" she thought. Then she laughed. "Maybe he saw the damn weather report," she said, as she wiped rainwater off her face.

She walked towards the four-car garage, and stopped by the garage door opener. She keyed in the code, the door opened, and there was the shiny new SL 600 Mercedes Benz roadster that her husband had given her for her birthday, with the hardtop secured tightly in place. It was bright red, her favorite color for a car. "He is so good to me," she admitted to herself, thinking not of the $130,000.00 gift, that was nothing special, but of the fact that her husband had the foresight and thoughtfulness to put the car in the garage in anticipation of the rain; that was sweet. She was still aglow after having spent a glorious night and morning with Ned. "We do not do things like that often enough anymore. We should find the time to share more moments like that."

The car was not usually kept in the garage. After all, "it never rains in sunny southern California," or so says the silly song. She realized she didn't even have to go outside into the rain. She could have simply entered the garage through the house. "Oh well," she chuckled. Her natural beauty was unaffected by a little rain.

Anna thought of their wonderful previous night and morning and how lucky she was. She began to reflect on her relationship with her husband. Some would say it was an unusual one; but she didn't care. For one thing, Ned was 57 years old. That, in and of itself, would not, necessarily, constitute unusual, although it's a start. Actually, there were many other couples in the neighborhood where their age difference was as much as 12 years, sometimes much more. What was peculiar here was that it certainly looked to the casual observer that these two truly cared about each other. People were jealous. She did not cheat on him, nor, he on her, or so it seemed. In their world, that was considered unusual. When they were together, although they could be mistaken for father and daughter, they truly seemed to be happy. Anyone could see that.

One other thing was slightly unusual. Ned, whose given name was Nadir, was from the country of Iran. He was a member of a small population native to that country in the Hollywood Hills. There were many people from the Middle East in the neighborhood, but not so many from Iran.

No one would guess him to be foreign born. He had striking good looks and spoke perfect English with barely a hint of an accent. Most people thought he was Italian, or Greek. Plus, he was always Ned, not Nadir, at least in the United States. At home he remained Nadir, and, make no mistake, although he had been "Americanized," after having lived in the U.S. for many years, no period of time living in this, or any other country, would ever completely eradicate the proud Persian traditions which had been instilled in him since birth by his family. These traditions had survived for centuries, no matter what name was given to his country by the West.

Ned and Anna met in college. Anna went to Southern Illinois University mainly because college was expected of her. She was, after all, not planning to be an astrophysicist. She just wanted to have fun; and SIU was well known as a place where fun could be had. When Playboy Magazine did one of their "Best Party Schools" features, the "honors" were awarded to mostly Big 10 schools, after which an asterisk appeared. At the bottom of the page it was stated that Southern Illinois University had to be excluded from the competition because the school had lost its amateur status and "gone professional" long ago. This suited Anna just fine.

Ned had an engineering degree from UCLA, but had come to Southern Illinois to do some postgraduate work at the university where Buckminster Fuller was formerly a fellow; he was interested in the geodesic dome, (he was considering putting a desert city under one) and to avail himself of the English as a Second Language program offered there. He moved into a small apartment in the same building in which Anna lived. They were neighbors, and met one day in the lobby by the mailboxes. They were attracted to each other, although Anna would not have admitted it at the time. She knew better. They began to spend time together.

They became part of a group of friends that always went out in a troupe. It was clear, among the others, that the two of them were becoming more than just friends. They always ended the night together, and, as time progressed, so did their relationship, all very properly and above criticism. They began to discuss the possibility of living together during the next semester. Whenever the subject came up, Ned always told Anna not to worry about it. He said he would take care of it. Anna took him at his word.

She would never forget what happened when they returned for the next semester. Ned had a little surprise for Anna.

"Do you like this place?" he asked with an unusually sly grin. They were standing in the parking lot that served the two charming three flat apartment buildings in front of them. The buildings had obviously been built by the same developer, a matched set.

"May I see the apartment before I answer?" Anna didn't understand. She smiled at Ned, unsure of what he was trying to say.

"I said… do you like the place?" Ned swept his arm, hand extended and palm up, across in front of him.

Ned had purchased the two entire apartment buildings. The top two floors of one of the buildings had been converted to a single apartment, which was beautifully appointed, and was to be their living quarters. The other apartments were for Ned's entourage. It seems that Ned had told Anna many stories about his home in Iran, but he had neglected to mention that he was actually a member of the royal family in his country, and wealthy beyond the imagination. Ned was actually a Persian prince! He had purposely hidden this minor fact from Anna, and all their friends, because he wanted to meet people that would like him for his personality, rather than his money and title. Anna decided that Ned had a noble purpose for deceiving her, and she would not be angry. After she had taken the grand tour, she demurely said, "I like it. I like it a lot." As a result of that decision she began a new and exciting lifestyle. In this lifestyle, you sometimes flew to France… for lunch.

Soon, Ned was proving the old adage that "money goes to money." Before he was thirty he had, personally or with partners, built part of the skyline of Houston, Dallas and Detroit.

They were young, incredibly rich, and very happy together, but they were not married, and Anna's one true love was not a citizen of the United States. It was the Cinderella story in progress, but it had a wrinkle. This was a delicate subject between the two of them. It was expected that Ned would some day soon, return to his native land, and resume his birthright among the ruling class of that country. However, if that were to happen, and Anna were to go with him, she would have to assume the status that women held in that country. In spite of the money, the wealth, the power and prestige, this was unacceptable to Anna. They, for the most part, avoided the subject entirely, but it always remained the undercurrent to their relationship.

Anna remembered how she would always say to Ned, "Honey, I love you from the bottom to the top of my heart, but I just cannot move to Iran with you. I will miss you every day, but if you leave, you leave alone."

Ned decided to solve the problem once and for all. He took a trip to Teheran. There he spoke with his father and his uncles. He explained that he was in love, which, frankly, did not mean much to his collective male family members. Love did not normally figure in to the decision process of picking a spouse, not in Ned's extended family. However, economic positioning and financial advantage did. Further, the country was undergoing a revolution. The political climate was unstable and dangerous, particularly for royals. Therefore, it was decided that Ned would become the family's United States operative. He would oversee and represent all of the family's financial interests in North America and the West, with particular concentration on the U.S. This was a display of great confidence in Ned, and he was very honored and grateful.

This decision by the family elders also made it possible for Ned to marry a U.S. citizen. In fact, it made a U.S. marriage imperative. Marriage to a citizen of the United States would secure, for Ned, resident alien status and later full citizenship in the Land of the Free and Home of the Brave. Things could not have worked out better. Anna often joked that she owed a debt of gratitude to the Ayatollah Khomeini for her marriage and resulting happiness. That joke was reserved for certain circles only.

When Ned returned from his trip, he proposed marriage; which Anna promptly accepted. The happy couple married in the Chicago area near Anna's parent's home. It was a truly beautiful "North Shore" wedding.

Shortly thereafter, they took up residence in Southern California where they began their storybook life. It seemed that the wrinkles in the Cinderella tale had been ironed out. Only one minor problem remained. Anna, it turned out, could not have children. This disappointed the couple for a time. As a woman, Anna was saddened by the fact that she would never know motherhood. Ned was secretly more affected by the news. He was a prince, after all, and was expected to produce an heir. He never let on to his true feelings, however. He did not want to unduly burden his new bride with such concerns. So, they resolved themselves to the situation, and filled their lives with other things, satisfying themselves with work, travel and each other; and they became the quintessential happy pair.

Anna came back from her moment of reflection, got inside her expensive little toy, and prepared, finally, to leave. She adjusted the rear view mirror, and cranked up the heat. She maneuvered the car backwards down the drive. A sensor automatically opened the ornate iron gate at the end of the intricate cobblestone, and she backed through it and onto the street in front of the house. The street was narrow and wound through the brush, trees and rocks of the Hollywood hills. The rain continued to pelt the windshield, and the wipers slapped back and forth. The heater was finally beginning to kick in. The warmth felt good. She had a chill due to the damp air and slightly wet clothes.

The car wound through and down the mountain road, passing other gated drives which led to other spectacular homes in the area. Anna could see the familiar views of the City of Angels, with its twinkling lights, as she negotiated the outer turns. The city was shrouded in a haze with clouds that obscured some of the distant lights. She never grew tired of the view. No one did.

Anna checked the digital display on the dash. She was late, even for her. She sped up slightly, but safely. She respected the tight winding curves, especially the outer reaches near the cliffs. "Isn't it funny," she thought, "that people feel safer on the inside turns. Although there are no cliffs, they are still dangerous. You don't get 'more dead' from falling off a cliff than you do from hitting a rock wall." She chuckled silently at her own observation. She began to go over in her mind the particulars that would be discussed during her meeting.

Anna's dedication to her work was legendary among those in her little niche of the world. She supported multiple charitable causes and was known as a "closer" when it came to insuring that a potential cash cow would part with big bucks in favor of her favorite charities. The guy she was meeting was supposed to be some kind of bigwig with money to donate; however, she had never heard of him. Ned claimed that he had heard of him when she told him of the meeting. He had said that the guy was truly wealthy. Anna almost canceled due to the predicted weather, but the guy was going to be out of town on an extended business trip or something. Anyway, he said he really wanted to meet on this particular evening, and she acquiesced. Now she was second-guessing herself. Something didn't seem right. Peering through the wet windshield, she stoically pressed on. No amount of rain or cold would stand in the way of a substantial contribution to one of her humanitarian causes.

The rain was steady which made for poor visibility. The clouds thickened and obscured more of the beautiful view below. This wasn't California weather. "What am I doing out here?" she thought.

Just then, Anna noticed the most unusual odor. It was so odd. She had never experienced such a scent. It seemed to fill the entire interior of the small two-seater. She wanted to reach for the button to roll down the window, but she found she couldn't. She realized her vision was blurred; her eyes teared, as she sat motionless, unable to move a muscle.

Once the car left the road, Anna could not hear a sound. Silence. She was conscious and aware that she could see a blurry picture of the Hollywood Bowl passing in her field of vision to her left. "How strange," she thought, "there's the Hollywood Bowl." That was Anna's final conscious thought. It took just eight seconds for the car to impact the next level of ground below. It seemed much longer to Anna. When it hit, the car buckled. Its frame bent. The steering wheel was driven into Anna's chest. The air bag was absolutely useless. Ribs cracked and broke and punctured her lungs. A large piece of jagged, broken glass from the windshield sliced through Anna's beautiful face, ripping her right cheek open and continuing down her neck, severing her carotid artery. In the movies, the car always explodes at this point, and a huge orange ball of flame rises amid black smoke in a spectacular scene of pure carnage. This didn't happen. Anna's little car simply came to rest on the side of one of the famed Hollywood Hills, a mangled, broken mass of steel, plastic, leather and glass, with Anna in it, dead.

2

" I HAVE TO WRITE A BOOK."

"What on God's green earth are you yakking about now? What do you mean, you have to write a book?"

"Well... I've always wanted to write a book. I've said that before. You've heard me say that before, haven't you? Plus, I don't think a person should go around saying that they want to do something; and, then not do it. People should do that which they say they are going to do, shouldn't they? You know...say what you mean; mean what you say...and all that. Isn't that the model?"

" Why would you want to write a book?"

" I don't know... money, power, fame, make a difference, make a statement...you pick a reason."

"Hold on...you have money. You once had some true power and some fame and you walked away from all of that. You have made a significant difference in the lives of many, many people. What's the matter, are you feeling unfulfilled, unloved?

" I don't feel unloved… I have your sorry ass."

"You don't think I love you, do you? I fucking hate you. You know that. You are a pain in the butt, pansy ass, tree huggin' liberal. I hate all you fucking people."

"That's what I'll do. I'll write a Bush bashing, tree huggin', pansy ass liberal book, just to piss you off… that will be fun."

Two old, dear friends are sitting at a bar in Key West, Florida. The bar is half indoors and half open air. Panama fans lazily spin above their heads, and palm trees and tropical foliage surround the place. There is a system of faded sea blue shutters that, in the case of a hurricane, will button down the indoor part of the bar quite well. The place has withstood many storms, and will withstand the next one and the next. The shutters are never closed at any other time. Behind the bar, partially built into the wall, is a large gold cage; and, in the cage are Ike and Mike, two brilliantly colored parrots that act like they own the place. Their vocabulary consists mostly of swear words and vulgar phrases which they both routinely squawk at unsuspecting female patrons. It is a little past 10:00 am. The air temperatures is 79 degrees, give or take a degree; neon flickers and reflects off the multicolored bottles lined up on shelves behind the beautiful, curvy, young barmaid. A Jimmy Buffett song is playing softly, almost imperceptibly, through the speakers of the in house stereo system. In other words, the two old friends are having their conversation... in heaven. At least that is the opinion of the, would be, author who is speaking again.

"I don't know what happened to you, man. In college you were practically a communist. You were progressive, open minded, inquisitive, intelligent. Now, you have gone all 'Dennis Miller' on me. I have tried and tried in vain to understand this transformation of yours. Try as I might, I will never get it."

"Get it...get it...there is nothing to "get." It is called growing up. It is called maturing. Further, I really dislike when all you 'bleeding hearts' try to equate open-mindedness, inquisitiveness and intelligence with liberalism, thereby implying that conservatives are not open minded, inquisitive or intelligent. Nothing could be further from the truth. It's you dipshit liberals that are closed-minded."

"It's not called maturing, it is called selling out, you old fossil, and you should be ashamed."

The barmaid, Ellie, sauntered over to the only patrons in the bar, having heard this diatribe, what seemed to her to be at least, a thousand times. She was polishing a glass and smiling.

" Ya know...ya'all sound like a couple of old ladies," she said. "Do you two guys realize that ya'all have this same damn conversation every damn day? Don't ya'all get sick of it? I do, in case ya'all were wonderin'. I get sick of it." She smiled again. It was playful banter. One of the parrots, probably Ike, squawked out something unintelligible, then clearly said, "Fuckin' hippie…fuckin' hippie." Everyone laughed.

The guy purporting to be an author is, Jack Patrick Donahue, often called Jigs by his friends and acquaintances. Actually, everyone calls him that, even people he doesn't know. Jigs is one of those guys, you know the type. Everyone seems to know who he is, even people he has never met. This is often a good thing, having lots of people know your name, having a reputation, but not always. Probably, O.J. Simpson would rather be anonymous these days. Of course, in the case of Mr. Donahue, he doesn't mind the reputation. His reputation is a good one. He is a familiar sight on Duval Street in downtown Key West. Most people like him. Most of the locals know him as " the crazy lawyer from Chicago that has that bar near the water." Everyone, however, knows him as a person that will help you out in a pinch.

His companion and friend had just finished emptying a shot glass full of Jameson Irish Whiskey and an eight-ounce "shorty" glass of domestic beer. Never mind that it is 10:00 am on a Tuesday. Whiskey tastes good to Willie at any time of day, on any day of the week, any time of the year. Beer too! Jigs glanced at his watch and shook his head with a smirk.

"Willie" is William J. Brennen, and these two unlikely travelers of life have known each other for more than twenty-five years. Willie is not "Bill". He is not "William". He is not "Will" or "Billy". He has been "Willie" forever and Willie he will stay.

At a very young age Willie had decided, with the help and influence of his sainted mother, that he would someday become a Catholic priest. He took all necessary steps in that direction, including serving as an alter boy, volunteering as a helper at the rectory and attaining the status of student extraordinaire. However, while attending a preparatory Catholic High School on the south side of Chicago, in his last year there, at the age of eighteen, and during an era (the early 1970s) when it was not uncommon to do so, someone offered Willie a tab of L.S.D. He took it. From that fateful day foreword, Willie knew that he would never become a priest, much to the dismay of his sainted mother. He had, as they said back then, "expanded his mind." However, as a result of his special efforts, he did receive a classical education, steeped in the liberal arts, history, literature, theatre, and science, both in Prep school and at the University of Notre Dame. As a result, Willie was a very well educated soul whom, some would say, had not fulfilled his complete potential. He had spent most of his career writing. He freelanced for many of the Chicago newspapers during his early years, but he never considered himself a reporter. He did do freelance correspondence work in Bosnia and El Salvador, but he always said he was not a reporter. Then there was the time spent in the Middle East during Desert Storm, but not as a reporter.

He has written many articles on many subjects in various publications, but what he did mostly, now a days, is work on "projects" with Jigs. People would sometimes ask the two of them for help on various issues, and they would try to help out. These adventures, and many times they were truly adventures, were affectionately called "projects". These "projects" kept life interesting for both of them, to say the least.

Willie pushed the two diminutive glasses forward on the bar and said, "Do this again, Ellie, would you please?"

The attractive barkeep strolled toward the bar and said, "How 'bout ya'all Jigs, more coffee?"

"Ellie, I would love some more coffee, you gorgeous creature. Plus, would you be kind enough to remind my conservative, old fart friend here of the time of day?"

"That would not make one little bit of difference to him, and ya'all know it," Ellie said.

"Yeah, I know," said Jigs. "I just pity his poor liver."

Willie raised his small empty beer glass in a mock toast, overstating his effort, as he said to the parrots behind the bar, "to hell with all of you… never get drunk, never get sober, that's my motto."

Ellie poured a shot and filled the beer glass from the draught spigot. She also poured a fresh cup of coffee from a glass coffee pot. "Ya'all know what? He's right. I've never seen him drunk, not even one little time." She returned the pot to the coffee maker hot plate and flashed her pearly whites at the two of them.

Ellie had the type of body that males from 15 to 50 and beyond could not avoid looking at, not so much like all the skinny ideal figures in the magazines and on the movie screens.

She was more the curvy type, like Marilyn Monroe, but clad in tight hip hugging jean cutoffs and a half tee shirt that exposed her midriff. There was three inches of air between the end of the tee shirt and the tan skin on her flat stomach.

The Panama fans gently moved the thick air around the quiet, dimly lit bar. Jigs had a lingering vice that he was not proud of…he still smoked. Therefore, the Panama fans also moved the smoke he emitted as it became one with the wet Florida air. For a moment, it seemed like peace was going to break out between these two bickering old friends.

You could hardly hear the haunting melody of the song "California Promises" in the background, but it was there, just enough.

"What I want to know is…how the hell can you support this buffoon in the White House?" Jigs was ready to get back into the mock battle.

Ellie just rolled her eyes and shook her pretty head. She raised her hands up over her head. "Here we go," she said in faux exasperation.

"Please, man, don't start. If you and your 'type' had your way, you would all attempt to start a 'dialogue' with the sons-of-bitches that attacked us on 9/11, you pansy. These guys do not respond to talk. Only decisive action will get their attention."

"Listen to yourself. You sound like one of them. Are you a 'neocon', Willie? Is that what you have degenerated into?"

"I would rather be considered a neocon than a tree hugging liberal, you tree hugging liberal."

"This is so sad." Jigs looked at Ellie and pointed at Willie. "You should have seen this guy when he was in college… You would have loved him."

"I do love him…and, I love ya'll too. I love both of you; and, although no one would ever suspect this, you two love each other." Ellie was wagging her finger at both of her friends. " Do you guys realize that someone might think ya'll are serious about the things that ya'll say to, and about, each other. Ya'll are like brothers. Why don't ya'll act like it and just quit?"

"Its true...we may be like brothers...but I won't have this old fart..."

Jigs' cell phone rang, a welcomed interruption. He excused himself and took the call. Willie and Ellie ignored him for a while, but after a few minutes, Willie noticed the look on Jigs' face and realized the call might be important. When Jigs closed his cell phone, he asked, "What's up." He was suddenly serious.

"Do you remember Anna Buckingham, I mean... Anna Khan?" Jigs didn't look happy.

Willie thought for a moment, and then he said, "Yeah...yeah, she was that really pretty- what am I saying, they were all really pretty- she was that really, really pretty girl that had some kind of a dilemma regarding a guy from the Middle East?" He was half making a statement, half asking a question. Then the memory became clearer and he said, "Yes, I do remember her. Why, what happened?"

"Well, she's dead." Jigs said this in a very matter of fact way, shaking his head slowly. It wasn't the first time he had gotten a call of this type from someone. People often called him at times like this. " That was her brother... remember him?"

"Yeah, sure I do. Rich kid. Daredevil. Skydiver. Windsurfer. He was in sugar…right? A broker of sugar and sweeteners." Willie was going back some twenty years.

" Very good," said Jigs. " Not bad for an old man. I guess the booze hasn't completely addled your brain." He was more serious again. " Apparently, there was a one car accident near her home. She lived in Los Angeles, in the hills. I guess her car went off a cliff. She was alone in the car. It was raining. The police see it as simply an accident. I guess accidents happen with some regularity up in those hills. Arthur, the brother, doesn't buy it. He says that she was way too careful and way too respectful of those mountain roads. I can't tell if it is grief talking, or if there is something to his suspicions. I will say this, though. She lived in those hills for a long time. She must have driven that particular road a thousand times, literally. Plus, she had a good head on her shoulders. She was no flake. She was smart… kind of like Ellie here." The mood lightened a bit. Both men looked at Ellie. She flushed slightly. " She was very unorganized, but smart… kind of like Ellie here." This caused some chuckles. Ellie pretended to slap Jigs. " I am not unorganized, ya' brat," she said.

"Anyway, he is asking us to look into this a little further. What would you say to a trip to California?" Jigs seemed distant. He was in another place. It was clear that he wasn't really thinking about what he was saying. He was in memory land.

"You know me, Jigs, I'm flexible," Willie said.

"How did you know this girl?" Ellie asked.

Jigs looked at Ellie. He seemed to be coming back to earth.

"Well, about a hundred years ago, when I was still in law school, I was living…"

"Get comfortable," Willie interrupted. "This could be a long one."

Ellie had a bar stool on her side of the bar. She sat on it, put her elbows on the bar and laid her chin in her hands. She looked like a little girl waiting for a story.

"…on the north side of Chicago in a high-rise condo right on the Lake. It was great. The place had a spectacular view of the lake and the North Shore. I rented, but it was still really cool. The building had an Olympic size pool, Jacuzzi, health club, plus, one thousand yards behind the building was Foster Avenue Beach. Remember that place?" Jigs looked at Willie with a grin. The mood improved. Willie nodded with a wry smile.

"I was on the elevator. It was one of the first gorgeous warm nights of spring. I was through studying, and I was going to go out and have a beer. It was pretty late, maybe 11:00 pm. I remember it was a Friday, so I could go out for a while. The elevator door opened, and two girls got into the elevator. One of them was very cute. The other one was B-E-A-U-T-I-F-U-L, just stunning. Blonde hair. Blue eyes. The whole deal. As soon as they got on, the beautiful one turns to me and says, 'Do you like M.D.A.?' Jigs turned to Ellie and asked, "Do you know what M.D.A. is?" She slowly shook her head.

"Well, I do not advocate the use of drugs of any kind…but, if you must do a drug, like if you have already made your decision to try a drug, and nobody can talk you out of it, and when I say 'you', I don't mean you, Ellie, I mean 'you' in the generic sense of 'anyone', if any person had already made that decision, then M.D.A. would be the drug to try. M.D.A. was the precursor to ecstasy, basically the same stuff, and, I have to say, it is pretty darn fun, I can't deny that…" Ellie was already laughing at Jigs' tortured sentence structure and uncomfortable bearing. She was not used to seeing him so off balance. She thought it cute that he was trying to be protective and parental, while telling a story in which he himself had used drugs.

"… Anyway, I said yes, and she said, 'Do you want to go to a party?' Needless to say, I said OK and off we went. The party wasn't much, basically a small group of snooty North Shore types, but she was cool. She seemed very nice. She had a beautiful body, long blonde hair, perfect smile, and a great laugh… "

By this time, everyone was chuckling, even Jigs. He was starting to sound like a high school kid. He went on. "So, after that night we started hanging out..."

"That is code for 'fucking'," Willie chimed in. "He should have said, 'so after that night we starting fucking."

"...Do you guys want to hear this or not?" Jigs was pretending to be frustrated.

"Well, were you?" Ellie asked teasingly.

"Was I what?" Jigs pretended not to know.

"Were you...f...ing?" Ellie was being cute.

"Of course," Jigs said, "But that's not important to the story. What is important is that I had met this really terrific girl. What I learned about her later, only made her seem more terrific. The first thing I noticed about her that was a little unusual was... well, she owned her own unit in my building on a high floor, a big two bedroom unit with sweeping views of the lake and city; this was an expensive unit. She drove a brand new BMW. The spread on her king size bed was made from rabbit fur. She had everything new and all of it high end, but she didn't work. I did not question this, but I wondered. I knew her parents had money, but I was pretty sure they would not just give her all that stuff. Soon enough, I got the whole story." Jigs looked off as if he was reliving times past.

"One night she just came out with it. She told me she had a boyfriend that she had been with all through college and afterward. He was actually some kind of prince, or royalty, in the country of Iran. She explained that she really loved him, but she could not go with him to Iran because they treated women like second-class citizens there. She did not believe that he was going to move here because he had actual 'royal' responsibilities in his country.

We talked for hours about the whole thing. She told me about a lifestyle that was pretty unbelievable, but I knew she was telling the truth. I respected her for being true to herself and her sense of values. Most people would cave very quickly in the face of all that money. I mean we are talking palaces, and shit. However, she had already decided to leave it all behind. She then went on to very matter of factly state that I was going to help her get through the whole thing, to help her get over him, as if I had no say in the matter. As it turned out, she was right. I figured that would be fine with me. This was a very beautiful... did I mention that before... very intelligent, very fun and funny woman. We did everything together. Snow skiing, water-skiing, biking on the lake, hand gliding, for crying out loud. She got into physical fitness, which became her passion.

I met her parents, her brother and many of her upper crust friends. They all met Willie here. This was in the days before he lost his mind, and started voting Republican. I played golf with her father and brother. We went to the family cottage in Michigan. We had plenty of sex, but we both knew that it was all...temporary. She still loved the guy...Ned, and I was actually fine with that. Truth be known, she was almost too good. She had energy and exuberance that was almost too much. She always said that if anyone could keep up with her, it was me, but I wasn't so sure about that. Then one day Ned came back from Iran. He had somehow worked things out with his extended family. He was staying in the U.S., becoming an American citizen, getting married...and that was that. I met him. He was nice. I remained friends with her brother and father, for a while. I went to the wedding. She and I have talked over the years. I have even done some legal work for her, here and there, and now...I guess, I'm going to go out to California and try to figure out if she was killed, and if so, who the fuck killed her. Isn't life strange." Jigs got up and started walking towards the Men's Room. He said over his shoulder, " Hey, Ellie, sweetheart, maybe it is time to have a beer, after all."

3

NED KHAN WAS INFORMED OF HIS WIFE'S death as he deplaned from his private jet in Houston, Texas. He had left Los Angeles earlier on the day she died to fly to Texas to attend meetings. There were plans to, once again, add to Houston's skyline. He was said to have been inconsolable. He immediately returned to LA.

The death of Anna Khan was reported nationally as a senseless and tragic automobile accident. The reason that it was reported nationally was perhaps more of a newspaper story than the tragedy and sadness that resulted from her untimely demise.

While most Americans did not know who Anna was, it seems that The American Cancer Society, Unicef, The American Diabetes Foundation, Jerry's Kids, MDA, and approximately fifty lesser-known charitable organizations, including Save Our Planet and many others that were dedicated to conservation, would miss her contributions and her tireless efforts in support of their various causes. It was just like Anna to be one of the nations leading philanthropists, but even more in keeping with her personality was the fact that she did all her charity work quietly and without fanfare. It was in this context that her death was reported in most venues, including in a piece done on "This Week with George Stephenopolous" in his "In Memoriam" segment.   Her work with both American and International Charities was compared in various articles and reports to that of Jerry Lewis, Danny and Marlow Thomas, Paul Neuman, Warren Buffet and Bill and Melinda Gates, yet, no one, outside of the organizations with which she worked, knew who she was or that she was such a great benefactor to so many. Of course, that was Anna.

The obituary in the Los Angeles Times was probably the most poignant, because it was local and more personal. After highlighting the accomplishments of her life, and mentioning the survivors, it ended with the simple statement: "All of LA has lost a dear and wonderful friend." This was the obit column, which was picked up in most papers nationally.

INTERNATIONAL PHILANTHROPIST ANNA KHAN
Anna Khan- 1962-2008
By: EDWARD ARMSTRONG

LOS ANGELES, Calif.---- Anna Buckingham Khan, who is know well in many circles, but particularly by local, national and international charitable organizations due to her tireless efforts combating poverty and in favor of energy conservation, died Monday. She was 45.

Ms. Khan began as a volunteer for the American Cancer Society in the early 1980s, but later became a member of the Board of Directors of that society. She was also a member of the board of several other charitable organizations and associations. She worked with so many various organizations and for so many causes that she was considered one of the country's leading and most beloved philanthropists. It has been said that there were no bounds to her dedication and generosity; with reference to causes she embraced.

She was raised in Winnetka, Illinois, the only daughter in a prominent "North Shore" family. Her father, William Buckingham, was a Sugar Broker, and his father, was a Sugar Broker, and Anna's great-grandfather began a sugar business, which flourished, particularly after he met, and became friends with, "Woody", a member of the Woodruff family. They owned a major interest in Coca-Cola in those days. The rest, as they say, was history. The family flourished as one of Chicago's finest and well-respected families.

She was a graduate of New Trier High School, in Winnetka, Il., and Southern Illinois University in Carbondale, IL. She was known among her contemporaries in humanitarian circles as one of the most beloved and respected members of their community.

Ms. Khan is survived by her loving husband, Ned, her loving parents, Bill and Jackie Buckingham, and her loving brother, Arthur Buckingham.

All of L.A. has lost a dear and wonderful friend.

———————————

The LAPD released a statement. It was for press consumption. It consisted of a copy of the narrative portion of the internal report by the officer first on the scene. It read as follows:

CITY OF LOS ANGELES

POLICE REPORT

At 19:47 hours on the date first written this officer, John Baumgartner, bdge# 345, herein R/O, arrived on the scene of an apparent traffic accident. Said accident was reported by one, Thomas Eggert, 5415 Sunshine Canyon Rd., Beverly Hills, CA., DL# 000-4323-6666-0087. Mr. Eggert was traveling upward and westbound on Laurel Canyon Dr. when he saw an automobile leave the road above him and fall approximately 300 feet landing about 500 feet from his position on the road. R/O encountered Mr. Eggert in an agitated and distraught state. He had arrived on the scene minutes after the accident occurred and was witness to severe injuries suffered by subject.

R/O approached the subject vehicle and viewed a F/W occupant, later identified as Anna Khan, 7744 Khan Canyon Rd., Los Angeles, CA DL# 111-4876-4444-6464, bleeding and unconscious. R/O called for paramedics and backup assistance. R/O attempted to speak with the subject occupant. She was unresponsive. R/O attempted to stop the bleeding to the subject occupant but could not reach her sufficiently to do so.

Paramedics and backup arrived at 20:07 hours and began working to revive the subject. R/O secured the area and attempted to question the single witness, Eggert.

Witness reported to R/O that he was traveling upward and westbound on Laurel Canyon Dr. when he saw a red Mercedes Benz automobile leave the road above him and fall approximately 300 feet. His attempts to help the occupant of the vehicle were unsuccessful. He notified LAPD by cell phone. He was unable to discern if any other vehicle was involved in the accident on the upper road. He reported that he did not see headlights on the upper road.

Subject/occupant, Khan, was transported from the scene at 20:34 hours by LAFD paramedics after having been extricated from the subject vehicle. R/O assisted the investigating detectives upon arrival on the scene. R/O left the scene at 21:42 hours after the investigation was taken over by LAPD detectives Harry, bdge#454 and Heater, bdge#552. Nothing further by this R/O.

SUPPLEMENTAL REPORT

LOS ANGELES POLICE DEPARTMENT

This report is supplemental to and amends the previously filed report submitted by this officer. The subject/occupant of the vehicle, which was in the accident that is the subject of this report, one Anna Khan, was DOA at Cedars Sinai Hospital. After a full investigation of the accident scene and the automobile, which was involved, no irregularities were determined to exist at the site or with the automobile. It is the position of the LAPD that no further action be taken regarding this matter, it having been determined that the incident being investigated was an accident, resulting in accidental death to subject, Khan. The subject body, together with the automobile involved in the accident, shall be released to next of kin. No autopsy shall be ordered or performed. No further action taken. End of supplemental report.

John Baumgartner bdge# 345

4

WHEN BUFORD TUCKER READ ANNA'S obituary in the Washington Post, he was at home in Ft. Meade, Maryland. He was unconcerned about her philanthropic efforts. That didn't matter to him. But, unlike most Americans, he knew who she was. He knew very well who Anna was. As he read on, he began to feel sick to his stomach. He tried to throw the paper across the room. Funny, when a person throws a section of the newspaper, it doesn't go very far, not unless it is rolled up like a paperboy does it. However, if one has just been reading the paper, and it is all opened up like it is when its being read, no matter how hard one tries to throw it, the paper just floats to the floor right in front of the thrower. That is what happened to Buford, so he looked really stupid. He felt really stupid as well. He then began to wonder just at what point his life had started to take this turn for the worse. He wanted to go back and do things differently from that point. He was actually pretty sure he knew the point. Then he started to wonder why he couldn't have seen this whole mess coming. If he could see the folly of his ways now, why the hell couldn't he have seen it in advance? Then maybe he wouldn't be in this fix. Then he started to ask God why things had gone wrong. Hadn't he been a good Christian? He humbly decided that he had, in fact, been a good Christian. Then he started to get mad at God, at Jesus! Why would the Lord let all this happen? He caught himself. "Jesus would not want such self pity," he said in a half scream, half whisper, with his head tilted upward. "We do not always know His will for us." Buford Tucker then fell to his knees, put his head in his hands, and started to sob uncontrollably. He could not believe he was doing it, but he could not stop doing it. *"What have I done?"* he screamed into his hands. *"What have I done?"*

Life was not always this way for Buford Tucker. When Buford was a young boy running around in the fields and the bayous surrounding Biloxi, Mississippi, he always thought he was lucky. The youngest of three children born to Bud and Luanne Tucker, he had an older brother, Jo Bob, whom he idolized, and a sister, Virgie, whom, although she was a year older, he protected and cherished. His mama always told him that he came in the year that Hurricane Camille attacked Biloxi and the gulf coast, and he had been attacking life the same way ever since. When Buford was in High School, he followed in his brother's footsteps, and lead the school football team as their quarterback. He loved football. He was also class valedictorian, and voted most likely to succeed. The girls literally chased him. All in all, he had a great life, no complaints.

Oh sure, his family didn't have much money. It would've been nice to have more material things. They had an older car and a small modest home, but his family made up for what they did not have in dollars, with what they did have in love, love of family, love of community, love of country and love of God. This was a familiar situation for many folks in the Biloxi area and along the gulf coast. The economy in the area was struggling. Many people were out of work. These were proud people. It was a hard life, but it built character. No one gave in to self-pity. They faced each day as a challenge with determination and fortitude. That was their way.

When Buford graduated from high school and turned 18 yrs old, he joined the 308th Port Security Unit of the United States Coast Guard Reserves in Gulfport, Mississippi. He did not do this alone. Several members of his graduating class, including almost all of his fellow teammates from the football team, joined him. This was a bit of a tradition in his community. Biloxi is a coastal community, and the boys, and some girls, felt a responsibility to serve. It was also a source of income for young men and women in a very depressed economy with little job prospects for the young adults. These kids would also get whatever jobs they could, and then they would contribute most of what they earned back to their families. Buford was no exception. He hoped he would be able to go to college someday, and his involvement in the Reserves would help along those lines. He would receive financial assistance from the government as a result of having served his country, but, at present, it was more important for him to help out at home.

Then things changed. In 1990, the United States became involved in a war to drive Saddam Hussein out of the tiny country of Kuwait. Buford was 21 years old. He was not astute in things political. He really didn't follow the goings on in the Middle East. However, he did love his country. He also believed in his Commander in Chief. If President George Herbert Walker Bush thought that it was important to intervene in this war, then it must be important. He, together with most of his Reserve buddies, transferred to active status. His unit was not scheduled to deploy to Kuwait, so he, and several of his buddies, arranged to be transferred to the Port Security Unit, Milwaukee, Wisconsin. That unit was scheduled to deploy to the Middle East. He was not going to sit out a war back in Biloxi, or Gulfport or anywhere in the States. He wanted to be part of the action.

While serving in Kuwait, Buford excelled, as he usually did, and he began to draw some very coveted duty. Buford looked like he was born to wear a uniform, and, quite frankly, he was. He had matured into a striking figure of a man, light brown close-cropped hair, square jaw, piercing blue eyes, athletic build. He was also a devout Evangelical Christian. He had the exact attitude and bearing the military looked for. He began to be given more and more visible types of jobs. He was chosen for color guard. He drove vehicles for and was aide to the highest-ranking officers. He was, to put it simply, a rising star in the military.

After Desert Storm and the completion of his active duty time, Buford returned to a very different Gulf Coast. Gambling had been legalized in Mississippi; and Biloxi, Gulfport, and the surrounding area, were fast becoming the "Vegas" of the South. It was incredible. His home turf had been transformed. The best part...everyone was working. There were jobs, jobs and more jobs. They were casino jobs, which would not be Buford's first choice, he was not a gambler, nor did he approve of the habit, but the prosperity that the casinos brought to the coast was undeniable. Even the preachers in the many churches in the area had to agree that working in a casino was not tantamount to gambling. After all, the collection baskets were getting filled again. It couldn't be all bad.

Buford, therefore, decided to return to reserve status with his original unit, the 308th. He would remain in the military, but he wanted to try his hand at a private sector job. It was at this time that Buford Tucker first went to work for The Grand Casino in Biloxi, Mississippi.

5

"SO, ARE WE LOOKING AT A MURDER here, or do you think it was just a very sad accident," Willie yelled out the question so he could be heard by Jigs who was below deck.

After a few beers, they had left the bar, and now were quickly stowing gear, and making preparations to lock down Jigs' forty-seven-foot Bertram Fishing Cruiser. The boat had to be readied for what could potentially turn out to be an extended absence by its owner.

When Jigs first arrived in the Florida, Keys, he immediately bought the boat. It had been a dream of his for a long time to move to Key West and buy a boat, which was big enough to live on. A large settlement on a terrible personal injury case made that dream possible. It never sat completely right with Jigs that his good fortune was the direct result of another's terrible misfortune. However, he had come to terms with the dilemma by telling himself that someone had to represent the client; and, that he, and his former partner, had represented the boy in the most professional and ethical way possible. This, by the way, was absolutely true.

During the years that Jigs practiced law, his practice was mostly limited to criminal defense work, although he would see all potential clients when they first made contact with the firm. One day an 18 year old young man walked into his office. He had made an appointment, but the purpose of the appointment was vague. This was a common occurrence. Often, people did not discuss their problems in detail over the phone with a secretary. As the meeting progressed, it became clear to Jigs that the young man sitting in front of him had, years earlier, been sexually abused by a Catholic priest. Jigs immediately called in his partner, and they both interviewed the client. Jigs' partner, Moe, took charge of the case on behalf of the partnership. Moe represented all of the personal injury clients that came into the office, and this case would be considered a personal injury or "civil" case.

The case became a huge matter, which put Moe "on the map" in the world of sexual abuse incidents among Catholic priests. Jigs worked with Moe on the case behind the scenes, but it was Moe's case. Moe was often seen on television pontificating on the subject of abuse by the clergy. It was, obviously, a serious subject, which seemed to become an epidemic over the years. When that case, and several other cases which were consolidated together for settlement, finally came to a close, Jigs' share of the legal fees was seven million dollars. Instead of plowing the money back into the firm, like many lawyers would, Jigs saw an opportunity to live his dream. After parting amicably with his partner, who went on to become very famous in his field, Jigs disappeared from the legal profession in the Chicago area.

Jigs moved to Florida, bought his boat, found a permanent slip with electricity, water, and cable TV in Marathon Key, about forty-five minutes drive from Key West. He was quite sure that he had moved into heaven. He lived right on the boat for the first two years… or so. Time did not mean as much in the Keys as it did in the North. Then he convinced Willie to move down to paradise, and they became the "dynamic duo" of problem solving. Most of the problems they were asked to get involved with were legal in nature, but they rarely involved courtrooms. That way, Jigs avoided wearing a suit, which he abhorred.

"Ya know, I'm not sure yet," Jigs was yelling his answer to Willie's question from below deck," but I'm very suspicious about this whole thing. Like I said before, this was a bright girl. I'm not saying that smart people never get into accidents…but… plus, her brother is absolutely sure that there is something fishy. I don't know… I guess that is why we are going there, to check it out, right?" Jigs appeared in the door to the cabin. He was carrying some extra rope and items to secure the boat. The sun shone on his tan face. His khaki shorts and white tee shirt were soiled as a result of climbing around on the boat and carrying gear. He stopped yelling. "Think of it as an excuse to go to La La

Land," he said in a normal voice. "It will be fun." He smiled. Willie simply said, "OK, sounds good to me." They both continued with their chores.

After he had been down in the Keys for a while, and had become an "honorary local" as he was called by the locals, Jigs got wind of an incredible deal on a piece of property right on the Gulf, on Key West. The property had several boat slips, a functioning tavern, and a large Florida-style ranch house, which wrapped around a beautiful outdoor, screened-in swimming pool. It took almost all of the money that Jigs had left, but suddenly, Jigs was an island property owner, and the proprietor of a small, but cozy, tropical tiki bar, complete with parrots. Actually, Willie and Ellie ran the bar. Jigs really just sat in it, and thanked his lucky stars.

"When we get out there, I think you should check out this husband / sheik of hers." Jigs was tying nautical knots.

" I am way ahead of you. I have already made some calls." Willie could find out anything about anyone. He could also find anyone, anywhere; no matter how hard they were trying not to be found. It came from his years as an investigative reporter, even though he never called himself a reporter. He had contacts everywhere; in many agencies, and companies, both inside and outside of government, state, local and federal. Also,

Willie was a master with a computer. He knew all the tricks and shortcuts.

"Oh really, looks like great minds think alike, except when you are thinking those ridiculous, right-wing, Republican thoughts of yours," Jigs said.

" Fuck you, lib," said Willie. Jigs ignored him. They were both still working on securing the boat. The water lapped against the hull, as the big boat rocked gently in its slip. It was a beautiful spot.

"Let's face it, this gal was well liked. Now, nobody can get through life without pissing off someone; but, it is my experience, that when someone is generally well liked, especially as well liked as this girl, one should look to the supposed loved ones for a motive to kill. Generally, casual, or even business, acquaintances do not generate that kind of emotional anger, at least not the kind that causes someone to commit murder. That much anger between strangers is only generated if they are driving in California traffic."

"You're right." Willie ignored the attempt at a joke. "If this was a murder...if she was killed...this whole thing was planned, very well planned. The cops out there don't suspect a thing. They checked out the car... nothing, no cut break lines, no tampering with anything mechanical, no phantom vehicle, nothing. They are absolutely convinced that this was simply an accident."

"Well," Jigs said, " let's get out there and see if we believe them."

6

WHEN NED KAHN ARRIVED BACK in Los Angeles, his wife had been dead for approximately seven hours. As it turned out, Ned was leaving the airport to go to Houston in his sleek private jet at almost the very same instant that Anna was leaving their home to drive into town. Now he was back. The round trip took almost seven hours. Ned had a car take him to the L.A. County Coroner's main office. He could not drive. This office was connected to the County Morgue, which is where Anna's remains were being held pending release to next of kin.

When Ned arrived, he saw Arthur, Anna's brother, sitting in the stark, sparsely furnished, waiting room. The walls were a drab industrial lime green; the lighting was florescent harsh. Arthur looked terrible. This was his only sister, his only sibling.

Arthur had long ago moved to the Los Angeles area, mainly to be near his sis', but also to be near the ocean. He lived in Huntington Beach, in Orange County. He had a beautiful waterfront home in Huntington Harbor. Right at this moment, however, he was thinking that he should have spent more time with his sister. They lived an hour, or so, away from each other, depending on traffic, and they did not see each other enough. He would have given back all his hours on a wind surfboard or skydiving for just one more day with her. These are the agonizing thoughts of the survivors of a deceased loved one.

Ned walked up to Arthur. They hugged. They both fought back tears and spoke in subdued tones.

"What do you know?" Ned asked. "I know nothing. I have been in Houston or on a plane. What do they say happened?"

Arthur began to tell him what he knew about the accident. It was becoming harder for him to speak. He was devastated. "This all happened by Laurel Canyon," his voice was hoarse and scratchy. " This is what is so hard to accept. You know how careful she was. She drove those roads all the time." Arthur turned away. He took a couple of deep breaths. When he turned back to face Ned, his face was determined and fierce. " This was *not* an accident!" He screamed a whisper through his teeth. "My sister would not just drive off of a cliff. Something else happened, I tell you, and I will make it my mission in life to find out what it was!"

Ned stood there looking at his brother-in-law. He was calm. He was tan. He was dressed like he had just walked off of a country club golf course, black polo, black belt, khaki trousers with a razor crease, not so much as a hair out of place. He then said in a level and somewhat authoritative voice, "It was an accident."

It was at that moment, that Arthur became confused. Did he suspect his own brother-in-law, his sister's own husband, of orchestrating the death of his dear Anna? He had no basis for this suspicion, no reason. It was in his gut. Why would he say that? With those four words...it was like lightning striking! Arthur was thinking to himself, not letting on to his feelings. "Didn't Ned just ask him what he knew? Didn't he say he knew nothing? How could he be so calm and self-assured? Why wasn't he falling apart? Why was he so quick to accept that it was an accident that killed her? Why wasn't he more upset? It was his wife, for Christ's sake. Why did he just say...it was an accident? How would he know that? He just got off the goddamn plane! Arthur knew Ned couldn't have killed her. He was not even in town when it happened. But, this guy had more money than God. He could buy *anything*!"

Then he stopped. He looked at Ned. "What was he thinking? Was he going crazy? Ned and Anna had always loved each other. Why would he do it? Why?" Arthur began to doubt his own theory of moments ago. He could not think straight. He decided to bring in a dispassionate, unbiased professional to look into the matter. He then decided to call Jigs Donahue. Jigs had a reputation for getting to the bottom of things. He solved unsolvable problems. "Plus," he thought, " I will tell him of my suspicions about Ned. I am not crazy, but I will let someone with a dispassionate eye sort this out."

"Yes, you are probably right," Arthur finally said out loud. "It is just so hard to accept. The whole thing is just too much."

"I will have someone investigate this further, if it makes you feel better…" Ned was just talking to talk. He was trying to console Arthur. "…but the police seem pretty sure…"

Both men started to walk towards the morgue, where they would have to perform the hideous task of official identification of the body. It was a formality. This was hell on earth.

7

BUFORD TUCKER TRAINED for four weeks to become a dealer at the Grand Casino in Biloxi, Mississippi. The flashy, fast-paced world of casino gambling was very foreign to him. He was basically a country type, a good ol' boy, and proud of it. However, he excelled in his class, as usual. The standard course, provided by the casino to ready its employees to hit the casino floor, taught students to "deal" all the games offered by the casino. This included the game of roulette, which did not use cards, but was still considered dealing. Roulette happened to be the game he was assigned to on his first solo day at the tables. Buford was nervous, but he felt ready. It was like game day back in his football days.

He had heard numerous stories about the amazing excitement and the incredible exhilaration that occurred at the gaming tables. However, he had never actually seen anyone gamble, at least not for real money. He had trained extensively, but not with money. They used chips and no one actually won or lost anything Plus, Buford was from the Deep South, the "buckle of the bible belt." Nobody gambled in his world. When he was on active duty, and in Kuwait, there were guys that played cards,

and "craps", but he didn't... not ever, and he didn't stay around
to watch them.

So, this was a new experience for Buford. He had been
spinning the roulette wheel for about an hour on his first day,
when a big, lug Yankee type, bellied up to his table. "This guy is
from central casting," Buford thought. He was wearing an ill-
fitting camel sport jacket that strained at the seams and jeans that
did the same. The guy was chewing on an unlit cigar and
sweating. He had the purple veins on his big wide-set nose that
resulted from years of drinking alcohol. He threw five one
hundred dollar bills at Buford, and mumbled, "Green and red."
He seemed pretty drunk.

Buford gave him 12 green chips, three hundred dollars,
and 40 red chips, two hundred dollars. Then the guy started
placing chips on numbers. He put all the chips out on the table
on various numbers, including double zero. Buford could not
believe that this man had just bet five hundred dollars on one
spin of the roulette wheel. It was the first time he had seen
anything like this. Buford spun the wheel. It landed on number
25. Sitting on number 25 was a single green chip. The Yankee
beamed. He simply said, almost under has breath, with a
clenched fist, "yes!" It was Buford's duty to pay the player eight
hundred and seventy five dollars. He mumbled through his cigar,
"All green." Buford pushed 35 green chips across the table, and
left the guy's original bet in place. "That was over eight hundred

dollars." Buford thought. He was amazed at how easy it was to win so much.

The Yankee then calmly put all the green chips on various random numbers. In some cases he put two or three or four green chips on a single number. People were starting to notice that the table was covered with green chips. Other people were playing their standard one-dollar chips, so the green chips stood out. More people stopped to watch. Buford said, "No more bets," as he was trained to do. He couldn't believe what he was seeing. Everyone was quiet. He spun the roulette wheel. When the wheel stopped on double zero, and everybody watching saw four green chips piled up on that number, the crowd erupted. More people gathered around the table. The Yankee just kept beaming, and he just kept winning. The crowd stayed and grew in size. Everyone cheered at the appropriate times. The Yankee was winning thousands of dollars. Thousands. This was fun to watch. Many people in the crowd bet on the same numbers as the Yankee by piling their chips on top of his, so they were winning too. Buford could feel his own excitement growing. Tiny beads of sweat were forming on his forehead. "I hope they can't see this," he thought. He wiped his brow. He was enjoying this more than he thought he should.

When the Yankee decided that he had had enough of an incredible lucky streak, it was four hours later. He looked at his watch and mumbled, "Color me up. Time to quit while I'm ahead." Buford was disappointed that the session was over. He had become part of the experience. The Yankee walked away from the table with more money than Buford expected to make in that entire *year*. Buford never forgot that experience. It had made his heart dance, just watching.

8

JIGS AND WILLIE DROVE TO FT LAUDERDALE. They could have flown, but they both still loved driving through the Keys, across the bridges, seeing the panoramic views of the water and the islands. It's such a beautiful drive.

They took a Jet Blue flight direct from Ft. Lauderdale to Long Beach. On Jet Blue, each passenger has his or her own personal TV. Jigs watched MSNBC. Willie watched FOX NEWS. They argued politics all the way to California. Everyone within earshot was bored to tears.

When they arrived in Long Beach, Arthur Buckingham was there to meet them. He walked up to them in the little airport and started making plans. He was agitated and spoke fast. He shook hands with both men and while doing so he said, "You'll stay at my house. It is 15 or 20 minutes from here, depending on traffic, great place, right on the water. I have extra cars, even a limo, I have great steaks, food, and booze if you want it, girls… yes girls, anything you want. There is a swimming pool, a pool table, boats, HDTV, anything, I swear to god. How do we handle your fee; do I pay you now? You guys have to help me. I know that there is something wrong about this whole thing…"

"Slow down," said Willie, "slow down, man..." Willie put his hands on each of Arthur's shoulders and held him at arms length. He looked Arthur straight in the eye. "Did you say you had booze?"

That broke the ice. They had not seen each other in years, but that got Arthur laughing. It seemed that no time had passed. These guys were never best friends, but they had shared some good times. They walked toward Arthur's black Cadillac Escalade. They had reverted to small talk and laughter. When they reached the car, Jigs said, " Oh wow, gas guzzler, huh?"

"Shut the fuck up, liberal," Willie said.

Huntington Beach is Southern California, incarnate. They drove past perfectly manicured lawns, down palm tree lined streets then, as promised, 17 minutes later, they arrived at a gorgeous sprawling ranch on a corner lot. What was extra nice about his place was that it wasn't on the corner of two streets. It was at the corner of two waterways. The house had water on two sides with freshly painted blue docks running the length of both. Several boats and watercraft of different sizes and types were tied up along the docks. It was Jigs' kind of place. " I guess people are still putting plenty of sugar in their coffee," Jigs said. " Nice digs."

The place was as nice inside as it was outside. When they all had beers in hand, they retired to the recreation room. It had a pool table with turquoise blue felt, that was the color of a Caribbean sea in the shallows, and lots of deep dark cherry wood everywhere. There was a huge 60-inch HDTV on one wall. They each fell into their own glove soft, deep burgundy leather chair. " Yeah...I guess we can hang out here while we are in town," Willie said, between gulps of cold beer.

" Just help me figure out what happened to my sister, and I'll deed the place to you." Arthur was convinced that something untoward had occurred.

"I will hold you to that," Willie was kidding but he wished he wasn't.

"I am loosing my mind... I suspect everyone. You guys have no idea. I loved my sister. Plus, my parents...I don't know if my Dad is going to survive this. He is pretty old. They both have broken hearts. Maybe it was an accident...I don't know." Arthur was obviously in terrible pain.

" How was her marriage?" Jigs was being blunt.

"Why do you ask?" Arthur sat up straight. He was like a dog that was responding to one of those silent whistles. This question triggered something in him that was perceptible by both of the other two men. "Do you guys think it was ...do you think Ned had something to do with this? Because, I have to say...I hate to admit it, but...Ned is just not acting the way I would expect him to."

Jigs took a very measured tone. "First, let's not jump to conclusions. Ned has never done anything to make me believe that he is a murderer. I did not know him that well, but it always seemed that he and your sister were very much in love. Let's face it, he left his country, where he was a goddamn prince I might add, became a citizen, all of that, for, or because of, your sister. However, if this was not an accident, then someone has expended a great deal of time, effort and money to make it look that it was one. They have successfully, and completely, fooled the police. This takes lots of planning and lots of cash. Now call me crazy, but I don't think that all of that occurred because she pissed off some member of the American Cancer Society. It is usually someone close to the victim that has a motive, so we cannot rule Ned out. You are not crazy, Arthur. The bottom line is this: When we find out why she was killed, if she was, we will know who did it. Then we will be able to figure out how it was done."

9

BUFORD TUCKER HAD BEEN DEALING at the Grand
Casino Biloxi for approximately six months when, for the first
time in his life, he gambled. He did not come to the decision to
do so lightly. In fact, he agonized endlessly over it. Truth be
known, he knew he was not supposed to do it. The act of
gambling ran contrary to his upbringing, to his religion, and to
his personal moral value system. However, he told himself that
he was just going to try it. He was not going to become a
"gambler." It was part of his job to know what it felt like on the
other side of the table. He had learned so much about gaming
that it wouldn't really be gambling. Most people that gambled
did not know how. He had become a professional. The excuses,
justifications, rationalizations and lies he told himself had
already begun to flow. Plus, he had never forgotten the
experience he had on his first night on the casino floor. That
Yankee won thousands. His family could really use that kind of
money. After all, he was the luckiest person he new. Why
shouldn't he try it?

It was grounds for dismissal for an employee of the
Grand Casino to be found gambling at the Grand Casino. This
was common within the gaming industry. Employees were often

barred from gambling at their own casinos. It was even true in some Las Vegas casinos. This rule was unnecessary as it applied to Buford. He would have been so embarrassed to be seen gambling, no one had to tell him not to do it where he worked. In fact, he would not even gamble in the same town, or area, for that matter. He traveled over 150 miles to Vicksburg, Mississippi. A new Harrah's Riverboat Casino had opened there, and Buford decided to go there so nobody he knew would see him.

When he arrived in Vicksburg, he went straight to the riverboat. He had $200.00 in his pocket. He told himself that he would not gamble with more, no ATMs or credit cards. He parked his car in the small, crowded parking lot, and walked towards the casino. It seemed like every square inch of the riverboat was covered with flashing colored lights. This place made the best decorated home he had ever seen at Christmas look paltry. His heart was racing. He could not believe or explain the feelings he was experiencing. It was a combination of guilt and exhilaration. He felt like he was about to rob a bank, or some such thing. It was incredible to him. This was a new experience. He liked it!

Buford could play any game in the casino. At least, he knew how. In fact, he thought of himself as an expert at all casino games. After all, he was a dealer; he new how the casino worked behind the scenes. However, he was so nervous that he just got some change, some tokens for the slot machines. He chose one-dollar tokens, and walked up to a dollar machine.

He could feel his heart in his mouth. He put three dollars in the slot. That was the maximum bet on that machine. He knew to always place the maximum bet. It increased your odds of winning. He pushed the button to spin the tumblers. The machine "sang" a very pleasant song. The tumblers stopped. Cherries. 7. 7. Nothing. He repeated the ritual. 7. Bar. 7. Nothing. Three more dollars. Bar! Bar! Bar!! Fifteen dollars fell into the tray at the bottom of the machine. He won! Already! The sounds were exciting. They were the same sounds he heard incessantly while he worked, which usually annoyed him, but they sounded somehow different now. He began to calm down. It was an amazing feeling.

He continued to drop coins three at a time into the slot. Sometimes he won small amounts, and coins clattered into the tray below. Other times the tumblers rolled round and round and ended with a silent click. "Maybe I should move to a blackjack table," he thought. He then dropped three more dollars in the slot. 7! 7! 7!! The machine started making a loud alert sound. DIT! DIT! DIT! DIT! DIT! DIT! DIT! DIT! Also, music was playing, loud congratulatory music. He looked around. His heart was really pounding now! "Oh my God." Buford stood back from the machine and just watched. Money was falling out and into the tray like crazy! Lights were flashing. He could not believe how he felt. A beautiful girl, wearing very few clothes, approached him. "Congratulations!" She said this right into his ear, so she could be heard over the din. He felt her breath in his ear.

Buford was no longer nervous. He was very excited, but not nervous. Everything was happening at warp speed. The pretty girl was counting *ten* one hundred dollar bills into his hand. She was explaining what had happened,   " ...You won the jackpot. It is $1199.00. That is so you don't have to report it...to the IRS. You must report amounts in excess of $1200.00. Less than $1200.00 is all yours. There is $199.00 in the tray..." She was leaning close, speaking right into his ear again. He could feel her breasts touching his arm, her breath in his ear and on his neck again. "Play that off," she said. She meant that he should play one dollar to roll the tumblers and clear the machine. When he did that, the noise stopped. He reached into the tray and grabbed a handful of tokens. He gave them to the girl. He did it again, and then once more. Then he said, "Thank you." She walked away, shaking her tail feathers.

Buford cashed in the rest of his tokens. He had never felt anything like the way he felt at that moment. He had $1112.00 in his pocket, plus $180.00 that he had not spent of his original stake. He all but ran out of the casino. He got in his car and drove away from Vicksburg as fast as he could without being arrested. He felt like he was making his get-a-way. He never went back to Vicksburg again in his life

10

After several beers, this reunited group of old friends had lapsed into reminiscing about times past and, inevitably, ultimately, reminiscing about Anna. Although she had not been gone long, it was time to begin to honor her memory, and what better way for three mooks to do that... than to make fun of her failings. They had been doing this for upwards of an hour. Telling funny stories about this wonderful gal, visiting times past. This was cathartic for Arthur, whom had been in a state of depression. He was telling a particular story about when they were kids.

"...And, when we were young, we were up at our cottage in Michigan most of every summer. Once, when she was first learning to water ski, maybe she was 9 or 10, she was up on two skies, and going along, not that steady though, and...she just started doing the splits...not on purpose...and her legs were spread so wide that she got a sprain and had to stay in bed for days after, but, what was funny, was that my Dad was filming this. Now, this has become a classic family story, because, she knew she was being filmed, and all she could think of at the time that she was being split in two... was to keep screaming, 'turn off the camera...turn off the camera'. Now, had she just let go of the rope…it would have been over, but she didn't want to be filmed falling. So, instead, she was filmed shooting the biggest beaver ever seen by man on earth. If she had been older, this film would have qualified as pornography. It was hilarious. She never lived that one down; because it was her vanity…her pride…she did not want to fall down on camera." Arthur had a look of both pride in his sister and sadness at her passing at the same time.

"Well," Jigs was speaking, " when we were doing our thing, whatever that was… I always thought I was…like…saving Ned's place…but anyway…when we spoke of Ned's country, or, if anyone mentioned his country, when we would hear it mentioned on the news or something, she would get all high and mighty if a person would mispronounce Iran. People always do, even news broadcasters, they still do it all the time. She would always say… 'It's not " eye raann"…it is "ear ron"… is that so hard? No wonder these people get angry with Americans. How would they like it if people pronounced the United States as the " you knitted stats," all the time? People here would get mad, right? How do you think they feel?'… The funny thing is…I'm sure she was right about that, and, that is probably still true today. People from Iran, and Iraq, for that matter, probably do hate it when Americans constantly mispronounce the name of their country."

That got Willie started. "Oh, are you worried about the feelings of the EYE RAANNIANS or the EYE RACKYS? Is this more left wing drivel from you, liberal?"

"Hey," Arthur asked, "do you guys really mean it when you get on each other for being liberal or conservative? Because, sometimes it sounds like you do."

"Of course not," Jigs said. " He is my oldest and dearest friend. I love the guy, even if he is a right wing asshole."

"Yeah…fuck off lib," Willie said.

"OK, enough of this blather," Arthur said. "How do we figure this out? How do we solve this thing? Was my sister killed? If so, who did it?

"Well," Jigs said, "do we know where she was going that night…and why she was going there, especially in that weather?"

"Yes…yes we do. She was going to meet a new client," Arthur said with authority. "I have her appointment book. I had a key to their house, and I went there after I got the news. I was the first person called, because Ned was in route to Houston, and, after I talked to the police, I just went there, I am not sure why… I just did."

"OK, sounds like you had good instincts," Willie was interested. "Who was she meeting? Do we know that? Do we know anything about this person?"

"Well," Arthur said, " his name was Jonathon F. Butcher, from Sherman Oaks. She was meeting him at the Pig'n Whistle, on Hollywood Blvd., and I cannot find out anything about the guy. It is like he disappeared."

"Don't worry about that," Jigs said. "Old Willie here can find anyone, anywhere. He can find out anything about anybody. He is uncanny. Don't do anything you don't want the world to know about, because, if he wants to, he will find out about it. Then the right wing red neck will tell everyone."

Arthur started laughing. "Do you guys ever stop, with the barbs?"

"Hell no," said Jigs with dangerous smile. "He deserves it. Plus, I keep thinking there is still hope for him."

" Let's take showers, and you guys can unpack. Then we will go out for dinner or something?" Arthur was stating what was really a question. " I will show you your rooms."

"Sounds great," said Jigs.

"I need to be in front of a computer for a few minutes," said Willie. "Do you have one or should I set up my lap top?"

"There is one in your room, man, said Arthur. " We don't fuck around here. I told you, anything you want, all the comforts of home. What shape and color do you want your girl to be, by the way?" He chuckled.

"Let's stick with the computer...and the booze...for now," Willie said. The three of them got up and started walking through the house. It was really a beautiful house.

11

BUFORD HAD NOT GAMBLED in a casino for over three years after the night he went to Vicksburg. The way he felt when he gambled, and the way he felt after he gambled, frightened him. The experience took him from abject guilt to total and spectacular euphoria and back again several times during the night. He was smart enough to recognize a potential problem. "That cannot be good for me in the long run," he reasoned. Not only did he avoid gambling, he donated the money he won in Vicksburg to his church. He also put in for a transfer off the casino floor to some other area of the casino. This resulted in, what turned out to be, a most fortunate and lucrative career move.

Because Buford had a lifelong immaculate record, together with recommendations from his former floor boss at the casino, and his commander in the Coast Guard Reserve, and because of his general reputation and standing in the community, he was offered a significant promotion into the front offices at the casino. He became a trusted member of management, was in charge of important aspects of casino operations, including the counting and movement of cash money within and outside of the actual casino building. Needless to say, this new position carried with it a great deal of responsibility, and a very significant increase in salary. Once again, Buford had excelled as he always did.

This new job situation allowed Buford to be in a position to propose marriage to his long time sweetheart, Juney. The couple had a wonderful wedding, a great Hawaiian honeymoon on Maui and Kauai, and they were soon the proud parents of a little boy and a little girl. Life was good for Buford Tucker.

Chief Petty Officer Tucker was also enjoying similar success in his military career. Buford was promoted at a rate faster than what would be expected for a Reservist, and he continued to pull exciting, coveted types of duty. He was meeting and associating with all the right people, and was continuing to be seen as a rising star, at least to the extent he could as a member of the Reserves. Life was very good for Buford Tucker.

He even was able to further supplement his income with sums he won from his various football pools, fantasy football leagues, and football betting schemes. You see...Buford loved football. Buford followed football all his life. Buford played football in high school. Buford was a quarterback. Buford understood football. Therefore, wagering on football was not gambling. Wagering on football was a science, and...Buford...was a football scientist. He was, without a doubt, the best football handicapper he knew, including the published ones and the ones on the Internet. He knew college ball, he knew pro ball, hell, he new high school ball, nationally. So, betting on football was not gambling. It was as simple as that. Plus, everyone he knew placed bets on football. The guys at work did. The guys in his Coast Guard unit did. Everybody did. He may have done it a little more frequently than some, and in amounts that were a little more "exciting", but that was because he was better at it!

So... Buford had resolved what he had rightly recognized as a potential problem, he, very simply, did not gamble. In fact, he was officially and publicly against gambling.

Just to be sure, however, Buford's football betting, which was not gambling, remained a very well kept secret, just in case there was a misunderstanding regarding the issue. Therefore, his betting was limited to the Internet, and to bets placed with a man, a bookmaker, that he referred to as a "fellow sports enthusiast," never in a casino; and, it remained a very private activity. No one else knew about it, not even his wife.

12

Jigs, Willie and Arthur piled into Arthur's Cadillac
SUV, and headed towards Los Angeles, passing some of
California's endless beaches, dotted with surfers and sunbathers.
The sun was low in the western sky, and heading for its nightly
dip into the ocean. It was a beautiful sight.

Inevitably, in Los Angeles, you must get on the freeway
if you want to get anywhere, then when you get on it, you go
nowhere fast. While sitting in traffic on the 405, they discussed
the case.

"It is a long shot, but we should, at least, ask around at
the restaurant where she was headed to that night," Jigs said. "
Maybe someone will remember something. It has only been a
matter of days. It is worth a try."

"OK, we are on our way there right now," said Arthur.
We can go there as easily as anywhere else. That is a good place
to eat. It has been there forever."

"I was checking, online, for a Jonathan F. Butcher from
Sherman Oaks. I found no such person. There was a John F.
Butcher in LA, Silver Lake area; he is a retired lawyer, and some

other Johns this and Jonathans that, but no Jonathan F. anywhere," said Willie. "It was a pretty cursory search, but I don't think I am going to find him, even if I search more thoroughly."

"What does that mean?" asked Arthur. "So what if you don't find him?"

"Well, it probably doesn't mean anything. Probably nothing... Of course, it could mean that it was a fake name. If it was a fake name, it could have been used to get her... your sister, to go to the restaurant, or...more precisely, to go out and drive, in the car, in the rain... Do you get what I'm saying?" Willie was just spit balling. "However, the police checked out the car. Nothing was done to it. The car was not tampered with. They can almost always tell, even after an accident, especially when the car did not burn, and hers did not burn... according to the report. So, let's not jump to conclusions."

"How the fuck do you know all this already? You just got off the damn airplane." Arthur was impressed.

"The Internet, man, the Internet is amazing. Give me a computer, and an hour, or so, and I'll tell you if you have a mole on your ass, or not." Willie was half serious so he didn't laugh. Arthur did though, loud and hard. It was good for him to laugh.

Jigs said through chuckles, "Yeah, Willie, here, is a real hacker. He is a magician with a PC. His politics are crap, but he is invaluable with a computer. "

"Fuck you, hippie...Hey! There's John F. Butcher's house!" Willie was pointing. He was only kidding. They were passing a sign that indicated an exit for Silver Lake. They were cruising on the 101, not as much traffic as there usually was. He turned a bit more serious. "I would like to get a look at that car, her wrecked car. Even if I can't do so right away, it must be preserved, somehow, without freaking out Mr. Khan. Can we get that done?"

" I will figure out a way," said Arthur. "Whatever you guys need."

When they arrived at the Pig n' Whistle, they pulled up to the valet to have the car parked. They all got out. Jigs was holding a $50 dollar bill in his hand, very obviously. He approached the valet kid. The "kid" was wearing a red jacket. "I guess they have to wear uniforms so you don't give your keys to just anyone walking by, but it must be hard for these guys. He was about 20 years old, a tough age to be wearing a bright red uniform jacket, not exactly a chick magnet," Willie observed.

"Were you working here two nights ago?" Jigs asked.

"Umm uh yes, yes I was." The kid was looking at Jigs' hand, holding the $50.

"Was it really busy that night?" Jigs was setting the stage. He was waving the $50 around a bit.

"Not real busy," the kid said.

"Are you going to be here for an hour or so?" At this point, Jigs was just teasing the poor kid.

The valet said he was working until closing. Jigs put the $50 dollar bill in the kid's hand. While he did that, he grasped the kid's hand and he explained in detail that they were trying to determine if a particular person had been at the restaurant on that evening, two nights ago.

"Think about everyone that you can remember on that night, would you? We will be out here after dinner. We may be able to tell you more by then. We are going to talk to people inside. Will you try to help us out?" Jigs let go of the kid's hand.

"I have a good memory," the kid said, as he lifted the hand that was holding the $50 dollar bill in the air and smiled. "I will do anything I can to help."

The three men were seated. Jigs asked the hostess if she would stop by their table, when she had time. She said she would. The place was like an Old English Pub. It was opened in

1927, lots of wood and brass with a Tudor look. It is a bit of a landmark in Hollywood. Sometimes they have live entertainment, but not today. This did not disappoint Jigs; he was there for information, not a show.

"So, what are we doing here?" Arthur asked over his menu.

"Well, we are hoping for a break. Please, let me preface my entire comment here, with a reminder: The police found nothing suspicious about the car. Having said that, if a pro were to 'arrange' for an accident, he would be sure to cover his tracks by following through with this meeting; because, if the plan failed, for example: if the 'mark'... in this case Anna... took the wrong car, or, somehow got a ride from an unexpected visitor, she could be tipped off if no one were here to meet her. That might alert her to a plot against her. She might take extra precautions for her protection, thereby making it harder, or even impossible, to succeed against her on a second or future attempt." Jigs started to smile. "Of coarse, it may be...that I just always wanted to eat here, and have someone else pay for it..." There was the smallest of chuckles from the others.

"Actually, if we came here and found true evidence that Jonathan F. Butcher was here waiting for her that night, we would then know that the meeting was not a ruse. Now, are those enough reasons for you?"

"OK, OK, I got it. You guys have done this before," Arthur said in retreat.

At that moment, the hostess approached them. "Did you gentleman want something?" she asked.

"Yes, thank you for taking your time...can you sit down? Jigs queried.

"No thanks, I better not. They don't like that here. But, what's up? I have a minute." The girl seemed genuinely interested. Perhaps, she had spoken to the $50 dollar valet. She was twirling her dishwater blonde hair with a finger, and standing with that hip cocked out like they do.

"We believe that two nights ago... there might have been a man in here waiting for another party that never showed up. Do you remember anyone like that?" Jigs had casually reached into his pocket while he was talking and pulled out his folded bills. He was simply holding them in his hand. It was not that obvious of a move; but Blondie saw it. She immediately started laughing.

"Oh, you must mean George Castanza." She was seriously giggling and looking at one of the waitresses.

"I'm sorry...George Castanza?" Her laughing was infectious. Now Jigs was laughing.

"Yeah, a guy comes in that night, and says he is waiting for someone else, but he would like a table. He orders coffee. Just coffee. He had a bit of an accent. I don't know what kind. I'm not sure. Anyway, after he sits for almost an hour, we started to make fun of him, quietly, of course, me and Kathy, my friend, over there. We were guessing that he had been stood up for a date. But, the funny thing was…he looked just like George Castanza, from Seinfeld, without the glasses. He was short, stout, chunky, and bald, a fireplug. We were saying… like…no wonder she stood him up. We thought the girl probably looked in the door, saw him, and took off." She was really laughing now. "He was not, what you would call, good looking. So, then he waits ten or fifteen minutes longer. Then he leaves. Bad tipper. Took up a table for all that time…asshole." She whispered the last word.

"Did he pay with a credit card?" Jigs was being hopeful, not thinking of the fact that he only had coffee.

"Heck no." Blondie looked at Jigs like he was nuts. "He just had coffee, I said."

"Of course, I forgot," Jigs apologized.

They each ordered burgers and beer. At this point they just wanted to eat something quickly and go.

Before they left the restaurant, Blondie got her $50 dollar bill. They all walked out, and stopped by the valet.

"Do you remember a guy from that night that looked like George Castanza, from Seinfeld?"

"Oh sure, the girls were talking about that guy. I remember that guy." The kid seemed glad that he might be able to help.

"Do you remember his car?" Jigs was fishing.

"Sure," said the kid. "It wasn't anything special, just a rental. I think it was a Buick Century, you know, midsize, white, plain..."

Jigs did not hear anything after "rental." "Are you positive it was a rental?" He wanted to be sure.

"Yeah, the keys were from Hertz. It had a decal on the bumper. It was a rental. Why, does that help you?" The kid seemed honestly hopeful that it did.

"Yes, it might, my car parking young friend. It just might. Thanks. Thanks a lot."

They headed east on Hollywood Blvd. the short distance to the 101. They looked at each other, each of them thinking the same thing. Why would a guy from Sherman Oaks be driving a rental car? They were all quite convinced that there was no Jonathan F. Butcher. It was becoming apparent to each of them that their thoughts on this matter were no longer mere suspicion or speculation. They all were beginning to believe that Arthur's gut was correct and that Anna was, in fact, murdered. But…Who? Why? How?

13

ON SEPTEMBER 12, 2001, THE WORLD was in shock. People were confused. People were dumfounded. People were angry. The list of responses and emotions was endless. Most people did not know what to think, what to do, how to respond or how to act. There were idiots that worked in high-rise buildings that were buying personal parachutes so they could jump out of their office window, in case there was a next time. That was not true of Buford Tucker, however. He knew how to act. Buford had been on the telephone with every high-ranking military contact he knew or could think of. He was determined and single minded. He had enjoyed the benefits of this great country. He had a terrific, high paying career, a beautiful devoted wife and a loving family. Therefore, he also had a duty. He knew what he had to do, and he was in the process of getting it done. In each conversation that he had, with each high-ranking officer to whom he spoke; he said the same thing. "How can I serve?"

All branches of the military were scrambling to respond to the horrendous and unprovoked attack on our homeland. Special units were being formed. Special duties were being assigned to the best of our military men and women. Buford wanted one of those positions. He wanted to do his part, and he thought himself qualified to help at high levels. The military agreed. Buford had always excelled at any task that had been given to him to perform. A Reserve Admiral that he had worked for and come to know and become friends with, recommended him for a position with the NSA, the National Security Agency. This would mean moving his family to Maryland, but that was the least he could do for his country, he thought. He would do anything that was asked of him. He would have gone overseas if asked. However, this recommendation and placement would allow him to stay with his family. It was a great opportunity. His wife agreed. She was of the same mind as her husband.

Buford had never lived anywhere except the gulf coast of Mississippi. He had served in Kuwait, but that did not count. Admittedly, it would be a sacrifice leaving his present job, and uprooting his family. However, he felt that he had no choice. That was how he was raised, when your country needed you, you must serve.

He and his family acclimated quickly to the area surrounding our nation's capital. Many government employees and officials, including a few members of Congress, lived in their neighborhood, so they were meeting interesting friends. Their kids were in good schools, and beginning to enjoy their life as children of a high-ranking government official. They were proud of their father. They did not know exactly what their daddy did, but they knew it was important.

He was accepted into the secret cliques, of the secret groups, within his secret agency. He immediately learned who the "right" people were and what the "right" activities were. He began learning as many foreign languages as he could, mostly Middle Eastern, particularly Farsi, because this was considered one of the "right" things to do. "After all, who had attacked us?" This would enhance his career opportunities, so he immersed himself in his studies of Middle Eastern language and culture. He was excelling in his new career in much the same manner as he had always excelled in all his life's endeavors.

14

THREE DAYS BEFORE ANNA DIED, Thomas Populous arrived on a flight that landed at LAX International Airport from Athens, Greece. He took a taxi to an offsite car rental agency that specialized in luxury automobile rentals. He had already reserved a particular type of car over the Internet. He drove off the lot in a bright red, brand new SL 600 Mercedes Benz roadster. It had only six thousand miles on it. He then proceeded to an area of town that was primarily zoned for small industrial buildings. He had paid, in advance, for six months rent on a vacant garage with attached offices. He had also made arrangements for this over the Internet. He had explained that he intended to do some light automotive repair in the leased space. The agent, with whom he had email correspondence, assured him that the place would be perfect for that purpose; in fact, the previous tenant had used the place for much the same type of business.

He stopped by an In n Out Burger and ordered two burgers, fries and a chocolate shake, which he always did whenever he was in Los Angeles. He just loved In n Out Burgers.

He had checked a bag when he flew, and inside the bag was a small tool set. When he arrived at his new office space and garage, he pulled the rented car into the garage. Even before he ate his food he had disassembled most of the ductwork around the blower motor for the heating system of the car. He was sitting on the front fender of the beautiful automobile examining the heating system, while he ate his burgers. Hey, it wasn't his car.

Thomas was not an auto mechanic. He knew a lot about cars, but he was not an auto mechanic.

When Thomas was at the University of Chicago, where he was attending on an academic scholarship, his name was Christopher Bloom. He has had many names since that time. He, like everyone else, took several liberal arts, general studies courses. It was during the study of philosophy, in a lower level philosophy course, that he solved, for himself, a dilemma, which would lead to his chosen career in later life.

Thomas asked himself: "If all of the great religions of the world, together with almost all accepted philosophic thought, whether religious or not, had as their primary tenant that, man, killing another man, was abhorrent and ran contrary to all civilized behavior, further, if God had given to Moses Ten Commandments, and those Ten Commandments were the ultimate laws for all mankind, and paramount among those laws

was the law: Thou shalt not kill. Then, how do we, the members
of what is supposed to be a civilized Christian society, explain
war, soldiers, paid military assassins, swat teams, paid prison
executioners, the death penalty, abortion and a host of other
"exceptions" to this, the ultimate law?" To Thomas, there were
no valid explanations and no valid exceptions. None. Not one.

The Commandment was not stated; "Thou shalt not
kill... unless... society thinks there is a good reason to kill". It
was clear and unequivocal. It said, *"Thou shalt not kill."* Period.
Not ever. These Commandments were not conditional. It does
not say... "Thou shalt not commit adultery...unless she is really
cute and sexy." It is not acceptable to covet your neighbor's
goods because these particular goods are really cool and you
really, really want them. The rules, again, are clear and
unequivocal. If you steal, you sin. If you covet, you sin. If you
commit adultery, you sin. There are no special exceptions or
dispensations for these commandments. Why would God make
exceptions to his most important commandment? The capricious
and arbitrary application of what were taught as, and what were
supposed to be immutable laws, made no sense to him. Thomas
saw these inconsistencies in religious and philosophic thought as
unexplained and unacceptable. This, to him, was man's hand at
work... not God's. No God would be that silly and inconsistent.
Only man would be that way.

At that young age, during his college years, Thomas formulated a philosophy of life of his own. It was very simple. Man, not God, had made up all of these rules and laws that he, Thomas, was expected to live by. However, man routinely altered, amended or placed conditions on these rules to suit the circumstances or, to suit what was thought to be necessities. Therefore, it was quite acceptable for him, as a man, to create his own rules, to suit his circumstances and necessities, as man, and mankind, had done throughout time. After coming to this revelation, Thomas decided, without personal moral contradiction, to pursue an incessant and sick dream of his. Who knows what causes a person to choose a particular course in life? For whatever reason, Thomas, or Chris, had always dreamed of one thing. Maybe he had seen too many spy movies in his life. Maybe he was simply miswired at the factory, like a serial killer or a child molester. No explanation was forthcoming, nor was one needed. Thomas had made his decision. He decided to become a contract killer, to offer murder for hire. He left school to pursue his chosen path. Thomas was smart; some would call him a genius. He excelled in his "craft;" and his reputation grew. Over the years, he had become, indisputably, without question, the very best in his field. Sadly, he had no shortage of "clients." He catered to the obscenely wealthy. It seemed that there was always someone among that class was looking to have someone else in their class "have an accident." Lots of business partners died "accidentally," as well as scads of spouses, uncles, old great aunts and various other rich relatives. Huge sums of money will invariably motivate people to do their worst. It has always been this way; and it will always be that way.

15

IT WAS BECOMING INCREASINGLY real to Jigs' mind that his once upon a time, erstwhile girlfriend, had been methodically, carefully, maliciously and, probably, professionally murdered. All of the early indications pointed in that direction, at least if you were naturally suspicious of the human animal like Jigs was. He had scene life from a different angle than most. He had scene its underbelly where nefarious plots are common. Maybe it was not crystal clear, maybe this guy in the rental car, the George Castanza guy, was waiting for someone else, who failed to show up, at the very same restaurant, at the exact same time as the planned meeting that Anna had, but probably not. It actually seemed like they may have gotten a break.

"What is the single most common reason for premeditated murder?" Jigs was thinking. There is only one answer to that question. Then he turned to Arthur and asked, "I know that Anna and Ned were pretty darn rich, but do you have some idea of just how darn rich we would be talking about?"

Arthur let out a laugh. " Ha! My sister and her husband have, uh, had, a net worth well in excess of a billion dollars.

That's billion with a "B". Well, Ned still does." A tinge of sadness entered his voice, then left it. "He was into everything, mostly building skyscrapers, but lots of other things too. Plus, Anna was actually making plenty, as well; and she was the savvy investor, between the two of them. Also, she inherited a great deal of money when our grandfather died. We both did. It all started as family money, from Iran, when they were first together in college; but Ned has been here in the U.S. for over twenty years. He became a citizen right after they were married, and Anna has added a lot of her own, so it is a good old fashioned American fortune."

"I hate to ask this, but was there any kind of pre-nup or anything like that?" Actually, Jigs was asking the obvious.

"Hell no. They were a team. They were lovebirds, more than most, I would say. They seemed to be the perfect couple. So, I believe the answer is no. Now, of course, who knows what goes on between married people? That's why I am not married..."

"Hear, Hear," the other two men said in unison. There was a knowing smile exchanged between them all. They all maintained that they greatly enjoyed the single life.

"...But, my sister and I were close, very close; she was my only family out here, my only sister anywhere, so, I think she would have told me." Arthur seemed very sure of his point of view in this regard.

They had arrived back at Arthur's home. Everyone decided to hit the hay early. That way they could get an early start in the morning. Soon, the house was dark, all except Willie's room. Willie was bent over the computer in the light of a single lamp, clacking away.

16

BUFORD TUCKER HAD FOUND HIS niche. Either the job at the NSA was made for Buford; or Buford was made for the job, it didn't matter. He loved being in on top-secret information and activities. He routinely had been given trusted assignments and projects, while the agency searched for the perfect permanent position that would match his skill set, together with the needs of the agency and his government. This position came into existence shortly after he joined the team.

Buford had studied more and worked harder on his tasks at the agency than he had ever done at any time before in his life. As a result of his efforts, he soon was, writing and speaking the language of Farsi fluently. Well, almost fluently. When he spoke it, he did so with a southern accent, which was hilarious, but he understood the language and that was what was important.

Shortly after taking office, and there is evidence that indicates, prior to the attacks on 9/11, President George W. Bush, together with members of his administration, devised a secret program, whereby certain types of surveillance techniques were authorized on specific telephone conversations, email communications, and other wireless correspondence sent, or engaged in, by both American citizens and persons who were not American citizens, within and out side of the United States of America. The surveillance in question was authorized to be conducted by the National Security Agency without having first procured a warrant from a special court, known as the FISA court, (Federal Intelligence Surveillance Act) in contravention to previous practice and, some would argue, existing law. This program was so secret; its existence was, at first, withheld from all, even the members of Congress. This program was right up Buford Tucker's alley. It suited him perfectly. The agency agreed with this sentiment, and assigned him to the program. So, Buford Tucker, and the perfect position for Buford Tucker, were matched. Buford felt honored and proud.

The program is reportedly administered in the following manner: First, The administration enlisted the cooperation of the major U. S. telecom corporations. Only one refused to help. The plan was simple. Every telephone conversation or email transmission that is engaged in by anyone... anywhere is now carried through fiber optic cables. If you simply "split off" of one of these cables, every word that is spoken over those cables is diverted to a new source, however all of those words also continue on to their original source as well. It is like when you want to have cable TV on more than one television in the house. The cable guy uses a "splitter" to route the cable signal to another TV. Once the cable guy does this, everything that appears on the first TV, appears on the second TV. Now, if you want to watch something different on the second TV than that which is being watched on the first TV, you have to have another cable box to decode the signal. If you do not use the second cable box, then everything that plays on the first TV will play on the second one.

It is really that simple. Once the splitter is connected to the fiber optic line, every single word that is spoken over that line is diverted and available to being monitored by anyone that has access to that line, which in this case would be the NSA.

Then huge elaborate "data mining" computers monitor communications, whether telephonic, email or otherwise. These mega-computers are programmed to separate and distinguish certain calls or communications, which have predetermined phrases, words or subject matter. The computers also separated calls or communications by their place of origin, or place of destination. This initial stage, results in the monitoring of the correspondence of hundreds of thousands of people, both citizens and non-citizens; however, no human person is actually "listening" to those communications. A computer is "listening" however; and the communications can be retrieved, because they are recorded, if the desire arose to do so.

If certain predetermined words, phrases or subject matter in a communication are identified by the mega-computer, such as "bomb" or "attack", then the communication is "flagged" or isolate by the computer.

At this point the communications are categorized by the mega-computer into predetermined threat levels. They seem to like "threat levels" over there in Washington. If, for example, a particular communication is taking place between the United States and France, and it contains the predetermined trigger words, it might be given a level 2 threat level. However, the same communication taking place between the United States and Great Britain may receive a Level 3 threat classification. It's all classified, as well it should be. One would hate to have to explain the rationale used in determining the levels. Level 2 and Level 3 threat classifications cause a printout to be generated by the mega-computer, which must be reviewed by a live person within twelve hours.

If a particular communication takes place between the United States and a country that has made the "watch list," the members of which change from time to time, a Level 1 threat level is assigned and that communication is "flagged live." It then becomes necessary for a live, human individual to immediately review the communication to determine if subversive or terrorist activities are indicated. It seems that a computer can't do that yet. Go figure. That is where Buford, and hundreds of men and women like Buford, come in. These individuals actually listen to or review the communications that the computer has "flagged." This process results in the review of tens of thousands of communications, most of which are just people chatting with each other. The large group of agents performing these tasks is broken down into teams. Buford became the leader of one of these teams.

Therefore, for most of the eight, or more, work hours in a day, Buford Tucker, and friends, sit with a pair of headphones on his or her respective heads, screening, or listening to, the telephone conversations and reading the emails of thousands and thousands of United States' citizens, all in the name of protecting America.

The national security implications and the top-secret nature of these communications aside, it was pretty mundane work. It was the importance of the work, and the top-secret nature of it, which sustained Buford's interest in his job, that and, sometimes, the content of the conversations to which he became privy. Sometimes, that part of the job was downright fun. For example, once Buford sat and listened to exactly what a woman was planning to do to her loving husband when he got home to her, this without censorship of any kind. She had no idea that someone was listening to her every word. The reason that the computer had "flagged" the call was that it was being placed between the U.S. and Saudi Arabia. The caller was an oil company vice-president who was temporarily stationed in Saudi Arabia; the person being called was his wife, at their home in

Saudi Arabia. The VP had been on an extended business trip back to the States, and his wife missed him. Boy oh Boy, did she ever miss him! The call was, quite simply, X rated. The woman left nothing to the imagination.

There was also the time when Buford got to listen in to some of the specific financial aspects of a huge business deal between a company located here in the U.S. and a company located in Pakistan. Discussions of large sums of money, during calls placed to certain foreign countries, would also cause a communication to be "flagged". Pakistan was one of those countries.

Once, he even got to listen in to a conversation between a very famous, right wing talk show host and his producer, while they spoke about a show they were planning, which was going to be aired later that week about terrorists and terrorism. Anytime anyone talks about "terror" or "terrorism" on a cell phone, Buford, or one of his co-workers hears about it. When the show actually aired, and Buford knew in advance what the guy was going to say on his show, he had a private chuckle.

Often, he would stop after work at one of the area's watering holes with other members of his team. Because all of his co-workers had top-secret clearance, they felt it was permissible to discuss some of the more interesting private conversations that they had become privy to among themselves.

Some of the stories were interesting. Some were just plain funny. They didn't mention names or anything. They were just stories. Besides, any one of them could be listening in on any call. The computer "flagged" or sent the calls randomly. If one team member got up to go to the bathroom, the computer would send the next "flagged" call to the next station. So, one was the same as the next, in their minds.

Once or twice, in the beginning, they learned information that caused a couple of their closest friends to make particular investments, lucrative investments. This activity became more and more commonplace as the team became more comfortable with the job and the incredibly lucrative nature of the information that was rattling around in each of their brains. It was " all in a days work." The longer they did it, the easier it became to talk about, among themselves, and the more fantastic the stories they had to tell. After all, this information would not be considered state secrets. It was nothing more than gossip, people's secrets, the stuff that drives "Inside Edition" and "Access Hollywood." They never spoke of any "top secret" information, no "terrorist plots" or anything like that. The never spoke to any unauthorized persons about the program, or shared any stories. Not even their wives or husbands knew the exact nature of their job. That was clearly not permitted, and they patted themselves on the back for keeping that rule sacred. But, some of the gossip was irresistible.

After the team had been together for over a year, the members had all become close friends. They had truly become a "team" in the best sense of that word. They could rely on one another. They were close knit and a bit cliquish. They made their meetings at the bar on Fridays after work a regular ritual. They called these get-togethers "Choir Practice." The name was borrowed from a book, "The Choir Boys", which was about a team of tough city cops.

At the bar, they could let their hair down a little, after the long week of being at what was a bit of a stuffy job. Lets face it; the NSA was not exactly known for its relaxed atmosphere. Much to the contrary, it was the kind of place that took itself a little too seriously, if anything. That was probably for the best though, you wouldn't want the place to look like a sixth grade class room, with spit balls and grab ass, while the members of the teams were listening in to America's, and the world's, most private communications.

Choir Practice was different. There the team had some fun. They had taken to having contests on who had the best stories about the best-overheard conversations. They would elect judges each week and everything. The teller of the best story drank free that week. What was funny though, was that the team would listen to conversation after conversation after conversation, and it was just people talking. It surly was not terrorists or subversives. Those guys pretty much knew not to plan attacks over the phone. So really all the calls that Buford's team listened in on were simply people chatting on the phone or in emails. They just happened to say the wrong word, or call the wrong country. However, Buford and his team were on the job, just in case some " stupid" terrorists decided to use the phone to make their secret plans.

Occasionally, it was necessary to report a call to a superior, due to "possible subversive" content, but, frankly, not very often.

The members of Buford's team were given special treatment, because the program was a pet project of the Bush administration. It was a very "secret" top-secret program. The program was being kept, not only from the public, but also from Congress. Therefore, they were the elite, among the elite. Buford liked that.

17

As THE SUN BROKE ON ANOTHER standard issue sunny southern California morning, three grown men were sitting around the poolside breakfast nook/ wet bar in gym shorts and tee shirts, scratching various body parts and clearing phlegm… not a pretty sight. Perhaps, there were other reasons why these three were not married. Reasons unrelated to their proudly proclaimed pronouncements of the previous day. The chilly rainy weather that had existed only three days previously, had long since moved on. Los Angeles was back to its old self, always perfect. A slight breeze blew through the palm trees that surrounded the pool area, and from where they were sitting they could see boats of various sizes silently motoring the channel at "no wake" speed, heading toward the Pacific Ocean. Gulls screeched overhead, and occasionally dove at the water. Arthur had pancakes, sausages and eggs sizzling on the stove in the kitchen; and the aroma wafting out was spectacular. They were each drinking hot coffee and Jigs was talking.

"…Yeah, and somehow you can see your way clear to endorse a party that would rather give our hard earned tax dollars to a few hundred fat cat, millionaire government contractors, that don't need the money, fuckin'war profiteers, so that they can all

shit into gold plated toilets, than to insure basic health care to
poor children."

All that was necessary to get Willie and Jigs started was
that they both passed a TV with the early morning news on it.

"Fuck you tree huger. You know as well as I do that,
although it sounds very altruistic to prattle on about the poor
children, this program is merely step one in a plan, by all you
fuckhead Democrats, to take this country towards a Canadian
style, European style, single payer, socialized medicine system,
that will ultimately bankrupt this great country. No one wants
poor children to go without health care, least of all me, but this
program is not the way. It is not working in those countries.
They all come here for their health care, if they can, and if they
can't, they wait in line for needed operations and treatments and
some die in the process." Willie sipped his coffee and sat back in
his chair.

"You know," Arthur said. "If someone was listening to
this incessant bickering between you two crazies, they might get
the impression that you guys hated each other. You sound like
enemies."

"Now that's funny you should say that, Arthur, it really
is. Do you know why?" Jigs' eyes were lasers. It was almost
intimidating. Arthur didn't answer. Instead he went in to check
breakfast, but he could still hear the conversation. Jigs went on.

"The discussions that he and I have are about issues that need to be solved. They are the pressing issues of our time. However, they cannot be solved by people who are enemies. This right wing dickhead here is my best friend, and although it may not sound that way, we will always be best friends. That is how it used to be between the statesmen and representatives that once actually solved problems in this country. They would vehemently and passionately argue the pros and cons of their most pressing issues on the floor of both houses of Congress by day, and then go out and have a beer together by night and, oft times, the solutions would be reached in the bar over those beers. One thing was sure; they did not hate each other. They disagreed with each other, but they respected each other. The only time when there was a division between the parties like there is today, was during the time leading up to the civil war. Get my point? Civil fucking war." Arthur was serving breakfast. It looked scrumptious. They all dug in. Through bites, Jigs went on.

"When I practiced law, I would argue the shit out of my case in court, and then see my opponent at a bar association meeting that night. There was no animosity. Hell, I dated a couple of the cute ones, when the cases were over. It was our job. He or she took one side. I took the other. The better we did our jobs, the more respect we had for each other. That is the nature of the adversarial legal system that our forefathers designed. It is the best system in the world. That system of arguing or debating issues also exists in our Congress, and it used to work. Then came right wing, and left wing, talk radio and the twenty-four hour cable news cycle, with their talking heads that, all in pursuit of the millions they earn, and in an effort to entertain, make it seem that you are actually supposed to hate those persons on the other side of the issue. It is fuckin' nuts! No one is as right, and no one is as wrong as these fuckheads would have you believe." Jigs stabbed a piece of sausage with his fork like he was trying to kill it. "Ya know, if someone is actually going to get apoplectic over a damn conversation, maybe they should stay away from politics. The reason Willie and I go back and forth like we do is because we love to do it. That is how we have fun."

"Really," said Willie. "I thought it was because you were a leftist hippie fuck, and I hated your tree hugging ass. Pass the syrup, please." That got a laugh. "Isn't this a pretty lofty conversation to be having at the crack of dawn over breakfast?"

"Crack of dawn? It is 8:45, not exactly the "crack of dawn," Arthur was mocking Willie.

"It is?" asked Willie as if he didn't know. "Hey Arthur, do you have any whipped cream?"

"Sure do, want some in your coffee? Arthur offered.

"Yeah… and could you pass me that bottle right there?" Willie was pointing at a bottle of Jameson's behind Arthur, on the shelf of the breakfast nook / wet bar. Willie was thinking Irish coffee. The other two simply groaned.

"What? Willie said as if he had just asked Arthur to pass the honey. As Willie poured a splash of whiskey in his coffee and topped it off with whipped cream, he said, "Oh, by the way, I have to go to Italy."

"What!" Both of other two looked up from their plates with a look of surprise and curiosity.

"Yeah, while you two old fogies were getting your required eight hours, I was surfing the net. It seems that there is a, yet unsolved, little incident that occurred over a year ago, in the foothills of the Italian Alps. It seems that an attempt was made on the life of a wealthy Italian socialite. The description of the accident sounded eerily similar to the one that we are interested in right now. Only in this case, the woman didn't die."

"What are you saying?" Arthur was dumbfounded and intrigued. "Do you mean to tell me that you found another... a similar accident...which happened in fucking Italy?"

Willie was smiling. "You sound surprised, Arthur, did you forget about the 'mole' analogy? You don't have one by the way."

Everyone laughed at this, and Willie was kidding about the mole, but he was very serious about the accident.

"OK," said Arthur. "Just what exactly are you saying?"

"Well," Willie put his fork down and rested his forearms on the table. He leaned forward to make his point. "There is a case pending in Northern Italy in which a very wealthy socialite type woman was involved in an automobile accident. She drove off a cliff, but she didn't die. When she came to in the hospital, she started screaming about having been drugged or something. She said that right before the accident she noticed a strange odor, and then she could no longer drive the car. To tell the truth, the local authorities thought she was nuts, or at least affected by the accident, but they checked out her claim. There was nothing wrong with the car. No tampering. They found no evidence of drugs left in her body. They found no evidence that a drug was administered to her, by way of a needle, for example, or any other way. However, she is a big mucky muck in her town, and her husband is a big mucky muck as well, so the case is listed as an attempted murder, which is unsolved, with no suspects, that is over a year old. So... I thought I should go and check it out. What do you think?"

"Well of course you should go if you think it will result in any information," said Arthur.

"I can't make any promises, but being there is better than trying to find out something over the phone or something like that," Willie said.

"Sure…he just wants a free trip to Italy," Jigs said with a mischievous smile.

"Jump in the lake, hippie…get a haircut." Willie responded.

18

BUFORD'S MOTHER WAS SICK... very sick. Buford had settled in at a job that he had come to love. He had several years on the job and had been appropriately promoted. He was "in with the in crowd" within a totally secret society. He was making more money. His wife and kids were adjusting to life in Maryland. They were happy and healthy. Life was working out wonderfully... and then...this.

His mother needed a transplant and Medicare considered the operation experimental; therefore, the procedure was not going to be covered. If she was to receive the procedure it would have to be paid for by supplemental insurance, which, of course, she did not have, or the family would have to pay for the procedure themselves. This was impossible, or so it seemed. All attempts to "reason" with Medicare had been expended.

Buford had already decided that he was going to do whatever it took to see to it that his mother would get the treatment she needed.

He had some money saved, but it was not nearly enough. In fact, if he had completely liquidated, he would still fall seriously short of the necessary funds needed for the entire procedure. He did, however, have what he considered his ace in the hole.

The up coming weekend had several college and pro football games which he considered "locks." These were games on which he was sure he could not lose, not the least of which was a game between the Green Bay Packers and the Chicago Bears. Now, Buford, under normal circumstances, would have bet these games, in what he considered a "reasonable" way. In other words, he would not usually empty his savings, and further borrow money, in order to make these bets. He would bet the games with money he had on hand, and pocket "reasonable" winnings. If the unthinkable happened, which sometimes did by the way, and he lost these bets; he would not lose "everything," so to speak. This had been his pattern, and it had been working fairly well for him. Unfortunately, desperate times call for desperate measures, as they say, and Buford had decided to "go for broke." He felt he had no choice. It was his mother! He had to do what he could.

Without first discussing this with his wife, or anyone else, for that matter, Buford embarked on his "well reasoned" plan. If anybody in Buford's life had known about the plan, they would have felt like they were waving goodbye to a passenger on the Titanic, but, nobody did.

First, on Wednesday, he went to his bank. He withdrew $30,000.00 from savings. His balance was now $1125.00 in that account. Then, on Thursday, he withdrew $3500.00 from his checking account, leaving about 80 bucks or so in that account. On Thursday evening Buford Tucker was holding in his hand all the cash that he and his wife had saved during their entire marriage. Buford looked at the money and felt his heart pounding, exactly like he had felt it pound years ago in Vicksburg, Mississippi. He was excited. All he could think about was how happy his mother would be when he told her that she was going to be able to have the operation. He could actually see the look on her face.

Unfortunately, Buford's plan had another layer. You see, in order for Buford to net enough money to pay for his mother's operation and, also, replace the sums that he had withdrawn from his accounts, which was part of the plan, he would have to "spread" bets, in amounts well in excess of that which he had, on different games, with his "sports enthusiast" and on different Internet sites. This was not a problem because Buford had been placing bets on games for a long, long time, and he had never defaulted in any way on any bet, in the past. The bookmaker, with whom he dealt, would take bets without him having to "front" the money, or pay it in advance, so he could make bets with money he did not actually have. He effectively had an account with his bookie, although he didn't call him that. In fact, his bookie owed him about $700.00 from previous dealings.

Then his account would be settled on the Monday following the games, unless you wanted to leave winnings in your "account" for future week's bets. Of course, loses were settled immediately on Monday. Let me restate that. All loses were settled on Monday. The Internet sites, however, required a credit or debit card account, with sums sufficient to cover all bets, on deposit, prior to accepting bets.

On Friday morning, Buford took some "personal" time, only four hours. He was owed about twenty-seven days. Buford never took off work unless he was "near death." He did not want his wife to be able to see the nature of this transaction on their credit card bill. She paid the bills. He did the banking. Buford opened an account at a completely separate bank from their usual one. He deposited $33,000.00 in cash. He kept $500.00 to use for miscellaneous office pools or any other personal bets, between friends, which might come up. Hey, any little bit would help, right? "Actually," he thought. "There are some suckers at work, not on my team, but there are some." He walked out of his "new" bank with a fully funded debit card. He checked. Before he returned to work, with the use of his cell phone and his laptop, Buford had placed bets sufficient to accomplish his goals. He bet just over $80,000.00 in various ways and combinations, with six games at the core of these bets. They were his sure bets. He walked into work feeling better than he had in years. He was already making plans about how he was going to tell his mom the good news.

19

THE MEMORIAL SERVICE FOR ANNA KAHN was what one might expect. It was somber and reserved, however it celebrated the life of a wonderful woman that had touched the lives of tens of thousands through her charitable work, and hundreds upon hundreds in a very personal way. Although Ned was Muslim, the service was Christian. She was waked over a period of three days, and it was very hard to actually get inside the funeral parlor on any of those days. Many of the rich and famous people sent their condolences. Those that were personal friends made their attempt to visit.

When Ned saw both Jigs and Willie standing with Arthur at the service on the first night, he seemed unusually surprised. Very surprised. Ned knew Jigs' reputation and his present business, and although he and Anna had been close friends in years previous, he did not know why he would come all this way for the service; and why would Willie be there at all?

Jigs walked through an elbow-to-elbow crowd and directly up to Ned to pay his respects. "I am very sorry for your loss," he said.

This was a very awkward encounter. Ned hadn't made a billion or so dollars because he was stupid. Jigs knew this. They eyed each other. Ned was impeccable and self-assured. That did not bother Jigs.

"Thank you for coming. I am surprised that you came all this way."

"Arthur called me. He is devastated. It was the least I could do."

"Yes, Arthur is not handling this well, as would be expected, but I believe he is imagining things."

"What kind of things?" Jigs was surprised that Ned was being this direct. He wanted to have this conversation, but not here, not now.

"Various things..." At this point, one of the other persons, there to pay their respects, walked up. "Excuse me," Ned said with a warm smile.

Jigs realized Ned was smart enough to know that he would not have to finish this conversation here or now. He was the grieving husband. No one talked to him for long at this place. Everyone at the service would come up to him at one time or another. Ned had simply stated what he wanted to say, and was now moving on. Jigs nodded, as other mourners surrounded the grieving husband. Ned nodded back. Then his attention was elsewhere.

Jigs wandered back to where Willie and Arthur were standing. He smiled. "What a cool customer. I don't know what to think about that guy."

"Why? What did he say?

"Well, he seems to think that our friend Arthur here is imagining things."

"Really, what kind of things?"

"That's what I asked him. We never got that far, and, believe me; he knew we would never get that far. That is why he said what he said; to fuck with me, the cocky prick."

After the service, the three musketeers, Jigs, Willie and Arthur headed, in Arthur's car to LAX. It was decided that Willie would take the trip to Italy.

It was another perfect night in La La Land, if you didn't count the fact that Anna was about to go in the ground. Yeah, if you didn't count that…it was perfect. They drove through the evening traffic in silence. Then Jigs spoke.

"You guys realize that the only people in the entire world who think that Anna did not have an unfortunate and tragic accident, are in this car… unless you include the killer, assuming there is one. You boys do realize this, right?" Jigs went on.

"And you both realize that we have not a single shred of evidence to the contrary, right? In fact, other than your gut feeling, Arthur, there is no evidence; none mind you, that this was not an accident. You both are getting this, correct?"

"That is not entirely true," said Willie. "What about George Castanza, and the absence of Jonathan F. Butcher?"

"Actually, that means nothing and you know it. That is, to say the least, weak. If all the cops in the world knew exactly what we know, not one of them would dare to investigate this case. You both know that this is true, right?"

"What are you saying, Jigs? Are you saying that we should just give up?" Arthur did not believe what he was hearing.

"No, Arthur, that's not what I am saying. I am just trying to put some perspective to this whole thing. Don't get upset."

"Don't worry Arthur, I've got your back. That's just the wimpy liberal talking; cut and run, that's all they know."

"Very funny, go fuck yourself, you old codger. Do you realize, Arthur, that you are listening to a man that now believes that the only purpose of government is to build a standing army? Forget the underprivileged, the infirm, the uneducated, forget anyone who isn't rich for that matter. You know he wasn't always this way. I don't know what happened to him."

" 9/11 happened. That's what happened. Do you remember any of that?"

"Yeah, yeah, yeah. Blah, blah, blah. Righty. Don't pay any attention to him, Arthur."

"Hey, Arthur, you said you had a key to your sister's house, right?" Jigs seemed inspired. "Maybe we could go over there and nose around, after we drop off this right wing a-hole at the airport."

"Well, that might freak out Ned, don't you think? He is home, you know."

"I don't mean tonight…I thought he was never home. We can do it when he is not home."

"What would we be looking for?"

"Oh, I don't know, phone bills, notes, a diary, fuck, I don't know, anything that might give us some direction."

"Hey, I have an idea." Arthur pulled out his cell phone. He started dialing a number. "When Anna traveled internationally, with or without Ned, which happened often, I sometimes would check her messages at their house for her. She gave me the code. They had people that worked for them at their offices, of course, but I would check her private home messages for her, just in case there was anything important."

He had listened to the recorded lady and was now pressing in the code to retrieve messages. The car strayed slightly from the lane.

"Hey, try not to kill us, huh? No wonder there is a law against using a cell phone in traffic."

"There are still two messages." Arthur was whispering like the recorded woman's voice on the other end of the line was going to hear him. Jigs and Willie looked at him like he was losing it.

"OK, the cleaners would be delivering their dry cleaning…yadda, yadda…" Suddenly, Arthur's face took on a look that was a cross between shock and elation. "Holly SHIT…its NED!" He pressed the speakerphone button on his cell.

"Hi, sweetheart, I am getting on the plane. I was just checking on you. Evidently, you went to your meeting. Good luck with that. This could be a good client. He's loaded. I'll see you in a few days."

"Arthur, may I ask you why you did not dial those numbers at some point in time sooner than just now?" These words came out of Jigs' mouth like syrup. Maybe he was being a little too hard on Arthur, after all, he hadn't thought of it either. When they say hindsight is twenty-twenty, boy, they are right. In this case it would have been helpful to dial the numbers sooner, but he hadn't. No sense obsessing over it. Arthur was shrugging. Jigs was smiling.

"Oh…. one more question…how can someone that does not exist, be loaded?"

Everyone in the car was smiling now…but it was not a funny ha ha smile…it was a knowing smile, like a kid in class that knows he knows the answer.

They were entering the airport grounds.

They passed the famous LAX sign, which has been seen in movies year after year. They pulled up in front of the Air Italia terminal.

"OK shithead, don't let any of that liberal commie socialism crap rub off on you while you're there. Bring us back good information."

"Yeah, yeah… take care of the hippy, Arthur. See you boys in a day or so."

20

As anyone might have guessed, Monday morning was not what Buford had hoped for or planned on. As he lay in his bed, not wanting to face the day, he relived a field goal scored with no time left on the clock, dropped passes in the end zone, and a collection of missteps and misjudgments that, frankly, had him considering slitting his wrists, literally. He could hear his wife and two children busily doing Monday morning things, oblivious to the pending catastrophe about to invade their lives, and turn it upside down. He could smell breakfast being cooked. He could hear kids talking about their homework and making plans for the day. To everyone else this was just another Monday morning. If only they knew.

Buford felt lost. He was not used to this feeling. Things always seemed to go his way. All his life, he had lived by the book. He had never broken a law, or made the kind of mistakes most people make all the time. Well, technically, placing bets with his fellow "sports enthusiasts" was breaking a law, but that was different. He knew football. He thought again of the coaching mistakes and the stupid errors made on the field in, not just one, but in almost all of his games. How could those guys have let him down, let his mother down?

"Honey, you better get moving, it is getting late." His beautiful wife was always thinking of his best interests. He could hear one of the morning radio shows, with one of the local hosts, squawking from the speaker on his night stand, as he slowly began to shake off the cobwebs, and head for the shower. "How do those idiots always seem to sound so gosh darn cheerful all the time?" He thought about how far from cheerful he felt at that moment. He looked at himself on the bathroom mirror. "I am getting old," he thought. He turned on the water. He put shaving cream on his face. He reached for his razor.

"The host of 'The O'Reilly Factor' on Fox News, and the same host of a nationally syndicated daily radio show on Westwood One, Bill O'Reilly, has been embroiled in a scandal involving a former female employee, who has accused the right wing pundit of harassment by telephone. There were accusations that allegedly included the suggestion, by O'Reilly, of the use of a falafel, together with other paraphernalia and/or gadgets. Now people...please let me stress... these are allegations and rumors. No facts have been ascertained. Why...why have no facts been ascertained? Well, there is a rumor, which addresses itself to that question as well. What, you might ask, is that rumor? Well my loyal listeners, the rumor is...that a tape of the conversation exists. Wow! A tape exists? How cool is that? Now we certainly can ascertain the facts, which, heretofore, have not been ascertained. You all might just be on the edge of your respective seats, or tightly grasping your respective steering wheels, waiting anxiously for me to play for you the infamous tape! I don't blame you, boys and girls! Further, I would like nothing more than to do just that! Unfortunately… unfortunately…I can't. Why not, you might ask? Why? Why? Why, Joey, why can't you play the tape? Well…it seems, and again this is nothing more than a rumor…it seems that Mr. O'Reilly has purchased the said tape…for *Ten Million Dollars*! Wow! He must not want us… me, or you, or anybody else… to here that tape! I wonder why…"

Buford stopped shaving. He did not really hear any thing else the cookey DJ had to say. "Ten million dollars," he whispered into the mirror. "Ten million…dollars." He said this again even more quietly. "I wish that conversation had come through my computer." That is when he realized that he had already heard conversations that were probably worth that much…maybe more. He had heard many men and women in conversations with, or about, their secret lovers. This, in fact, was quite common. It was the topic most often discussed at Choir Practice.

It was much more than that, however.

He had heard a man that was a CEO of a Fortune 500 company speaking to his wife about how he was worried that a corporate rival had found out about his propensity to dress in woman's clothes. Everyone at Choir Practice thought it was hilarious that he was speaking to his wife. Evidently, his wife did not mind that he had this habit.

He had heard born again Christians that were secretly degenerate gamblers. There was the pastor of a church who was a raging alcoholic, and refused to admit it, or treat his problem. As a result, he was into the church's till for thousands. Once he heard a trust fund college student that was purchasing term papers. This kid would lose his endless meal ticket if he were caught. Oh, very common among the conversations were admissions to operations, penile implants, breast augmentations, plastic surgeries, and, the best, sex changes.

All of these, and thousands more, secrets unknowingly shared with Buford Tucker, and his team, simply because they had said the wrong word or phrase during their telephone conversations. Then, after they say that wrong word or phrase, and they are "flagged", they go on to say everything and anything one might say during a private conversation with a loved one or a confidant. In America, people believe that they can do that without concern, and that used to be true. It no longer is.

Buford took a shower and finished up getting ready. "It's funny; the best of plans are made in the shower," he thought. Isn't that true? People compose their best speeches, closing arguments, and apologies in the shower. Everyone makes plans in the shower. Buford was no different.

When he walked into the kitchen, he smiled warmly at his wife. "I love you, sweetheart."

The kitchen was well lit and cheery with yellows and baby blues. Little blue ducks were on the wallpaper. Clearly Mrs. Tucker read "Country Living" magazine. He sat down at the antique white table, and picked up the glass of fresh squeezed orange that his wife had waiting for him.

His wife looked at him. "Of course you do, honey, I am your guardian angel. You want some eggs?"

"I'll have some toast, but I am running a little late. I have to make some stops on the way to work."

"Really, anything I can help you with?

"No, honey, work stuff."

Buford knew what he had to do. He needed money, and lots of it. He had no intention of watching his loving family go down the tubes, or causing it to happen. Plus, he still had every intention of seeing to it that his mother got the procedure she needed. Life meant tough choices. Buford was in the process of making one of those tough choices.

As soon as he left his driveway, Buford picked up his cell phone. He pressed the button for contacts, scrolled down to "Sport" on his list of contacts, and pressed, "send".

"Hey Billy, this is Buford... Yes, yes, you are right, it was not a good weekend, not at all... Yeah, I know how much it is...Yeah; I know it is a lot... That is why I called...I need a week, just run the vig...Yeah, I know how it works... Don't worry...have I ever given you a reason to worry? Yeah, just run the vig...I will see you one week from today...ok...no problem. Thanks." He slapped his cell phone shut. "Billy the Bookie, what an asshole. Who the fuck calls himself, Billy the Bookie," uncharacteristic words for such a Christian.

Buford had just bought himself some time, at great expense, financial expense, moral expense... great expense. "Vig", as you may know, means vigorish, or, very high interest paid in illegal gaming; but, truth be known, Buford was about to lose much more than mere money.

21

THOMAS POPOULAS SAT LOOKING at the various pieces of the heating vent system for the Mercedes he had leased. He had made a list of the items he would need. He had called a cab, and he was getting ready to run some errands. There was the sound of a car horn from the front of the building. He went out and got into one of, what seemed to be a very few, taxicabs in the fair city of Los Angeles.

"I understand that there is a Hertz Rental place not too far from here?"

The taxi driver nodded his assent. "There is one about a mile and a half from here."

"Let's go. That is our destination."

Mr. Popoulas walked in to the car rental agency as Thomas Popoulas, from Athens, Greece; and he walked out of the agency as Thomas Gazdik from Ino, Wisconsin, a small town just west of Ashland, in the Bayard Peninsula. When he left in a nondescript white Buick Century, Thomas Popoulas no longer existed, nor would he ever exist again. He counted four of the exact same cars that he was driving within a couple of miles. He wanted to blend in. He did.

Mr. Gazdik had in his wallet a Wisconsin drivers license with his picture on it, a slew of credit cards from various banks with his name on them, a social security card, pictures of his nonexistent family, even several tattered little bits and pieces of paper and worn business cards with the phone numbers of people he had never met or seen. He had had a small bonfire back at his new temporary office and garage. Into a waste bin went all of the items that had identified him as Thomas Popoulas. He sat and watched those things burn, while he read the owners manual of his other rented car, the Mercedes. He stirred the ashes until not a single unburned speck of paper remained.

Tom Gazdik's errands took him from one store to another. He leisurely strolled shopping malls and strip malls, passing by specialty shops of every stripe, searching out each item on his list. He saw so many specialty shops and emporiums, he was sure that he would soon pass by the scotch tape store from Saturday Night Live or the Left Handed store from the Simpsons if he walked any farther. He had a little trouble finding paraffin, but eventually he had everything, and he returned to his local home away from home. He bought a 13-inch color television for $89.99 and made his customary stop at an In n Out Burger before he arrived back at his office. He was one of the few people left in the world that still loved to watch network

TV. During the day, he actually watched soap operas, or at least had them on while he worked. He just loved television.

22

JIGS AND ARTHUR DROPPED WILLIE at the airport and headed back to Hollywood to resume the arduous task of attending the wake of a deceased loved one. Arthur's, and Anna's, parents were going to be at the wake this evening. As they drove through LA traffic, Jigs brought up a point.

"Your parents are going to be at the service today, right?"

"Yeah, that is going to be tough on me. My mom…I don't know…she just is not dealing with this well, at all."

"I have a dumb idea… Ned will be at the wake. He has to be…why don't we stop by their house before we go to the service? You get my drift?"

"I do have a key right here." Arthur pointed to the key chain hanging from the ignition switch. "But… do you think that is a good idea?"

"No! I just said it was a dumb idea. What are you, fuckin' deaf?" Jigs was laughing while he said this. He then got serious. "However, the longer we wait, the less likely we are to find anything. I was really surprised that we were able to hear that message from Ned. I would be willing to bet that it has been erased by now. I don't know what we are looking for, but you would be surprised how effective good old-fashioned snooping can be. Sometimes, you simply stumble onto great information if you put yourself in the right place at the right time. It is like sending your kid to Harvard or Yale, no matter how stupid or uninformed he or she is, if they are where the knowledge is, chances are they stumble onto some of it. Of course this is not a fool proof process."

The news was on the car radio and the broadcaster was mentioning President Bush. Jigs was pointing at the radio. "Obviously…but, for us it would be worth a try."

So, they began heading towards Ned and Anna's home in the Hollywood Hills.

As they approached the home where Arthur's sister had lived for so many years, they had to pass the very spot where Anna had met her untimely demise. As they passed the spot, Arthur felt a surge of sadness, then anger. There was evidence that his brother-in-law had been the reason for her death. It was circumstantial in nature, but it was evidence nonetheless. He was still plagued with questions. Why would Ned do this? How the hell do you make someone drive off a cliff? Who was his accomplice? Was he crazy? Was he simply grasping at straws, trying to make sense of a senseless situation?

The ornate iron gate which guarded the driveway leading to the Kahn home was equipped with an automatic opening system which could be activated by a device much like a garage door opener; or, one could walk up to the gate and activate it with a key to the house. This system was put in place in case the opening device was lost or its battery went dead. Arthur had lived with his sister for a short time when he first moved to Los Angeles, and he was waiting for his home to be decorated and readied for him to move in, so he knew this.

Arthur jumped out of his car and ran up to the gate. He cast a long shadow in his car's headlights on the dark mountain road. There were crickets chirping and a slight breeze rustled the dry desert brush and the short trees along the roadside; otherwise it was silent. They were far enough up in the hills to be completely out of earshot of any street sounds emanating from the busy city below.

The key slipped into the slot and he turned it. The heavy iron gate parted and slowly creaked to the fully open position. Arthur ran back to the car and pulled it through the open gate and up the dark drive towards the house.

The house was as dark as a house of this type ever gets; however there were bright coach lights on either side of the mammoth oak entrance doors, and there were several lights on timers inside the house that came on automatically at sunset. There were other lights, which illuminated the driveway at this point. It would be all but impossible to approach the house without being detected by someone inside the house. His sister had domestic help when she was alive, but none of the people that helped out in keeping the house up, and the pool clean, and the grounds trim and cut lived on the premises, at least when Anna was alive. They did not know if Ned had made other arrangements this soon. They both doubted it, but who could be sure. No car was in the drive in front of the house.

"So...this is how really rich people live." Jigs was speaking in a normal tone, however his voice seemed to boom out and echo throughout the entire canyon and surrounding hills, due to the amazing silence that existed there. Both of them started to laugh because it sounded so loud.

"Well, so much for sneaking up on the place or anybody in it." Jigs was giggling like a teenager pulling a Halloween prank. "We better give up on the plans to become cat burglars, huh?"

"There is no point trying to be stealth, and, frankly, no reason to. If someone is here, we will be meeting them in just a minute."

"Right." Jigs was looking at the huge house and its grounds. "What I can't get over is...how rural it seems here, when we are such a short distance from the second largest city in the entire country. I guess that is why all these wealthy folks live here, huh? It is pretty nice up in these hills... I would miss the tropics though, and the water." It sounded a little like Jigs was trying to convince himself of this statement rather than asserting it.

They both approached the front door. Jigs reached for the doorbell and said, "What the heck, you are the fucking brother here for Christ's sake...this is silly." He rang the bell. "We can be here, right? We are not trying to sneak around."

They waited. Tic. Tic. Tic. No one came.

"Now we *are* trying to sneak around." They were both giggling like schoolboys. "OK, lets get serious here." Jigs was actually trying to convince himself to do so more than anyone else.

Arthur slid the key into the lock and turned and pushed the door. It opened silently.

"Someone is pretty good with an oil can. Aren't big doors like this supposed to creak?" Jigs was whispering, but he could not seem to take this whole breaking and entering thing seriously.

The house looked like a dimly lit layout of a Better Homes and Gardens photo shoot. Jigs followed Arthur through the expansive rooms. They headed directly for his sister's home office. At one point they were passing an area where the pool could be seen. It was lit from beneath the water. There was not a ripple on the surface. The pool was surrounded on three sides by dense tropical vegetation. On the side of the pool that was without plants, you could see miles of the spiraling city below and then… the Pacific Ocean. Breathtaking.

They reached the door to Anna's office and they were about to enter when they both heard the sound of what sounded like muffled footsteps.

In spite of all the previous levity they both felt their hearts jump into their mouths. They looked at each other for confirmation that the sound was really there. They both nodded at each other. Jigs could feel his heart thumping. The "fight or flight" response was automatic. They had both stopped in their tracks. Not a sound.

Suddenly, the cat shot by.

They both started laughing again. "Mustafa…Jigs…Jigs…meet Mustafa. The cat was gone again. Arthur turned the light on in his sister's office.

"Fuck this, man. This is my sister's house, right? I used to live here, for crying out loud. Lets stop this sneaking around crap. Ned is at the goddamn wake. Nobody else lives here. We are acting like criminals."

"Do you know if she kept a diary?"

"She never said one way or the other. What else are we looking for?"

"A diary, a calendar, notes, appointment books, I don't know, man. Use your head. We want to find anything that will give us a lead. Check her computer."

"You know, this is not like it is supposed to be. My sister was not this neat. This office never looked this organized when I lived here. Either she had a complete change of personality, or someone has cleaned this place up. Now, the big question is…was it a maid…or was it someone else?"

They both continued to rummage through the private things of a special human being. It naturally made Arthur sad to see all the little things that were particular to his Anna. There were things that reminded him of her personality and special gifts. It simply made him more determined to find the truth. They had been snooping for about a half- hour and were about to give up the ghost, when…

"May I ask you two what you are doing in here?"

It was Ned. He was impeccable as usual and filling the entire doorway to the office.

"Hey…hi, Ned…you know…this a truly beautiful home you have here.

23

ONE OF THE PROCEDURES THAT were in place with reference to the proper performance of Buford Tucker's job at the NSA, was that if Buford, or a team member, detected a conversation where subversion, or, God forbid, terrorism, of any kind, was suspected, a background check was immediately ordered by Buford, as the team leader, of the suspected individual. This report would be generated through collaboration between the NSA and the FBI.

A preliminary report could often be generated, if high priority was requested, within hours of the request. This became a routine procedure. There were agents assigned full time to these requests. If no background checks were ever ordered, the very program itself might be subject to the criticism that no intelligence, whatsoever, was being generated by the program. Therefore, it was made clear to the members of all of the teams, through very subtle methods that these requests should be made on a regular basis. That way it looked like the program was churning out scads of potentially actionable intelligence, in case anyone were to check. (Of course, this would require that someone actually be told about the program, someone like a member of Congress or a member of the Press. Perhaps they were planning to tell someone like that someday.)

Once the person requesting the report read through all of the private information of the subject of the report, and determined that no threat existed from that individual, the report was supposed to be shredded; at least that was the official policy. There was no enforcement of this policy, however. None.

Therefore, Buford made several of these requests every day, some days ten, some days twenty, some days more. It was among the most routine aspects of his job. It was one of the indicators that he was doing his job. Normally, he would review the report, determine that the individual was not a threat of any kind, and then he would shred the report, as proscribed by the official policy. Occasionally, there would be what was considered to be a potential threat indicated. These files would be forwarded, through proper channels, to Buford's superiors for further review and consideration. Buford, and the members of his team, would rarely hear anything further regarding the matter, unless, of course, a national terrorism plot against the United States was uncovered as a result of their efforts, and the whole thing was played out in the newspapers and on television. This did not happen very often. Like never.

So, on any given day, hundreds of these reports were requested and generated by the participants in the program, the

NSA, the FBI and related alphabet agencies. Keep in mind that Buford's team was only one of many such teams. Each of these reports would typically contain the name, address, social security number, telephone numbers, telephone records, email addresses, email records, job status, marital status, military records, criminal records, credit records, bank records, medical records, IRS records, citizenship status, immigration status, together with any and all other information thought to be pertinent by those generating the report, including a picture, if available.

These reports were generated about US citizens as well as non-citizens. Obviously, the reports were less complete on non-citizens. One might think that having hundreds of reports with this kind of information about US citizens floating around would be a concern, a cause for consternation, but it wasn't. You see, only trusted members of the US government saw the reports, so it was not a problem…really.

When Buford arrived at work, still affected by his talk with Billy the bookie, he had a new purpose in life. When he put on his headphones that day, it was like he was putting them on for the first time. If some foreign idiots were to be stupid enough to speak about their plans to attack America over the telephone, no problem. Buford would have heard them and personally put an immediate stop to those plans, but quick; however, that was no longer Buford's primary focus. Buford was now a man obsessed. He was going to find an individual that was rich… and had something to hide.

This did not take long.

By 1:00pm that day he had two prospects. By 5:30pm that day he had in his hand complete background checks on both of them. Because he was team leader, Buford had a small office. Most of his co-workers had cubicles. It was one of those kinds of offices where the walls on two sides were glass. Buford looked out at the busy bustle of the very official, very secret, very professional expanse of desks and cubicles that made up the greater office outside his own. Everyone he saw was dedicated and busy; totally focused on keeping America safe from attack. No one was paying any attention to him in his office. Buford opened his brief case and dropped the two reports, containing incredibly complete personal information about two United States citizens, into the case. Nothing happened. No bells went off. No lights or sirens. Nothing. That was the first time Buford had ever decided to bring work home with him. It would not be the last.

Buford walked out of the office on that day just like he did on every other day during all the years that he had been employed there, nodding and waving and saying his "good nights" and "see you in the mornings" to everyone that was interested. He got into his Chevy Impala and drove away from the office. He joined the rush hour traffic that plagued the greater Washington DC area each and every day.

Before heading home, Buford had some stops to make. First, he went to his "private" bank. This was the bank where he deposited funds that were used for football bets. He also had a debit card, which was issued by this bank. He went straight to the vice-president, whom he knew, and made arrangements to lease a safety deposit box. He sat in the private room adjacent to the safety deposit boxes. Here he was free to peruse the files that he had in his brief case.

Buford opened the first report.

Dennis Van Wyck was the CEO of an international distributor of auto parts. He had recently closed a deal with a company in China to set up plants there, which would result in earnings to his company in the hundreds of millions of dollars. To celebrate this coup, he and his assistant stopped over in Tai Pan where they spent three glorious days sight seeing by day and canoodling by night. There would be absolutely nothing wrong with this scenario, except that his assistant was a twenty-eight year old recent graduate of the Wharton School of Business. She was on the fast track to an upper management position with the company, partially because she was a graduate of the Wharton School of Business, and partially because she was canoodling the boss, who was a fifty-one year old father of three, with a forty-eight year old wife. Actually, they had to cut their little mini-vacation short because Mr. Van Wyck's youngest daughter was in the school play. He could not miss her performance.

The assistant told the entire story to her real boyfriend in a telephone conversation which went on for twenty-five minutes, complete with references to her boss as "Dennis" and "Mr. Van Wyck." Sadly, she properly identified the great business success that they had maneuvered as a coup. The words "coup" or "coup de tat," when spoken during an international telephone conversation, will get the conversation "flagged" every time. She was a chatty little wench that had a boyfriend that did not seem to mind that his girlfriend was "canoodling" her boss in order to advance her career. In fact, he seemed to encourage it, and demanded to hear all the details, to boot! Go figure.

Rather than order a complete background check on the assistant or her boyfriend, the actual participants in the telephone conversation, Buford got the skinny on the CEO. As it turned out, Mr. Van Wyck was a very successful man, financially speaking that is. He had a net worth in excess of ninety million dollars. He had been filing joint tax returns with his wife for twenty-four years, which was one year more than the age of his eldest son. He was a registered Republican, a Methodist, and a member of the Board of Directors of four other corporations. He belonged to two country clubs, one outside Atlanta, where he and his family lived, and one in Naples, Florida. He was a model citizen, if you forgot about the canoodling.

"Boy, those FBI guys are thorough." Buford actually said this out loud to no one as he sat in the privacy of his little room. "I will never look at a telephone in the same way again," he thought while he devised his next step.

Buford opened the second report.

Dexter Washington was drafted in the first round by the Miami Dolphins. It was the culmination of a life dedicated to the game of football and to physical fitness. Buford felt a connection to Dexter in that he had played and followed football all his life. One might think that this connection would make Buford less likely to extort money from him. Such was not the case. Although Buford had the complete report in front of him, he only needed to know one thing about Dexter, which he discovered during the conversation that he overheard between Dexter and the other party to whom he was speaking. Dexter, it seems, was taking steroids. He was speaking to a man in Cuba. Buford had an opinion about athletes who took steroids. He was against it. He did not believe that a person should have an unfair advantage against others who did not feel that they should defile their bodies. This opinion was actually a long held grudge, which Buford had held since high school; therefore, Buford was going to secretly enjoy the process to which he intended to subject Dexter.

Buford was aware that Dexter had received a ten million dollar signing bonus as part of a twenty-five million dollar five year contract. He also had read that one of Dexter's first purchases was a $200,000.00 Jaguar, which Buford considered a waste of money. The mention of drugs during a telephone conversation to Cuba, or anywhere else for that matter, will cause the call to be "flagged." The Bush administration knew that any information learned about drugs or drug transactions during a conversation, which was monitored without first having procured a warrant, would be inadmissible as prosecution evidence in a court of law. However, that was never the purpose of the program as it pertained to drugs. The administration simply wanted to know about people in power who took drugs. Information is power in the world of politics. That might explain why the program was begun prior to the attacks on 9/11. The policy turned out to be very good for Buford Tucker and very bad for Dexter Washington.

Buford decided that he would only demand from his prey an amount, which was to them inconsequential, comparatively speaking of course. The same amount would be his salvation. He agonized over the details. Above all, he could not get caught, obviously.

Everyone at the office was aware of Buford's mother's illness. His second stop on his way home was at the travel agent that was used by the agency, to book himself on a flight to New Orleans and to book a rental car to drive to Biloxi. Everyone would assume that he was going to see his mother, and this was part of his purpose, but he had other reasons to go to New Orleans.

He went home to explain to his wife that he was going to visit his mother for a couple of days. His wife was surprised he had not gone sooner. He went with her blessings. His team members all agreed that it was high time he took the trip. The office would survive without him for a few days. They could see the wear and tear that his mother's illness was having on Buford. The trip was considered a good idea by all concerned.

When he arrived in New Orleans, Buford secured a car and drove straight to the French Quarter. Since Katrina, there were more homeless and hangers on in the area just on the peripheries of the Quarter than ever before. Buford spotted a guy sitting on a stoop that he thought might serve his purpose.

"Excuse me sir, may I speak with you for a moment?"

The guy that Buford was talking to was slightly better dressed than many of the others he had secretly sized up from his car. He had clean faded jeans and a red button down shirt. He had a fresh haircut and a shave. The neighborhood in which he lived was run down, but it was not affected by the floods.

"Would you like to make $500.00 for an hour's worth of work?"

"Hey, I ain't no fag man, move along."

"It is nothing like that, sir, nothing like that at all. Do you have a social security number?"

"Of course I do. What the fuck do I look like?"

"Please give me a moment of your time. You won't regret it. It will be the easiest $500.00 you ever made. I promise."

The guy stood up slowly and ambled up to the car. He now seemed intrigued.

24

BOTH JIGS AND ARTHUR HAD THE sheepish look of kids caught in the act. Kids get tongue-tied, clasp their hands behind their back and kick their toe into their heel. "Awe shucks, Mister. We didn't mean nothin' by it. Honest." These two were adults, however, and could think pretty well on their feet.

"Ned, my parents are going to be here tonight. We just stopped by to pick up something personal that I could give to my mom. You know a picture, a recent picture, or something that she could hold on to, I don't know, something." Arthur wasn't completely lying, not completely. He really had thought about bringing something to his mother, at some point.

"Your parents are at the funeral home, wondering where you are, Arthur. Moreover, if you wanted an item from inside of my house, you might have said something to me." Ned was eying the two men in front of him. There was not one person in the room that had any misconceptions about why they were all there. Ned didn't believe Arthur's story for a second.

So, it was official. Ned was suspected, and he knew it; and the two guys that suspected him, knew he knew that they suspected him. It was like an old Colombo episode. The bad guy always rubbing the crime in Colombo's face, daring him to prove that he did it, and Colombo having to prove the case inside of an hour and before the credits rolled. Now it was time for the mutual two-step.

"I'm sorry, Ned, I didn't think. I will always think of this as my sister's house. I have a key, you know, I didn't think. We practically had to drive by here on the way to the funeral parlor...so... again, I apologize."

"Yeah? Well maybe you would like to buy it? Because, I think it will be up for sale soon. I am considering moving."

This statement had implications that went far beyond the conversation they were having. Jigs and Arthur looked at each other.

"Really..." Arthur said. "Where...When? What do you mean? When did you decide that you were moving?"

"Yeah, Ned, I was just saying how beautiful this place is. Why would you want to leave here?" Jigs was really just talking to talk. He had a pretty good idea why Ned would want to move, far, far away.

"We have been considering it for some time, actually. I am surprised Anna didn't mention that to you, Arthur. By the way, you won't find much of anything in here. I have gone through most of everything that was in here. I have put together some personal items that you or your parents might like to keep. Those items are being delivered to you at your home, Arthur. Then, I had Maria, my housekeeper, straighten up the office. So, why don't we go out to the deck by the pool? Lets get out of this office, at least. As long as you two are here, do you want something to drink? No reason to be inhospitable, right?"

Ned stepped aside from the doorway to the office, and extended his arm like an usher. It was clear that they were being relocated within the huge home. They did not have a choice. The search of Anna's office was over.

As the two "visitors" walked passed Ned who then followed and escorted them through wide halls and gorgeous rooms out to the deck by the pool, Arthur continued his questions about Ned's apparent plans to move from the LA area.

"Ned, I just can't imagine you living anywhere else, you guys have lived here forever. Where would you move to?"

"I haven't decided. I have looked into the south of France, some Caribbean locations, also I have considered moving home to Iran. I really have not made any kind of final decision."

"Somewhere without an extradition treaty," Jigs was thinking and almost said, but didn't. Instead he said, "France is nice." He looked at Arthur and smiled. They were standing near the pool, looking out over the great expanse of the sprawling city and then...the endless blackness of the Pacific Ocean. "The political climate in Iran may not be very receptive to a naturalized US citizen. Things are a little volatile over there, are they not?"

"Thanks for your concern." Ned was being a bit sarcastic. "Why don't you let me worry about that, Jigs?"

"When did you start thinking that you were going to move, Ned?" Arthur was not buying this assertion by Ned that "...he was surprised that Anna hadn't mentioned it."

"We had been considering it for quite some time. Did either of you want something to drink, by the way?"

Both men were shaking their heads, looking at each other. Finally Arthur said, "As you said, Ned, my parents are probably wondering where I am, plus we don't want to tie you up. Again, I want to apologize for barging in here like we did. Perhaps we should go. What do you say, Jigs?"

"Yeah, I'm sorry too, Ned, if we freaked you out."

They all started heading through the sprawling home towards the front door. Then Ned said, "Well, in spite of the circumstances, it was good to see both of you. I will catch up with you at the funeral parlor. I am actually going to have something quick to eat." They had reached the front door. All were sick of the faux pleasantries. All simply wanted to end this rather uncomfortable chance meeting. Then Ned said, "Arthur, I don't wish to be indelicate, but is there a reason that you would still need that key?"

Ned was standing with his arms folded across his chest. He then unfolded them and extended his hand, palm up.

Arthur clumsily reached into his pocket, and pulled out his key chain. He removed the key from the chain, and dropped the single key into the palm of Ned's hand. "Of course," Arthur mumbled. "I cannot think of reason. I'll call you if something comes up."

"That would be best." Ned's teeth were white against his tan face. He was smiling warmly, as if nothing unusual was happening. "What an asshole" Arthur was thinking. Of course, he was smiling too.

Jigs and Arthur got into Arthur's SUV. Arthur started the car then turned to look behind him and through the rear window to back down the drive. Jigs looked at Arthur and Arthur looked back, and they both...absolutely cracked up. In short order, the each had tears in their eyes from laughter.

"What an unbelievable fuckhead!" Arthur said through hysterical high-pitched laughter.

"I never liked that guy." Jigs felt like he was at camp making jokes about the camp counselor.

They slowly backed down the tightly pieced cobblestone drive. As they got further away it was darker until they reached the narrow road at the end of the drive. The road was dimly lit with streetlights very intermittently placed. They had not driven far when the magnitude of their "visit" set in. The laughter stopped.

"Is there any question left in your mind that we just talked to the son of a bitch that had my sister killed, or am I crazy?

"Arthur...he surely was acting strangely, taking a key back that you have had for, what, fifteen years, twenty years; however, I still have a question...why? Why would he do it? There is no evidence that there was anything wrong with their marriage, is there?"

"No...no evidence."

"OK, then, why would he do it?"

"I don't know. Obviously, there would have to be a reason we do not know about, right?"

"Right. Further...there is an incredibly loud clock ticking...an omnipresent clock...because no one thinks that she was killed… except us. Without a motive, or some evidence that this was not an accident, we have absolute shit for a case against him. If he leaves the country…this case is over. We are through, and that guy will fly away in his private jet, and never look back, whether he did it or not. So, we have to answer two questions. Why would a guy have his wife that he apparently loved, killed? And…how the fuck do you make a person that is intelligent, savvy and responsible, drive off a cliff and leave no sign that it was done? Plus, we have to answer these questions before this guy leaves the country, or those questions…are moot. So…no problem…right?"

This elicited unenthusiastic chuckles from Arthur. He looked at Jigs and slowly shook his head.

"Oh…by the way…with the exception of taking back the key to his house, Ned really hasn't done anything to cause him to be suspected of doing anything, much less killing someone. I'm guessing that if we went to the police with what we have…they would very politely say…'Why don't you two nice rich guys go get another hobby.' "

"You are not painting a very pretty picture."

"Don't worry, Arthur, last time I checked, it is impossible for a non-existent person to be 'loaded.' You have me on your side, for what that's worth, and you have Willie, and that is worth a lot… He is sadly misguided in his political views, which is truly a shame...such a shame..." Jigs shook is head slowly, like Willie had been diagnosed with cancer, or something. Arthur could not help but laugh silently... "but he is great when it comes to this business of figuring out what happened in seemingly unsolvable situations I have had some luck along those lines as well...so...anyway...Speaking of Willie...why don't we see what's happening in Italy."

25

BUFORD WATCHED THE TALL BLACK man walk towards his rental car. He was approximately thirty years old, good bearing, confident air, intelligent look. "This guy will do as well as any other," he thought. When the man was leaning into his passenger window, he said.

"I have a favor that I want you to perform for me. It will seem, and it is, a bit clandestine, but it is not, in any way, illegal. It will take about an hour. When we are done, I will drop you off right here, and you will be $500.00 richer. I'll even buy you lunch if you like. Why don't we take a ride? I will explain on the way."

"I don't like this shit, man…"

Buford reached into his pocket and pulled out five one hundred dollar bills. He fanned them out and pretended to fan his face with them. The guy opened the door and got into the front seat. They pulled away. They began to drive without direction for a time. New Orleans mid-morning traffic was reasonable, tolerable. Buford reached into his jacket pocket and pulled out his official NSA government identification card and badge and handed it to the man. "It is real, don't worry. Go ahead and look at it. What's your name?"

"Dallas," the guy said as he examined the ID, "Dallas Johnson. What the fuck is this shit all about, man?" Mr. Johnson seemed more at ease after looking at the badge. He handed the folded wallet back to Buford.

"I want you to open a post office box for me. I have something that I want to have delivered to me, and I don't want to have it traced back to me."

"No, man, ya'all want it traced back to my black ass. Man, is ya'll crazy? Pull this car over, man. Let me out of this muther fuckin' car, man. Five hundred dalles ain't worth no stretch."

"Why don't you here me out before you jump to conclusions. First, you all are never going to go back to this box in your life. Now, it is not illegal to have a PO Box, right?"

"Yeah, thas right. So what?"

"OK. Now, if you have a box, you cannot control what someone sends to you, right? If someone sends you something improper, you cannot be blamed for that, arrested for that, or bothered about it, unless you pick up the item. Well, you are never going to pick anything up from this box...I am. If I open a PO Box under my name, my social security number, it would be "flagged." What I mean is, it would likely be reported immediately, because I work for the NSA. All I need is a box, which is available for a delivery, and is not reported prior to the delivery. Get my drift, here? You open this box, and then you forget about it. You never return to it. We are going to pay for six months in advance. I pay that, of course. When it expires, it expires. If you get a letter alerting you that the box is about to expire, you throw it away. If anyone ever asks you why you had a box in the first place, you tell them that, because of the flood, you were not sure where your address would be, and you did not want to miss any mail, especially government checks, which may be due to you because of the flood."

"Man, this don't sound right."

"Look, there are thousands of displaced people that are in need of an address down here. You are just going to be one of them. I have thought this through. You have no risk. Besides, if you are ever questioned in any way, about anything, at any time, you simply tell them the truth. You have no risk, whatsoever, and I am guessing you can use the one thousand dollars. I hear things are pretty rough down here."

Buford had reached into his pocket and pulled out another five one hundred dollar bills. He had expected some slight resistance to his plan. To him, this was like a "sure thing" football bet. There was always some risk, but this was a good bet. He would risk the thousand bucks to insure his overall plan.

"If I ever is approached by anyone…"

"If you are ever approached by anyone, you tell them the truth. If it ever gets to that point, they will believe you, because they will have my balls on the chopping block. Don't worry. It will never happen. It will never get to that point."

Mr. Johnson needed the money… badly. He looked at the bills in Buford's hand and said, "Where do we go to do this thing?"

The two partners in crime had traveled aimlessly for a time and had found themselves on the edges of the infamous ninth ward. It looked like a war zone. Buford stared out the windshield in disbelief. "I had no idea…I didn't realize…my god." He looked at his passenger. "This is really not a sight I really expected to see. We have heard it was bad but this is…really not good." He thought of his mother. "Are Biloxi and Gulfport like this?"

"Actually, the Gulf Coast, 'specially near the water, is gone. Plum gone. The buildins' is gone, man. Flat."

"My mother and father are there. I am on my way to see her."

"Well then ya'all 'l see, won't ya?"

Buford headed back to slightly higher ground, and civilization. He spotted a Mailboxes Etc. in a strip mall, and pulled into the parking lot in front of the store. He took note of the address and location. "Lets do this," he said with conviction.

After a time, the unlikely pair were sitting back in the car. They had rented the largest box available. Buford paid the six-month rental fee in advance. Dallas Johnson dropped the key into Buford's hand, and Buford forked over ten one hundred dollar bills, as promised. They stopped at Miccie D's, as Dallas called it, for burgers and Cokes, to go. Buford dropped Dallas off at the same spot he had first picked him up, and said thank you. He drove away and never saw him again in his life.

Buford headed east on Interstate 10, towards Biloxi. Luckily, Buford's parents were not right on the water. The house was still standing. However, this was going to be a harder visit than he had originally planned. The storm had taken its toll on everything he saw as he drove. It was worse than he had imagined, worse than the national media had reported. It had not looked this way on the Gulf Coast since the year he was born.

When Buford arrived at his mother's home, he found more than he had bargained for. It was just like his mother to underplay her illness. That was their way. The whole family, the whole neighborhood, the Gulf Coast, hell... the whole South, they were always... stoic. There was always an attempt to be strong in the face of hardship or adversity, sometimes to a fault; but it was a way of life that had traditions, believed in honor and believed in God. Who could criticize that?

However, it also solidified in Buford the abject determination to proceed with his plans. No doubt remained. When he saw the state of his mother's illness, when he realized that she and his father were too proud to reveal the true nature of the problem, for fear it would inconvenience their son, he became single minded. Nothing would dissuade him. Nothing. His mother would have her operation. He would return to his home and his job with a single purpose.

26

ARTHUR HAD NOT SEEN HIS mother cry for at least twenty years and he could not remember ever seeing his father cry. The experience was not pleasant, especially when you consider the fact that Ned was just across the room during the end of the evening. He showed up about an hour after Arthur and Jigs and then acted as if nothing had happened. Jigs and Arthur acted the same way. They stayed until the crowd had thinned and Arthur's parents had left, then they escaped.

"If it is 11:30pm here, what time is it in Italy? Where did he go…Milan?"

"Jigs, I don't think he is there yet, or, if he is, he just landed. Let's let him have some time to find something out."

"We do not have time to screw around, you know. If that prick, Ned, leaves this country, we can kiss him goodbye permanently. You do realize this, don't you?

"Yeah, I do. In the morning I will call my broker and…"

"I realize you rich people have a special relationship with your brokers, but is this the time to be thinking about investing money?"

"...you did not let me finish...so...in the morning I will call my broker. He has his ear to Wall Street better than anyone in the nation. He is a rich guy's broker. Harvard man. He hears things others don't. He hears things before they happen. I will ask him if he has heard any rumblings about Ned's company or Ned's holdings. If Ned is thinking about moving, he may also be thinking about moving money, selling assets, changing the structure of his financial picture. When someone as huge as he is moves around, the street hears about it. My broker hears the street."

"Why you little detective you..." Jigs was smiling and teasing, but he was actually impressed. This was a very good approach, which he had not thought of. "That is a very good idea, isn't it? Willie is rubbing off on you, man. So, that is the plan. I like it. After that, we call Willie, or he calls us, and we know a lot more than we do right now. I guess it is bedtime, huh? Would you like to head home, or would you like to paint Los Angeles red? I'm Irish. We go to the bar after a wake."

"There is red paint from me in every crevasse of this town. Plus, the financial world starts early here. New York starts

at 8:00am, right? That's 5:00am to us. I will wake you at 4:30."
It was Arthur's turn to tease.

"Yeah, why don't we just head home? I've seen LA."

When Jigs first opened his eyes the next morning, he smelled coffee and bacon. It was still dark outside. He looked out of the window next to his bed and saw the early morning sport fisherman silently motoring by, making their way through the channel that passed just outside at the edges of Arthur's property, on their way to its mouth where it connects to the open sea and then, ultimately, to the waters that are home to the marlin or tuna or wahoo that they sought. The silhouettes of the big and small crafts as they slid by, lit only by red and green running lights, moved slowly past the black palm trees contrasted against the gray-blue predawn sky. Jigs farted into the clean white sheets and decided he better get up.

He came out to the poolside breakfast nook/ wet bar, scratching his ass, hair askew and yawning. He saw Arthur, showered, fully dressed and talking on the telephone.

"What the fuck, Arthur?"

Arthur looked up with what looked to be excitement on his face. He punched the speakerphone button on the telephone and said, "Jim Labuda… meet Jigs Donahue; Jigs…listen to this. Tell him what you told me, Jim."

"Hello there, Jigs. Arthur tells me only good things about you. It's nice to finally meet you, in a manner of speaking."

"Arthur lies, Jim, don't believe him."

"We actually have mutual friends back in Chicago…I have heard of some of your exploits before…"

"Enough small talk Jim," Arthur interrupted, "tell him…talk."

"My, my, my Arthur, aren't we a little curt in the early morning hours," Jigs teased.

"OK, OK…well…as I was telling your rude, excitable friend, Jigs, when Arthur called and started asking the questions he was asking about Ned Khan, and Ned Khan's business interests, I was absolutely shocked. I really cannot tell you how surprised I was. Because, he was speaking about things, and he seemed to have information about activity, that only the fewest of the few truly inside people on Wall Street have. I mean no one is aware of these apparent plans of Mr. Khan. If they were aware, it could cause ripples that could upset some markets. Now, I must stress that we are all, and by "all" I mean the parties to this phone conversation together with any other astute investor that may be privy to this information, speculating. However, within the last few days, I have been watching Mr. Khan secretly and silently consolidating many of his own holdings."

"Wait till you hear this, Jigs." Arthur could not contain himself.

"Yes… well…this consolidation of assets is unexplained. It does not make any sense, from a business point of view at least. It actually looks like he is making moves without consideration to the financial consequences. That is why I was so thoroughly flabbergasted when I received Arthur's call. I had just been working on trying to figure out just what Mr. Khan had up his sleeve. It is my job to know these things, you see. It is not like Mr. Khan, or his organization, to make capricious or frivolous business decisions. Some of these recent activities undertaken by Khan and his people seem to be of that nature."

"How have you come by your information, Jim?" Jigs was curious.

"From conversations like this one. Someone hears about certain stuff and passes it on to me. I speak with another person and he tells me about more stuff. I keep my ear to the ground and learn even more. Then I put all that stuff together, and I wind up knowing the most about all this stuff."

"Well put…were you an English major at Harvard?"

"Very funny. Actually, "stuff" is a term of art. It means that you don't really want to be perfectly clear."

"Touché Jim, OK, so what does all this stuff mean?"

"Of course no one can say for sure what is in a person's mind, however, if I had to venture a guess…"

"I'll tell you what it means." Arthur loudly blurted out before Jim could finish. "It means that this mother fucker is not 'considering moving' as he so obscurely stated. This son-of-a-bitch is picking up stakes and running. That is what it means. The prick."

"Apparently, Arthur can in fact 'say for sure what is in a person's mind.' Why don't you tell us what you really think, Arthur?"

"Based on the very sketchy information that Arthur and I have discussed during our conversation this morning, and based on the fact that Ned could experience comparatively small losses, but losses nonetheless, if he continues on his present course, I would say that Arthur has very succinctly stated one plausible explanation for Ned's actions."

"So," Jigs queried, "you are saying that Ned may be consolidating so that he can sell off his interests for cash, and then disappear?"

"That is a possibility. Actually, that is likely. I cannot think of another explanation for his actions."

"Well, we can't let that happen now, can we?"

27

BUFORD TUCKER LEFT THE GULF Coast determined to do what it took to save himself and his family from financial ruin, not to mention avoiding serious physical injury to himself from Billy the Bookie or his minions, and to insure that his mother received the treatment she needed. Nothing would stand in his way. He felt his back was up against wall. He flew home from New Orleans and retrieved his car from long term parking at the airport. He drove straight to his "private" bank and went immediately to his safety deposit box upon arrival.

When he was secured away in the private viewing room attached to the safety deposit box department at the bank, he pulled out the files, which he had obtained regarding Dennis Van Wyck and Dexter Washington. He reviewed both files and took notes. The files contained all addresses and a complete list of all telephone numbers of each man. He took detailed notes so he had available to him all of the salient points set forth in each file. He paid particular attention to the names of the other players in both of the men's sordid activities.

When he left the bank, it was cloudy and threatening rain. The gloomy skies accentuated his dour mood. He realized that his choices were limited and he did not like feeling this way. Buford had a very sick mother who needed expensive care. In an effort to help, he had created an even more pressing situation. He had lost the nest egg that he and his wife had squirreled away and become indebted to men who were not willing to negotiate the debt, to put it mildly. If he did not follow through with his present plan, he would not only suffer physical injury at the hands of the "sports enthusiasts," but, after having received his beating, he would still owe the money and he would be exposed at the NSA as having been involved in illegal gambling. The agency did not respond well to this type of information. He would be given his walking papers post haste. He would be out of the job, which he had come to love. He and his family would be destitute. His mother would be no better off. His course of action seemed clear. He had only one choice here.

He could not believe he was contemplating these thoughts. He had lived his whole life in an above board manner. He had a stellar record on every count, however it was viewed. He was a devout evangelical Christian, a loving and devoted husband and father, and a respected and dedicated leader in the work place. "I am not a bad person; I am a good person." He refused to let himself believe he was turning to crime. "Necessity is the mother of invention. This is a necessity." This was not an overstatement or misstatement, and he had no intention of pissing his reputation or his or his family's lives away. Period.

The car in front of him stopped quickly without an apparent reason.

"Pay attention to the fucking road!" He screamed this out the window like a New Yorker. He was not being himself. He was immediately appalled at his own behavior. He had to fix this problem. It was consuming him. He saw a strip mall with which he was familiar. He knew that there were pay phones inside the mall. He pulled into the parking lot and parked the car. He walked into the mall carrying the notes that he had taken at the bank. He was imbued with resolve and determination. He stopped at a newsstand and bought a coke with a twenty-dollar bill. He requested extra change for the phone and approached the phone bank. No one else was nearby. People did not use payphones anymore.

"Mr. Van Wyck, I am glad I caught you." Thank God for cell phones, Buford thought. "Please listen to every word I have to say before you respond in any way. I know about your relationship with Kathy Kroening, your assistant, more specifically, I know about the tryst that you all had with her in Tai Pan. Do I have your attention, sir?"

After a long silence, Buford heard a very tentative response.

"Yes…yes, you have my attention."

"Can you talk, sir?"

"I can talk."

"Again, please listen to what I have to say before responding. Sir, I am a Christian man. I have no desire to harm you. I have no intention to cause you harm or pain. However, I am in trouble and you can...and will...help me solve my problem... I have information that, if exposed, would ruin your life. I can cause your life, as you know it, to end. You will lose your family, your job. You will lose everything. I am faced with similar circumstances, I know it is a terrible feeling, and, believe it or not, I am sorry to be the one causing you pain...I just have no choice. Therefore, you must do the following:

Place $100,000.00 in a compact package tightly wrapped in plain brown paper. Make it look like standard business mail. I don't have to add that the bills must be non-sequential and unmarked. Mail the package to this address. "Do you all have a pen, sir?"

"I do."

"D.J. Inc. 141 Robert E. Lee Blvd. #603   New Orleans, Louisiana 70116. Did you get that, sir?"

"I did."

"Please understand, I know everything about you, sir. Everything. For example, your wife's cell phone is 111-555-1111. Her email is pattyvan1@yahoo.com. Your board chairman is William McGrath whose cell phone number is 111-222-5555. His email is w_mic@gmail.com. Do I need to continue, sir?"

"No, you do not."

"You all are a very intelligent man. Perhaps that is how you have amassed a net worth of ninety million. I ask that you think this through before you act rashly, sir. If I am arrested for anything, or bothered by anyone, as a result of our conversation today, the subsequent press coverage of my confession or my press conference, will defeat the purpose of your trying to do anything other than to comply with my request. You will be exposed... Then there is the other option that you might consider. If I were to die, or disappear, then someone would open my safety deposit box. The letter in there would speak as loudly as I ever could. Is there any reason for me to go on, sir?"

"No, you need not continue. I understand."

"The amount I request is meaningless to you, comparatively speaking. To me it is my salvation. Now...we come to the most important part of this telephone conversation. I must convey to you that you all will never hear from me again, provided you comply with my request... I am not a bad man, sir. I am a good Christian man. I would not be doing this if I did not have to do it, I assure you. Just do what I ask. You will never be bothered by me about this matter, or any other matter, again. You have my word. I must receive the package no latter than this Friday…Do you have any questions, sir?"

"I don't believe I do."

"Do not disappoint me, sir."

Buford hung up the receiver and ran to the public rest room, where he promptly vomited.

28

JIGS AND ARTHUR SAID THEIR "thank yous" and their "good byes" to Jim Labuda. They all promised to keep each other informed as to any new information to which any one of them became privy. Over breakfast, Jigs and Arthur continued to discuss the state of affairs, as they knew it. The morning fog was apparent in the early dawn light, which crept across the channels and inlets that were in view off Arthur's poolside deck. Boats continued to putter bye, as Southern California was waking up.

"What time is it in Italy?"

"I think it is about 3:00pm on today's date. I don't know. My sister used to be the one that could answer that question. They traveled so often and so extensively that she always knew the time everywhere."

"Well, I am surprised we haven't heard from Willie, especially if it is mid afternoon where he is."

As if on queue, Arthur's telephone rang.

"Your ears must be burning," Arthur said as he spoke into the wireless phone. "We were just talking about you...No, actually, we are both up. We have been up for quite a while. I am putting you on speaker." Arthur pushed the button for the speakerphone and Willie's voice could be heard.

"…Put the tree hugger on with us," he was saying.

"Hey, fuckstick, are you a communist yet? I figure a day or so in any part of Europe and they would have you by now."

"Not likely, however, I went by a hospital a while ago. There were lines of sick people around the block. It looked like a Rolling Stones concert."

"Yeah…right."

"So, you guys have probably been sitting around on your asses, waiting for me to solve this case for you, right?"

Jigs looked at Arthur and smiled.

"You got it…Arthur ordered in those girls he had promised, and it has been booze and broads ever since you left. You know…its LA. We had one for you, but she's also with me now. I guess these two gals were friends before they got here…cuz they sure are friends now."

"Just thinking about something like that is going to wind you up in the hospital with a heart attack, old man, let alone doing it…Now…tell me what's really happening back there, leave out the pathetic, old codger fantasies. "

"Actually, you have to get back here, man. We are pretty sure Ned has plans to fly away, for good. He has been moving his financial holdings around…positioning them for a sell off…Oh, and you can thank Arthur, here, for that little tidbit of information. He has become a regular Sherlock Holmes."

"Really, Arthur, you sleuth you."

Arthur was smiling proudly. "Yeah, I don't know how you two guys ever get anything done. All you do is fuck around. I thought I should lend a hand. So you two could save face."

"Hey, thank you Arthur."

Jigs asked in a slightly more serious tone, "So, what have you heard, dickhead? What do the Italians know?"

"Well…as it pertains to their case here…they know exactly what happened…they just can not prove it."

"Really…do tell."

"It seems the husband of the woman that took the header off the cliff and lived…well…he is kind of a twit. He only has money because his wife has money. He only has prestige because his wife has prestige. Wait, that is not exactly true…

This guy's name is Davisimo Lombardi. When this guy was young, Davisimo was one of these Italian gods. He was one of these guys that looks like a model, only better, with the thick black wavy hair, dark swarthy skin, deep dimples, square jaw. Actually, he is still pretty much of a heart throb, I guess."

"Hold on a second," Jigs interrupted. "Did you turn gay since you left here? Not that there is anything wrong with that...but...I'm just curious."

"Fuck you, hippy, I am trying to make a point here. Shut it..."

Jigs and Arthur were laughing silently.

"...so, this guy meets the daughter of one of the richest men in all Italy. She is smitten. They get married. Mr. Lombardi goes to work for daddy at one of their largest companies. He actually does very well. He is considered, by everyone that matters, as a truly innovative manager and CEO. They actually write books about his management style. He is revered in the Italian business community. But... no matter how well he does, no matter how many books they write about him, or awards he wins, or how much money he makes, he is always second fiddle to his wife. She is treated like a princess. He becomes rich, but the wife and her family are wealthy...really wealthy. He is always just the husband to the star. Do you get my drift, or am I going too fast for you?"

"We're with you…keep talking."

"Well, as you might expect, Davisimo, who has an ego the size of the Alps, is not happy; but he cannot do anything about it because he will lose his connection to the golden goose. The detective here, who is very good by the way, hypothesizes that Mr. Lombardi decides he would rather be the grieving widower of the magnificent princess than the husband of the magnificent princess. This would give him favorite son status. He would become the family's only living connection to their dead princess. There would be all this empathy. This is the convoluted logic of those obsessed with money, I guess. Of course, the death of the fair one has to be the result of a tragic accident."

"OK, sounds interesting, but I can hear you leading up to something, like, how this all relates to us. Am I right, or is this just story time?"

"Sit tight, lib…listen. My new best friend, Detective Anthony Biancafiore, tells me that there is a phantom, a myth, a guy whom is known by law enforcement all over Europe… and in the United States, but, evidently, a little more so in Europe, that is famous, or infamous if you prefer. Interpol knows about him, the FBI, all the alphabets. This guy is a contract assassin that no one can catch. They don't even know his name, because his name changes constantly. They certainly don't know what he looks like. No picture has ever been taken. This guy is right out of a spy novel. The only reason they know about him at all is because of his methods. From time to time they see what they believe to be his style, like this time, this case here in Italy. They are sure this guy was involved, but their hands are tied. Once Interpol discovered the same prints at two separate accident scenes. They are pretty sure they belong to this guy, but there is no way in hell they can prove anything. The two victims might have had the same mechanic, just as easily. He is always considered, however, when wealthy wives, husbands or business partners die accidentally.

The closest they ever got to this guy was in France, when a sad excuse for a husband to a dead heiress that died in an accident, spilled his guts. The only problem was, the guy never saw or talked to the operative. The job was contracted through a web of connections that breaks down after you investigate the first few levels. All this dunce could tell them was that he transferred a million Euros to an offshore account, and the job got done. He would not have ever been suspected either; except that husband had a horrendous attack of conscience. What an idiot. They were grateful, however, because they had an opportunity to check out his handiwork, his style, if you will. All of this leads up to the following: Detective Biancafiore believes, well actually he says he is sure, that the attempt on the princess here is the work of this guy. They call him John Doe "the Great", pretty funny, huh? Further, Anthony says that if Anna's case were his case, he would believe that the same John Doe "the Great" was suspect, based on what I have told him."

"What do you think of all this? It sounds a little far fetched, to me. Or, do you believe this theory is sound?"

"Oh, the theory is sound, all right. There are a lot of very smart law enforcement types all over the world that believe that this guy is real, and that he has been responsible for several "accidental" deaths to persons where big, big bucks are involved. Do I think the guy is used as a scapegoat when no other answers are available? Absolutely. No question. Anytime you have a legendary figure, a phantom type, they get tagged with every unsolved crime that fits their pattern. Having said that, is it possible that our case could involve this guy? It very well could...Now, I have an appointment to talk with the would be "victim" in this Italian case, the princess, who, by the way, is still with her good looking husband, and does not believe any of this shit...After that, I was going to fly back there. What do you guys think?"

"We want you back here, Wil, don't ask me why we want an old fart Republican anywhere near us, but we do. As I said, it is starting to look like Ned may be planning to make a move, and...we can't have that now, can we? So, get your ass back here. We miss you."

"Yeah, right...now you sound gay."

"See you in…what…fifteen or twenty hours?"

"That sounds about right, I'll call when I get there."

29

BUFORD SPAT OUT THE LAST of the remaining bits of peanuts that he had had on the plane, and washed out his mouth with water again and again. He looked in the mirror. His face was as red as a beet, the veins at his temples bulged, and tears dripped from his eyes, although he wasn't crying. He splashed cold water on his face. Slowly, he could see his features returning to normal, now that he seemed to be through wretching. He hated this whole sordid business. However, he had absolutely no choice in the matter, in his view, and he was preparing to go back out and do the same thing again with reference to Mr. Washington. He shook off the effects of his bout with nerves. He once had the same experience before. It was in anticipation of a big playoff game. It was nothing. Buford walked out of the public restroom as if nothing unusual had happened. He approached the bank of payphones. Again, nobody was around.

"Mr. Washington, I am very glad I caught you. I have something to discuss with you. Do you have a minute?"

"Who the fuck is this and how the fuck did ya'all get this number?"

"That doesn't matter, sir. What does matter is that I know that you are buying, presently in possession of, and regularly taking anabolic steroids. I guess you would have to call this a shakedown. I think that is what it is called. That is what it is called, isn't it, sir?"

"Fuck you, man. I don't take no steroids, man. Who the fuck is this?"

"Mr. Washington, this is not a debate. I did not say that I think that you are taking steroids, if ya'all were paying attention; you will remember that I said that I *know* that you are taking steroids. Now, I will assume that the fact that I also seem to know your personal private cell phone number is, at least in part, the reason why you all have not hung up on me. I also assume that the other reason you have not hung up on me yet is because…you know as well as I do that you are taking steroids and you don't want me to tell anyone about that fact. Now, if you are smart, ya'all will listen to what I have to say. It will be surprisingly painless, I assure you. Do I have your attention, sir?"

Silence. No "click," just silence.

"Your dealer's name is "Ice." His real name is actually Malcolm Jackson. I bet even you did not know that. His cell phone number is 222-333-4444, and he makes deliveries to you at the house you all bought for your Mama at 2121 W. Argyle St.

right there in Miami. If I had to, I could produce a recording of a phone call between you and Mr. Ice. I do not expect to have to do that, however. Again I ask you, sir, do I have your attention?"

"I fuckin' hear ya'all, muthur fucker. What else does ya'all have ta say?"

"Well, there is an answer to that too. But first, I have to indulge myself...I played football in high school. I love football. This conversation will not be a discussion about the use of anabolic steroids. I just have one thing to say, on a personal level... You should be ashamed of yourself. You all have this unbelievably wonderful opportunity to play this absolutely incredibly great sport. Please don't degrade it, sir... Ok, that was what you call an aside. This is what I actually called to tell you. You are to place $100,000.00 in unmarked, non-sequential one hundred dollar bills in a tightly wrapped plain brown package. Make it look like a business package. Mail it to this address. Do you all have a pen, sir?"

"Hoed on...hoed on...OK, give it to me."

"Mail the package to D.J., Inc. at 141 Robert E. Lee Blvd., #603, New Orleans, Louisiana 70116. Make sure it goes out immediately. I must receive it no later than this coming Friday. Now, I understand that you all are probably concerned that I might keep doing this to you again and again. Don't worry. I am a Christian man, sir. I have children and a wife. I am not a bad person, sir. I am not a criminal. However, I am in very deep trouble. I need this money. This amount is insignificant to you. To me... it is my salvation. I didn't, and still don't, want to be doing this. I do not want to harm you in any way. This is a one-time thing for me. You have my solemn word. I have read about you, sir. I know that you too are a Christian. There have been articles about how you take care of your Mama. This whole matter has to do with my mother as well. She is sick. I would not do this unless I had no choice. You will be free from me after this one time. I swear to almighty God. Just do what I ask. If you do not comply, I will have no alternative but to ruin your life. Play the tape all the way to the end, sir. If I were forced to expose this little secret of yours, it would not be at all good for your career, to say the least. Think about it. I have two words to say to you...Barry Bonds. You just paid twice this amount for a damn car. It really is not worth taking a chance on any other scenario. The pain that would result would not be worth the risk. If you do not do this, there will be a shit storm in your life that you will not enjoy. Everything you have worked so hard for...gone."

"You muthur fucker..." And then Mr. Washington was gone.

Buford walked from the strip mall in a calm confident manner. This time he had no urge to puke. Like everything else in life, except marriage, it got easier the second time around. He had no idea what would happen next. He simply figured he would know soon enough.

30

TOM GAZDIK A/K/A THOMAS POPULOUS was accepting deliveries. He had ordered several items over the Internet, which he could not pick up with his rental car. "Next day delivery is a godsend," he thought. The delivery trucks were coming and going. He ordered a bed and box spring that he positioned on the floor of the office section of his rented space near the bathroom. He also had another delivery guy wheel in a chest style deep freezer. That went in the garage area near where the Mercedes was parked. He had ordered a cheap desk and chair, which went in the office. Each time a delivery arrived, he was dressed a little differently. He wore hats, sunglasses, different things…just different enough.

When he was alone in the rented building, he would watch TV or work on his computer. He also had what he considered a "hobby." His "hobby" had a direct connection to his work. One might say it was essential to his profession, but others that performed similar services did not usually have the same "hobby." They simply paid others to provide the items that Mr. Gazdik's hobby provided. Tom did not trust others. He was a perfectionist. He felt he could do anything better than anyone else. Plus, he got a kick out of his "hobby." Some guys collected baseball cards. Tom collected identities.

Tom only worked occasionally. His jobs would usually take less than fifteen days from planning stage to completion. Often much less. The rest of the year he sometimes traveled, but most of the time he was a homebody. It wasn't so bad. He lived in the Cayman Islands, close to his money. He liked that he received special treatment from bankers that were famous for giving special treatment to the rich and famous, worldwide. He got extra special treatment because he was a local. He often required this type of special treatment. Some of his transactions had to be kept very confidential. It was easier to get the treatment he needed as a local. Tom was like that. He left nothing to chance. Nothing.

This attention to detail applied to his "hobby" as well. Tom would peruse the major newspapers of the world on line. He liked to be well informed, but he actually would pay particular attention to the obituaries. Sometimes, he was checking up on his own handiwork, but that was rare. He did not need the obits to tell him of his own exploits. What he was looking for were deaths in which the date of death was within one year of the date of birth. When he found one of these sad entries, he would make a file on his computer containing all of the vital statistics.

When he first began his "hobby" he had to short circuit what has grown into a more perfected version of this "hobby." Now, when he does travel, he stops by the bureau of vital statistics, or the office of births and deaths, maybe the office of the clerk of records, whatever applies, in the county or burrow or town or city where the birth was recorded. He buys a certified copy of the certificate of birth. They usually cost about two dollars. Sometimes, they are free. That is when the fun begins.

Tom begins a file on each "person." Then he waits. When the "person" is approximately ten years old or so, he applies for a social security number and card in the U.S., or its equivalent in other countries. Then he waits some more. At about age sixteen, his person may get their first job. It varies from one "person" to the next, just like in life. He slowly, methodically and purposefully builds their lives. He rents apartments, gets credit cards, opens bank accounts for his "persons" all over the world. They have jobs, file taxes and, in general, exist. Over the years he has created approximately twenty adults, with many more growing up to replace the ones that have disappeared. When he is stopped by the police for a ticket, for example, he actually is the "person" that he has currently assumed, complete with back-story and work history. He is a meticulous soul. He is careful. The expenses he incurs in giving life to his "persons" are a cost of doing business. It is money well spent. He can afford it.

Unfortunately, the government began a program of assigning social security numbers to children at birth. This has made his little system unworkable in the United States. This does not bother Tom. He has enough "persons" to last him until he retires, for which he is beginning to make extensive plans. It would seem that he was heading for a very long and pleasant retirement.

31

FRIDAY MORNING WAS PLEASANT. Buford's household was as it always was. The kids were getting ready for school, his wife was making breakfast and he was getting ready to fly back to New Orleans. Two trips inside of a week were unusual for Buford, he normally went to work and only to work, but these were unusual circumstances. Everyone understood, however, his mom was quite ill, and that was the apparent reason for his trip. He sat with his wife over bacon and eggs. He looked at her and at his children as they scurried around prior to the arrival of their school bus, and remembered why he was doing what he was doing. He had no remorse or second thoughts about his true plans. He was doing what men had always done, no more no less. He was protecting his family. Nothing else mattered.

A taxi appeared in their driveway. Buford kissed his kids and then his wife. He grabbed a small carry on bag and ran out to the cab. He would make his flight with time to spare. The flight went without incident and arrived in New Orleans on time. He rented a car and headed into The Crescent City's mid-morning traffic.

Buford had no illusions about the danger and the potential catastrophe into which he was heading. He had no idea if one or both of his victims had alerted the authorities. He could be walking straight into a trap.

As he drove and got closer to the Mailboxes Etc., he could feel the adrenalin starting to course through his veins. It amazed him to realize how physiological this experience was becoming. His heart was racing and his senses were keen. New Orleans was always muggy, but his perspiration was not due to the humidity. He pulled into the parking lot of the strip mall that was his destination. He saw the sign for the Mailboxes Etc., and he pulled the rental car into a parking space that was far enough away from the entrance so that it was not obvious that he was planning to patronize that particular store. He turned off the engine and focused on the entrance to the establishment. Then he sat. He did not take his eyes off of the doorway. He could see inside. He sat some more...just watching. He then began to pay particular attention to the parking lot. He looked at each and every shopper. He looked into every car parked in the lot. He fully expected to see a nondescript car of some sort, perhaps a Ford or a Chevy, with two bored men in it, one reading the paper, the other staring out the window, coffee cups on the dash board, like in every bad cop movie he had ever seen where a "stakeout" was depicted. He did not see anything like that. Nothing.

Buford thought of walking towards the mailbox store and suddenly being surrounded by men and women with guns drawn and yellow signs on the backs of their black tee shirts, which exclaimed FBI or SWAT, and screaming at the top of their lungs…"Get on the ground…put your hands behind your back!" Although this image made him shudder, it was quickly replaced with the image of his wife and two kids being forcibly evicted from their home in Ft. Meade, with all the neighbors staring and pointing. He did not like either image, however it made him realize that those were his choices. What a mess… He then realized that there was a third scenario. He could walk into the store, pick up his packages, and walk out, without incident. He reached for the door handle, and opened the door to his rental car. He stepped out and began walking towards the store.

Buford's eyes were darting all around. He was looking in every direction. He walked slowly but purposefully towards the entrance. There was nothing unusual… yet. As he approached the doorway he could see inside the store. He knew the layout. He had been there before. This time, he was looking for irregularities, movement, an unusual person or two hanging around. No one. Nothing. He kept walking.

Buford entered the store. The clerk on duty was a man about thirty years old with salt and pepper prematurely gray hair, slightly overweight, and a big toothy smile. "Hello sir, may I help you with anything…or are you just going to your box?"

Sometimes, these guys overdo the greeting, in an effort to be oh so friendly. This guy certainly fit that bill. Buford did not mind. He was just glad that no guns were drawn in his direction. The clerk was standing behind a counter. Behind him were shelves covered with boxes of different sizes and shapes. Also behind the clerk was a door that evidently led to a back room. That door worried Buford. Anyone or anything could be back there. Buford simply nodded at the guy and pointed at the adjacent room where the mailboxes were. The clerk understood.

Buford walked directly up to box number 603. He stuck his key in the slot and turned. It was at this moment that Buford felt both the most excited and the most vulnerable. His heart was beating through his chest. He was sure anyone with ears could hear it pounding. It was that loud inside Buford's own head. He could see something in there. He could feel pins and needles all over his body. He reached in and pulled out a package wrapped in plain brown wrapping paper, with no return address. Just block letters...DJ, Inc. and the address. There was more...junk mail? How can there be junk mail already? Buford looked through the mail, trying to look nonchalant, but his hands were shaking. Just ads, the kind everyone gets. There was a large trashcan that was placed near the mailboxes specifically for the purpose of accepting the junk mail. He tossed the items into it. He kept the package.

It was in his hands, this package. He could feel its firmness. He was disappointed that there were not two of them, but he was quite excited that there was one. He began to walk towards the door. As he passed by the clerk, he smiled. That is when it happened.

"Excuse me sir, did you just come from box 603?" The clerk was smiling the same plastic smile that was on his face when Buford walked in. No change, nothing to indicate his intention. Buford was not sure if he was going to pass out or fall down. He could hardly breath and he could barely feel his legs. One of the two had to give. All he could do was to nod at that stupid toothy grin.

"Do not go anywhere, sir. Wait right there." The clerk then took two steps to his rear and opened the door to the back room about ten inches. "Mailbox number 603," he yelled into the opening.

Everything was happening in slow motion. Buford looked at the exit door to the store. He could see shoppers blithely walking by. He could see cars in the parking lot. He could see his rental car. He could see the blue sky and the green trees that surrounded the parking lot. He could see freedom. He felt trapped. He thought about bolting for the door. He did not know what to do.

A pretty girl about eighteen or nineteen years old with red hair and freckles appeared in the doorway to the back room. She smiled a winning smile at Buford and then she handed a package wrapped in plain brown paper to the man with the teeth. "Here it is," she said, and then she faded back into the room behind her. The door closed.

"This one would not fit into your box, sir." The clerk was holding the package out so Buford could take it from him. Buford let out an incredible rush of air and immediately took in another. He looked like he felt, eyes wide, mouth slightly agape, a deer in headlights.

"I'm sorry, sir, did I startle you?"

Buford did a magnificent job of pulling himself together. "Yes, I'm sorry, I was not paying attention to you. I was concerned about that second package." He pointed to the package in the man's hand. "It is important. I did not know you all stored them back there. I thought it just didn't come. Thank you very much." He took the package from the clerk.

"Yes, sir, when a package will not fit into your box, we store them back in the back room..." The guy was still talking when Buford left the store. He walked across the parking lot to his rental and got in. His heart was still pounding and his breath was short, but he was beginning to realize that all he needed to do now…was start the car and drive away. That is exactly what he did.

———————

By the time Buford had reached Interstate 10, he was beginning to experience an incredible euphoria. The nervousness that had plagued him during his escapade was being replaced by a sense of calmness that he had never felt before in his life. The only time he had felt anything close to this feeling was when he was leaving Vicksburg, Mississippi years ago, after he had hit the jackpot on the slot machine. This was like that. Only, this was much more serene.

When he left Vicksburg, he was going back and forth between guilt and this feeling of euphoria. For some reason he was not feeling the guilt this time. Not at all, not this time. He had stopped looking in the rear view mirror about three miles back. He had accepted that he was not being followed. He had actually convinced himself that God had let this happen because that is what God wanted. God wanted his mother to have the medical treatment she needed and deserved. God wanted his family to lives their life in a state of relative happiness and peace. They deserved it.

What was amazing to Buford is that he had not even opened the packages yet. He knew what was in them. The packages were just lying there on the passenger seat. $200,000.00! Everything he needed. No more did he have to be obsessed about Billy the bookie and his goons. No more concerns about how his mother would receive her operation. No more worries about money. He actually would have money left over, a lot of it. All of the fears that had threatened to give him an ulcer... evaporated. Poof. Gone. He started to laugh out loud. It was all better. Problem solved. Two telephone calls and...Problem solved... Thank you Jesus!

32

THE THREE MUSKETEERS WERE reunited at the Air Italia terminal at LAX. Jigs and Arthur sat waiting for Willie in Arthur's black Lincoln Executive Series sedan. Arthur's company had purchased the limo to take advantage of the fact that limos had special entrances and egress at the airport. It was a semi stretched version of the classic Lincoln. He had a driver, but they did not bother him for this pick up. Arthur drove. Jigs teased him.

Willie exited the terminal door and headed for the car. He had been alerted as to what car he should look for when he called. He jumped into the back seat and said, "Home, Jeeves."

"Have you slept?" Jigs was not really concerned, but it is what people said.

"What the fuck do you care, lib?" Willie actually did look tired. He had been up for hours. "Actually, I slept on the plane. What's with the limo?"

"My company picks up some very big bigwigs, Coca Cola, Pepsi, General Mills, Seagrams, etc. etc. Plus, we get to use the limo lanes. It was just cost effective for us. We don't worry about the car being late. We often fly out of Signature Flight Services; therefore, we go at odd hours…"

"I really wasn't looking for a company history, Arthur. What's all this about Ned trying to fly the coop?"

"Arthur's broker confirms that there is some significant activity in the financial world of Mr. Ned Khan. He believes, as do we, that it is an effort to consolidate and divest."

"Well, we have to fuckin' stop that shit, don't we?"

"Yeah, we sure do… How about you? What is all this spy novel crap, a sinister, shadowy, phantom figure? Are you buying all this shit?"

"Actually, I do. It fits. Ned has that kind of money. He travels in those kinds of crowds. You know…the kind of crowds that would know about a secret professional, phantom killer that works only for rich guys… What I cannot figure out is why. Why kill Anna? Have you guys gotten any closer to an answer to that question?"

"No, not really."

"So, Arthur, what are you doing, Mr. Limo driver? Are you working your way down the ladder of success?"

Everyone laughed.

"Where are we going...my house?" Arthur was playing his part.

"Well...I could use a drink..." Willie was only half kidding.

"What, no booze on the plane?"

"Of course there was booze on the plane, but that was over an hour ago...friggin' Customs... takes forever."

"Willie, open that cupboard type door right in front of you." Arthur was smiling at Jigs.

"Arthur, don't encourage him," Jigs said.

Willie opened the fine mahogany door and said, "Hey...I like Jack Daniels." The other two looked at each other and shook their heads.

"What?" Willie was smiling and pulling the bottle together with a cut crystal glass from the cabinet. "Is there ice...oh, of course, I see it here...you rich guys have it made, don't you?" Willie got some ice from a built in ice bucket that was full of cracked ice. Everything was built so as to limit the ability for anything to move around while driving. "Arthur, this is nice." He sipped his drink.

"Did the "princess" shed any light on this situation?" Jigs asked.

"Not really. She swears that someone slipped her a mickey or something. The only problem with that theory is that the cops investigated every person that could have gotten close to her. Each person has been with her for years, all trusted employees, and, of course, her husband, whom she does not suspect. She and her husband are still together, so I hope he is not the guy. She said she smelled something strange in the car. The only problem…they found no evidence of drugs in the car or in her. I will say this, though. Detective Biancafiore, whom I respect, thinks the cops that responded to the initial call…did not follow through very well because they thought she was crazy…or drunk. Therefore, evidence was not preserved. Some of the investigation could have been bungled. Biancafiore believes there was an attempt on her life and he likes the husband for the perpetrator, by proxy of course, but any evidence that might have existed of that is long gone. Although they list the file as open, they are only doing that to placate the "princess's" wealthy family. Nobody is working the file, and probably nobody ever will."

"So…we know nothing new, except that there is a real cool professional killer out there that we need not fear because he only does business with billionaires."

"That is not a fair characterization, dickwad." Willie sipped his drink. He was exaggerating the elite way of drinking from a crystal glass with his pinky finger extended. "In our set of facts we suspect the billionaire husband. We know, however, that he could not have done it because he was on a damn private plane. So, my rather exhausting little trip provides us with information that gives us an explanation for how it got done."

"Well, if you put it that way."

"That is the only way to put it, hippy."

"OK, who do you know at the LAPD?"

"I know several guys who are good detectives, but the guy we want to talk to is my buddy Detective Mark Roth…Why, do you think we have enough to get them interested?"

"Presentation, presentation…don't you think? If we present it right. We are going to need a cop on our side, and soon. If this asshole, Ned, is going to try to sky, we need a cop. Will this guy work with us?"

"Oh yeah…you will like this guy…you too, Arthur. He will fit right in."

"Well, set up a meeting. It's time."

———————————

The next morning Willie arranged for a meeting with Detective Mark Roth of the Los Angeles Police Department. Willie had known Mark for years, dating back to his days of freelance reporting. Willie never referred to himself as a reporter. In fact, he often went out of his way to deny ever having been one. Arthur wondered why. "So Willie, why are you so hell bent to distance yourself from the Forth Estate?"

"What...are you writing a book?"

"We are going to be in this traffic for quite some time. I was just curious. Don't get snotty on me."

"OK...OK...sorry, Arthur. Lets see...well...in a nutshell... I used to believe that being a journalist was an esteemed profession. The very concept of the Forth Estate...and I think even the hippy over there agrees with me on this one... being a journalist made you part of the checks and balances that have been established for this great nation's form of government. The idea that a free press watched the persons holding office and held them accountable, gave me chills. Especially, when I read my own article... the first time I had a published story in the newspaper. I was joining the same profession as the great reporters, the great men that kept this country strong. I was joining the free press. I was proud... Then came the eighties, and cable news, and paying for news stories, and millionaire newsmen, and "newspersons", and "access", and book deals, celebrity "news" and celebrity "reporters" and "Rush" and "Sean", hell, I could go on and on. Just about the time that the movie "Broadcast News" came out warning against where the profession, and the assholes in it, were all heading, that was when the whole profession turned into whores, most of them anyway. There were always some that seemed to be keeping the faith, but fewer and fewer every day. It seemed to me that a lot of these guys and girls made a conscious decision to emulate the William Hurt character rather than the Albert Brooks character... like none of them got the point...   It makes me sick...shit...I don't want to get up on a soapbox...let's leave it at this...I am no longer proud to say that I am a journalist and I don't know how most of the so called journalists today can look at themselves in the mirror...so...I don't fucking say that I am, or ever was, a journalist anymore. Does that answer your question?"

"OK...a simple 'all journalists are fags' response would have sufficed."

"I'm sorry, Arthur, I don't mean to preach. I just feel strongly about that issue."

"No...no...Willie...I agree with you. I do. I was just trying to be funny...unsuccessfully."

"Arthur...you are always funny...funny looking." Willie whispered the last two words.

"Now boys, let's get back on the issue at hand. What are we going to say to this cop?"

Silence…then some laughter.

"Don't worry, I have this one," Jigs said with mock conviction.

They pulled up in front of the precinct, jumped out and headed toward the front door, piling into the amazing world that is inside any precinct headquarters. It was a sea of desks and uniformed and plain clothed officers moving in every direction. And it was loud. There were donut boxes and coffee cups half full of stale coffee strewn about. There were obvious suspects being questioned and obvious complainants actively complaining. If they were not in an actual LAPD precinct it could have been a movie set. They headed towards what seemed to be the main desk, and talked to a cop straight out of central casting. He was overweight, balding and gray, except the hair growing out of his ears... that was jet black.

"Hi, we are looking for Detective Mark Roth…He is expecting us." Jigs was the first to speak up.

"See that door, right there, marked 'Investigations'? Go through that door. There is a receptionist about thirty feet in. Tell the girl. I believe he is in."

"Thanks." They all walked through the door as directed. As soon as they got inside they saw a tall, lanky, handsome man with blonde slightly graying hair talking on a telephone at a desk about thirty feet inside the door. The guy waved at Willie and motioned them all in. He hung up the phone.

"The receptionist is on break. She is a civil service employee." Then under his breath he said, "I wish I got as many breaks…" Then loudly he said, " Willie Brennen…how the F are you?" The guy looked around as if to check for any women. Then he said, "How have you been you old fuck?" He had a big winning smile that creased his face with laugh lines. He had a big time California tan. This guy looked like he spent a lot of time on the golf course, or on a boat, or both. He walked toward them and grabbed Willie's hand with a death grip.

Jigs…Arthur, this is Mark Roth. Mark, this is Jigs Donahue and Arthur Buckingham. They all shook hands and Mark led them to his office.

"So…I am told you guys have information about a case?" Mark was pointing to chairs and closing the door behind him.

"Mark," Jigs began, "Arthur here is Anna Khan's brother. Are you familiar with her case? She was a woman that was killed near Laurel Canyon when her Mercedes went off the road. She was a favorite of many charities, very wealthy woman. Do you recall her case?"

The detective sat down in his large leather chair behind his small cluttered desk.

"Forgive me Arthur if I sound at all disrespectful. I am very sorry for your loss. Having said that...my answer to you, Jigs, is this...of fucking course I fucking recall that a fucking young, fucking beautiful billionaire fucking woman fucking died in my fucking district. What the fuck do I fucking look like to you...some kind of fucking asshole?" The detective had the look of pure furry in his eyes. He was staring at Jigs with what seemed to be abject contempt. Jigs was taken aback, to say the least. He looked at Willie for some help. Willie was staring at his shoelaces. Jigs looked at Arthur. He seemed very interested in the ceiling. It was starting to get more and more quiet in the room. Jigs had no idea what to say. It was becoming increasingly uncomfortable in the office with each passing second. "This guy is a little touchy," Jigs was thinking. He was actually starting to get angry, both at the cop and at his so-called friends. He didn't come here to be yelled at by this son of a bitch. Jigs was about to speak his mind when Mark spoke first.

"I bet you are a fucking hippy...to boot."

Jigs looked at Willie...then at Arthur...then at this detective. "What the fuck?"

Willie was first to crack. He started with the kind of laugh that you try so hard to hold in that it just gets worse. Then Arthur broke.

"You pricks," Jigs said to everyone in the room. That is when the laughing started in earnest. Willie said very quietly, "Gotcha lib."

"Arthur, you are a party to this. You must be. I would expect this from the Bush lover over there…but, you Arthur? You?"

Arthur could not stop silently laughing.

"Plus, a member of LA's finest. You should be ashamed, sir. Ashamed, I say."

More laughter.

"I called Mark to inform him of the purpose of our visit. We talked for a while. You deserved that you leftist son of a bitch." Willie was calming down.

"OK…OK, that was fun, but lets get down to business. Jigs, I'm Mark. Willie tells me you guys think that Anna Khan's death was not accidental. I have the file right here. I have reviewed it. Why don't you fill me in on why you guys think what you think; because, I have to say, based on what I see in this file, it looks like an accident to me."

"We believe that it was designed to look that way. Let me start at the beginning." Jigs was collecting his thoughts. "Immediately after Anna died, Arthur saw Ned, her husband, and Arthur was not impressed by his reaction to his wife's death. Ned was, in Arthur's opinion, way too quick to accept that Anna's death was an accident. He called Willie and I to get a dispassionate point of view. We came here and we first went to the place that Anna was heading on the night she died to see if we could unearth any leads there. We discovered that a man that looked like George Castanza had waited at the restaurant at the exact same time as that of Anna's appointment..."

Mark was curious so he interrupted. "Excuse me, Jigs. How did you guys know where she was heading? We did not have that. One of our investigators asked Mr. Khan for that information, and he said he did not know where she was going or who she was meeting."

"See...now...that is exactly the kind of thing that has got all of us so suspicious that Ned may have had a hand in this..." Jigs was pointing at Arthur and Willie indicating that they were all in agreement on this issue. They were nodding. "We all heard Ned say that he knew whom she was meeting and that that person...to quote him...'was loaded'...meaning rich."

"What do you mean when you say that you all heard him say that? When did you hear him say this?"

"Let me go back. Arthur, being her brother, had access to certain things. One, he had a key to the Khan's home. Two, he had the password for her voicemail. Arthur went to the Khan home immediately upon having been informed of Anna's death. There was really nothing else for him to do at the time. He was sad. He went there. He found and took with him her appointment book, which indicated that she was meeting a person named Jonathon F. Butcher at the Pig n' Whistle..."

"Now, that could be considered tampering with evidence of a crime, and why didn't you come to us, Arthur?" Mark had interrupted again.

Arthur was shrugging his shoulders.

Jigs continued. "He couldn't have been tampering with evidence of a crime. You guys didn't think it was a crime... and we are coming to you now. We are here now. Right?"

"OK...forget that...go on." The detective was now taking notes.

"OK...so...where was I...oh yeah. So, we went to the Pig n' Whistle where we found out about this George Castanza guy. This guy had arrived at the restaurant at the very time Anna was supposed to arrive. He told the waitress and the hostess that he was waiting for another party. The party never showed. He left. Then, some time later I might add..." Jigs looked at Arthur with a knowing smile. Arthur looked helpless "…Arthur called Anna's voicemail. We all heard a message, left by Ned for Anna at a time we believe to be within minutes prior to her death. It was on speakerphone so we all heard it. Ned was talking about the meeting that Anna had and the guy she had it with."

"See now…that is just the kind of thing that perks our interest…here in the law enforcement community…ya know…when we discover that someone lied to us. Now, here I sit looking right at a note in this file where it says that Ned didn't know nuthin' about the person she was meeting or where she was going. Perhaps he would like to explain that little inconsistency."

"I don't want to tell you your business, but there is more, and this little tidbit may cause you to want to wait to ask Ned any more questions."

"What is that?"

"Well, it would seem that Mr. Khan is making plans to move away from this fair city. He told us that. Plus, he has been moving most of his money around…We think…in an effort to consolidate his rather extensive wealth and possibly divest most or all of his holdings here in the United States. Then he would be liquid. He could disappear."

"He could run his business from anywhere. Why would he divest?"

"It would be harder to run his business from Iran, especially if we wind up in a war with Iran. Plus, if he turns out to be a suspect in a murder case, and he becomes a fugitive, some of those assets might be subject to seizure, right?"

"You think he would go there, to Iran?"

"He has royal blood. Maybe he has worked out a deal with his relatives. However, I don't know if the royals are that welcome in their own country these days. I don't know. It is all speculation at this point. However, we thought it was time we got you guys involved. Although we are speculating, some of the guesses sound plausible. It is becoming easier and easier to believe the speculation."

"That was a good decision, coming to us. What else do you have?"

"Willie, the conservative old man here, whom seems to have converted you to his evil ways of harassing me, has recently been to Italy. He went there to chase down a possible lead. He found out that there exists a contract killer who seems to limit his services to the very, very wealthy, a mythical figure, of sorts. Our Mr. Khan could have employed this guy. Again, speculation, nothing more, but it is based on some investigation and thoughtful reasoning. All of what we have at this point is speculation. However, we believe that it is all leading up to something, and we believe that our time limitations are shrinking by the day. With each day that passes we get closer to possibly losing our suspect forever. Now, based on what you have heard so far, do you have any thoughts or an opinion?"

"Yes I do. I hate it when a person lies to me or to one of my people. If what you guys are telling me is true, and I have no reason to doubt that it is, it would seem that our friend, Mr. Khan, has done just that, lied. That alone would make me curious as to why. But, I still do not see a motive, not that one is absolutely necessary. It would make me more comfortable if we had one, though. We like things neat…you know…means, motive and opportunity. We have means and opportunity, if you accept the paid assassin theory, but no motive. What we do have, however, is more than enough for me to reopen this file, and to put a couple guys on it. You guys have me on your side, for whatever that is worth. I don't like people who lie to cops. There is usually a reason why they do it."

33

BUFORD STAYED IN BED A LITTLE longer this Monday morning. Like last week, the kooky DJ was in the same manic mood that always characterized his show. Like last week, his wife and children were doing what they always did in the morning, making breakfast and getting ready for school, respectively. Like last week, the sun was peeking through the curtains in his bedroom. This Monday morning was different than last week, however, very different. Only one week earlier to the minute Buford was considering suicide, literally. Today, he was fantastic. No worries. Last week he hated the kooky DJ. Today he thought that he was hilarious, the funniest guy on the radio. Last week he was sure his life was fast coming to an abrupt end. Today...life was great. Everything was copasetic.

Buford began to review the reasons why he felt the way he did. Well, his mother was going into the hospital to receive the treatment she so desperately needed later that week. He had an appointment to see Billy the bookie, and he was not concerned about life or limb. Billy would be paid in full before Buford arrived at work that morning. The money that he had lost in his attempt to afford his mother's treatment was back in the bank, together with an extra $25,000.00. An extra $25,000.00!

Buford was almost giddy. This all was the result of two telephone calls, and, surely…the love of Jesus Christ.

It seemed that Buford had dodged a bullet. He had been very close to personal disaster. This was causing him to make some tough decisions, to rethink past practices. Although he had been placing bets on football games for years, and it was something he loved doing, he decided right then and there in the comfort of his warm bed that he should not continue to do so. It was a bet on a slew of football games that had put him so close to the edge. What concerned him the most was how close he had come to jeopardizing his family's future. So it was official, no more non-gambling bets with "sports enthusiasts." He would have to find another hobby. He did by the way.

While driving to work, Buford could not suppress the feeling of excitement that he was experiencing. He had just pulled away from a Dunkin' Donuts where he had met with one of Billy the bookie's goons and had given him a manila envelope containing over $80,000.00 in cash. He kept thinking about the fact that he had successfully procured an amazing amount of money without a hitch. His plan had worked. He was a man that had never stepped outside of bounds, never broken the rules. His entire life was the quintessential "straight and narrow." Now, he had just met with a real "goon." Yet, he felt good about himself and what he had done. Was that a good thing? Was he heading in a wrong direction? Buford decided that as long as he kept his cool, he was not. He was convinced that his Lord and Savior, Jesus Christ, had smoothed the way for him. So, he felt great. He walked into NSA headquarters with a smile on his face and a melody in his heart.

Six months had passed and Buford had remained true to his decision to refrain from placing bets on football. His mother was on the mend following surgery and her prognosis was good. Life had returned to normalcy and Buford was happy about that. He did, however, miss the excitement of days gone by. In spite of the fact that he and his family's lives were put in peril during those days, the experience did create a level of excitement that he remembered fondly. Occasionally, he thought of how easily he had obtained such a large sum of money. When he allowed himself to do it, he rather enjoyed reliving the whole incident. He did feel that doing so might be unhealthy. Therefore, he didn't do it often. One thing became true though, and he could not deny this; he listened to every "flagged" call with a slightly different focus. He now heard the "secrets" as well as he heard the "plots," or potential plots.

It was in this context, and with this mindset, that Buford Tucker heard a conversation that would alter the course of his life, and the course of other's lives, forever. It was not a conversation full of subversive content or one that indicated impending danger to the people of the United States of America, as one might expect, given the position he held and the job that he was charged with performing. It was nothing like that. It was simply a telephone call between a man, his wife and their young twelve-year-old son. Yet, this particular conversation would prove to be the single most important telephone conversation he had ever had the misfortune to overhear.

The day started like any other day, same kooky DJ waking him up to face the day, same breakfast scene with his loving wife and adorable children, same drive through the crazy rush hour traffic on his way to work, same mundane greetings to his coworkers and subordinates on his way to his office. It was no different than any other day…really.

He was seated at his desk reviewing computer print outs from the previous night. He had been doing just that for about an hour when a lower level analyst, named Ellen knocked on his door. "Mr. Tucker, we have a high priority 'flag', which is being transferred to you, sir." All that meant was this: A call that contained several of, or all of, the criteria indicating a need for immediate review was being routed to Buford, as team leader, to check out. It happened every day. It was nothing special. "OK, Ellen, send it through at your convenience," Buford said nonchalantly. "Thank you."

Buford put his headphones on, and waited. Soon he heard the first words of a conversation, part of which was in the language of Farsi. "No wonder they sent this to me." Buford could hear all the parties changing from English to Farsi at will. There was a man, a woman and a young boy. The man was in Los Angeles. The boy and his mother were in Teheran. Ellen walked in with a printed report, which was generated to give the conversation context. Buford winked at Ellen as if to say..."Thanks." He then began to concentrate on the conversation.

" ...How is my favorite twelve year old boy?"

"I am fine, Father. I miss you. When are you coming home?"

"I miss you too, my son. I will be there soon, very soon. Someday you will have to travel for business and you will understand why so much time must be spent away from those you love... How are your studies coming along?"

"I am doing well, Father, all high marks. Did you get my email with the attachments?"

"Of course I did. Your grades are all very good. If you keep it up you will have a better average than I did when I was your age. You should be proud of yourself, son. Very proud."

"Thank you, Father. I am proud. In most classes, I have the best average."

"That is true, and soon you will have the best average in all your classes. Am I correct?"

"Yes, Father. That is my goal."

"Good for you, my boy. Now, you go and study. I need to talk to your mother for a bit, OK?"

"Yes, Father. I will see you soon, right?"

"Yes you will. You will see me very soon. I love you, my son."

"I love you, Father."

Buford heard the "click" of one of the receivers on the other end of the line. Then the woman's voice was heard…and the man's.

"When are you coming home, Nadir? Your son needs you here."

"Sonia, you know my situation. Please do not make me feel worse than I already do. I know I have a duty to my son. I know this."

"You do not seem to understand how important these years are to the boy. A boy who is a prince, I might add. He needs his father. This is the age…"

"I was not born yesterday, Sonia. I know these things only too well. I am a man, but I was once a boy of twelve. I know he needs me. You do not understand the ways of America and Americans. I am a naturalized American citizen. Therefore, I am bound by the laws of America."

"You can obtain a divorce. That seems to be the favorite pastime of Americans. You say that always. It is as common as marriage. One follows the other in America. You know this. You must do something on behalf of your son…"

"Silence! I live in California, woman! You truly do not understand Americans. A divorce would cost me…cost us…you and me and our family… over $600,000,000.00! Can you understand that, Sonia?"

Buford was mesmerized by what he was hearing. He motioned for Ellen who was outside his office. He lifted his headphones up off his ears so he could hear himself talk. "Order a complete background check on this guy…and…expedite it. Highest priority."

"Do you have something?" asked Ellen.

Buford shook his head. Then he shrugged his shoulders. He whispered, "...I don't know. Just do it. OK?" She scurried off. Buford returned to his headphones.

"...What am I supposed to do, Nadir? I cannot be a mother and a father to the boy."

"I will be there in two weeks time. I have business that will take at least three weeks, perhaps a month. I will spend time with him then. I will begin a process of coming there more often and for longer periods. I love the boy. This will all work out."

"But...Nadir..."

"No more, Sonia. Not now. We will speak about this matter at length when I am there. Right now...I must go at this time. You may tell him of my visit in two weeks. I will call tomorrow to speak to him. You are doing an admirable job, Sonia. I do not say that enough. You are a good mother... and wife.... Good-bye...Sonia."

"Good-buy, Nadir. I will speak to you tomorrow."

The conversation was over. Buford removed his headphones. He sat there silently for a few minutes trying to digest what he had just heard. No matter how hard he tried, he could not believe his ears. Did he just hear a conversation between a United States citizen that had a wife in California and another wife and son in Iran? He felt an all too familiar feeling of excitement overtaking his whole body, that physiological response that he had grown to hate and to love at the same time. It was like New Orleans all over again. It was just like the feeling he had when he was on his way to the mailbox store. Was this guy a...billionaire? Who was he? Iran? Wasn't Iran a member of the axis of evil? What did all this mean? Jeeeeesus."

Buford did not have to wait long to get some answers to these questions.

Shortly after lunch Ellen was back in Buford's office holding a file that was over two inches thick. "That wasn't hard," she said. "This guy is pretty well known in the business community, especially the international business community. He is truly a billionaire. He is a citizen. There you are. You have pictures and everything."

"Thank you, Ellen. Thank you very much. I will call you if I need anything else." Buford didn't say this in a dismissive way. He said it in an encouraging way, with emphasis on the "you." She blushed and smiled as she left his office. He was a good manager. Now, he turned his attention on the file in front of him.

The guy's name was Nadir "Ned" Khan of Los Angeles, California. He was a graduate of the University of Southern California and Southern Illinois University. He was a naturalized citizen of the United States of America. He was originally from the country of Iran where his family was Persian royalty. He was a Persian prince. He was married to one Anna Buckingham Khan from Illinois. The combined wealth of he and his wife is estimated to be in excess of a billion dollars. He and his wife are the majority shareholders in N&A Holdings, Inc. as well as a myriad of other international corporations, limited partnerships and holding companies.

Buford read page after page of this rather extensive and complete document and as he did, one thing became increasingly clear to him. Other than Ned Khan himself, Buford was probably the only person within the United States of America that knew that Mr. Khan had another wife and a twelve-year-old child. Nowhere in the pages of that document, which was prepared by both the National Security Agency and the Federal Bureau of Investigation in cooperation with each other, was there a mention of anything like that. Not a former wife or an illegitimate child. Nothing. Chills ran up and down his spine. He could hear his heart beating inside his chest. "Talk about a secret," he silently mumbled to himself. "My God."

34

As Jigs, Willie and Arthur walked out of precinct headquarters it felt to each of them that they were doing everything they could to close in on the person that they believed had caused the death of dear Anna. They all got into Arthur's big SUV.

"What's next?" Arthur did not want to leave any stone unturned.

"Well, we have covered most of our bases; however, I do think we have another step we can take." Willie was thinking out loud.

"What would that be?' Arthur asked.

"I have a friend that is an air traffic controller. I think we should pay him a visit, if he is free. He would be able to keep an eye on any plans Ned might have to fly away from this fair city."

Jigs was smiling. "Yeah, he cannot leave town without filing a flight plan. Good idea Wil."

"What do you know about it, tree hugger?"

"You forget how long you and I have been doing our thing. I can anticipate your thoughts on a matter."

"You can't anticipate shit, hippy."

"Well, let me ask you, is that the reason that you want to meet with an air traffic controller?"

"Yes."

"Well?"

"Well what?"

"Well...I was right."

"You are never right. You are left. Therefore, you are wrong."

"I am not going to dignify that crap."

"Arthur, head for your little airport."

"You mean Long Beach?"

"Yep."

"OK."

"Stop this shit. Talk normal."

"OK."

"Jeeeeesus."

They headed towards the airport through suburban L.A., each of them snickering. Finally, Willie said, "Don't worry Arthur, we have this guy, Ned. He is not going anywhere. Wait till you meet Tim Keefhaugher. When this guy was a kid, and other kids were sneaking off to meet with girls or sneaking into the movie theatre to watch "R" rated movies, this guy was sneaking off to watch planes land and take off at the airport. He eats, thinks, and dreams…airplanes. He loves them. He always has loved them. This guy will not let Mr. Khan leave here without our permission. You would be surprised at what these controller guys can do. He once told me about a dude that lost money on a sports bet. The next day the guy won all his money back by not allowing the team, on which he had lost money, arrive in the next town where they had a game. He kept diverting them. They had to forfeit the game. This guy is cool. He did not proclaim himself as the guy that made the bet…but I know better. You will like him."

"Ned flies out of Long Beach at Signature Flight Services."

"That is what I assumed. Our friend will know if the son-of -a-bitch is making plans to skid addle. Like I said…don't worry."

———————

They arrived at Long Beach airport and traveled around to the special entrance for Signature Flight Services. Jigs wanted to get a look at the lay of the land. Signature Flight Services is where the truly rich go to catch a plane. There was a small "terminal" of sorts. It is actually a small building where movie stars and corporate heads wait to board their private jets. One of the many nice points of having your own jet is that there is almost no security. Plus, you don't wait for your plane; your plane waits for you. Then, when you arrive…you leave.

Willie called his friend Tim and they agreed to meet in the parking lot near the tower. They drove over and when they arrived at the lot, a tall, good looking middle-aged man with black hair and a moustache was waiting and waving to them. Willie jumped out and walked up to him and they exchanged a warm handshake and pat on the back.

"So, how have you been, fly boy?" Willie was saying as Jigs and Arthur walked up after parking the car. Willie pointed to them and said, "This is Arthur Buckingham and Jigs Donahue." They all shook hands. "Arthur is the brother-in-law of Mr. Ned Khan, the guy we spoke about, and this is an old washed up hippy, so don't pay any attention to him."

Tim laughed. "This guy always calls me a hippy too. You must be left of Attila the Hun, Jigs. That is all it takes, nice to meet you. As for your brother-in-law, Arthur, he is in and out of here all the time. We know him and his plane."

"Yeah, he travels all the time," Arthur said.

"Hey, while I am down here I thought I would get a quick bite. Are you guys hungry?"

"Is it good food?" Willie really didn't care but he asked.

"No, actually. It is edible. That's about all."

"OK, let's go have some edible food."

As they walked towards the small terminal where the restaurant was, Jigs could not help but ask Tim why he too was the butt of Willie's right wing barbs.

"Well, that is simple…we all, and by "all" I mean air traffic controllers in general, most of us anyway…despise his all time hero…Ronald fucking Regan."

"Holy shit, you say that out loud…right in front of him?" Jigs was loving this. He had an ally. "You mean to say that you do not revere the 'Great Communicator'?"

Willie was laughing silently. He obviously had previously had this conversation with Tim.

"When they renamed Washington National Airport, Regan National, most of us refused to call it by its new name. I think that you could safely say that *I do not* revere the great communicator. That, by the way, is the only nice thing they could say about him. He could talk…I will give him that…he was an actor. However, in my opinion, a more apt name for the son-of-a-bitch would be the 'Great Shill.'" The guy was nothing more than a mouthpiece for the rich and the corporate interests in this country. They needed someone to speak for them, so they hired an actor to act like a president."

"Oh…I like this guy. Where did you meet this very intelligent man, Willie?" Jigs was having so much fun with this. They had arrived at the sandwich stand inside the terminal. They all ordered burgers and Cokes and sat down at a little table in front of the greasy spoon. The burgers were great, just what they needed. Hundreds of travelers passed by as they ate and talked, oblivious to the men and their conversation.

"I interviewed him at the time of the air traffic controller's strike."

"Yes he did. That is when I lost my job due to Ronald fucking Regan."

Willie almost stood up to make his point. He was talking through a mouth full of burger. "You lost your job because you and your fellow "communistas" were trying to shut this country down by striking one of the most important industries to business that exists. You can't shut down air travel. That would shut down commerce."

"Funny, I thought that was the point of collective bargaining. I thought that collective bargaining created and, for many years, maintained the middle class in this country. I thought the ability to ban together and show the true worth of the workers in an industry...to bring to the attention of all...the importance of the men and women that actually do the work, was the very point of a strike...or was I mistaken?"

"I think that was a pretty concise statement of the purpose of collective..."

"Don't you try to put your two cents into this discussion, lib," Willie interrupted. "He does not need your help." Everyone was smiling because they all knew that Willie was freaking out about this challenge, not only to the anointed leader of the modern conservative movement, but also to some of the most basic tenants of the conservative point of view. "Ronald Regan was simply trying to avert economic chaos."

"Ronald fucking Regan was a strike buster with the bully pulpit of the presidency, nothing more. Oh, and by the way, it is the policies that began during the Regan years that are about to drag the middle class in this country into the gutter. Reganomics. Supply side economics. Trickle down theory.

NAFTA. WTO. Fucking conservatives will still tell you that tax breaks for the rich and for corporations will stimulate economic growth and result in a "trickle down" effect to the middle class. Oh really. The only problem with that theory is that when you give tax breaks to the rich and to corporations...THEY FUCKING KEEP THE MONEY. It does not "trickle down." That is why the relative difference between the income of the common working man and the corporate CEO has gone from five or six times more than the worker to, get this, three hundred times more than the worker in the last twenty years. THREE HUNDRED TIMES MORE. Are they fucking nuts? It is now commonplace for a CEO to make $150,000,000.00 per year, sometimes $300,000,000.00. Oh, and one more thing about the 'trickle down' concept, in order for the theory to make any sense at all, the tax breaks, or the money saved thereby, has to 'trickle down' to the worker in the form of new jobs that offer fair and honest wages, right? The theory claims that all will do well as long as the rich have the money to invest. The investments will create jobs. 'A rising tide raises all boats.' Sounds good, right? Only problem...the jobs are not being created here. The jobs are being created in China and Mexico and other such places where they can pay workers one dollar a day, if that. The 'trickle down' effect is trickling down right into China. A rising tide does raise all boats...but the boats have to be in the fucking water. The American worker is not 'in the water.' Therefore, the theory sucks. It does not work...in my humble opinion."

"Oh…I like this guy. You are a smart man, Tim. You are a very smart man." Jigs was ecstatic. "You think he is smart…don't you Willie?" Everyone was chuckling. All looked in Willie's direction.

"Fuck all you guys. You are all a bunch of lefties, I guess." Actually, Willie was laughing too. Nobody enjoyed the banter back and forth more than he did.

"Well…let's talk about the reason we all came here to meet…what do you say?"

"Good idea, Arthur."

There they were, four guys sitting casually eating burgers and plotting to prevent a billionaire Persian prince from leaving Los Angeles. No problem. No problem at all.

35

BUFORD TUCKER HAD A PROBLEM. He could not stop thinking about Ned Khan's secret. He thought about the information that he had rattling around in his brain when he woke up in the morning. He thought about the information that he had rattling around in his brain when he went to bed at night. He thought about the said information time and time again throughout the day. He thought about Ned Khan and Ned Khan's secret, more often than he thought about sex. One might say he was distracted, or single-minded or even obsessed. Anyone would say that, if they knew. Of course, he kept his thoughts to himself.

One of the most prevalent thoughts of all the thoughts that streamed through his mind was simple. He had easily convinced two men with similar net worth, to give him $100,000.00 each. He was careful not to ask for too much from either man. When you ask a man with $10,000.000.00 for the sum of $100,000.00, it is like asking a man with $1000.00 in his pocket for $100.00. Buford always believed that this amount would not cause the "donor" undo concern. It was, to him, a small amount. It was, to Buford, his salvation. The thought that would not leave Buford's mind was this: If you ask a man with

$1,000,000,000.00 for the sum of $1,000,000.00, it is like asking a man with $1000.00 in his pocket for $1.00. The amount was not just small; it was miniscule to this man. It would, however, change Buford's life forever. Buford asked himself over and over again the following question: Would a man with an incredibly volatile secret pay the equivalent of $1.00 to keep his secret... a secret?

Buford could not help but think about how his family would benefit from the sum of $1,000,000.00. His kids could go to the college of their choice, no questions asked. They also could have the advantages that he had not had. Plus, he thought of his loving wife. He could make her life so much better, and, God knew, she deserved it.

He also thought endlessly of his deep abiding faith in a power greater than himself. He knew that extortion or blackmail or call it what you will, was a form of theft. Instead of a gun, one simply uses information to force the money from the victim. Information can easily be as dangerous as a gun. He knew what his Pastor would say if he asked him about his dilemma. So, he didn't ask. He had long since rationalized the taking of $200,000.00. Every time he saw his mother, he was further convinced he had done the right thing. "The Lord works in mysterious ways." He had come to believe that Jesus had not wanted his mother to die. People of faith sometimes have to twist reality to make their faith fit with reality. That is why they call it faith. Why else does a paramedic save lives through the use of science and medicine, or a lawyer save his clients through the use of long standing precedents and legal theory six days a week, and go to a church and speak in tongues on the seventh.

Then, in May of 2007, Jerry Falwell died. It was actually the cause of a revelation in Buford, an epiphany of sorts. He watched the television coverage with his wife and children, mostly on Christian channels, but sometimes on the networks.

Buford had always considered Reverend Falwell a great man. Not only a great man of God, but a great man. Falwell was credited with helping to elect Ronald Regan president of the United States, and for helping to ignite the conservative revolution, which was apparent at that time, and which Buford supported. One thing became very clear to Buford as he watched the reports chronicling his life; the Reverend Falwell began and sustained his rise to prominence and power on the contributions of his church going followers. Often these contributions were made with money that his followers did not have to spare. Yet, he made no apologies for the way he lived. His ministries were taking in multiple millions of dollars and the Reverend lived like a multi-millionaire, right down to the private jet plane and the handmade tailored suits. He was often criticized for doing so, but he maintained his right to do it.

Buford decided, wrongly or not, that it was part of Jesus' plan that a man of God, a true Christian, could be very rich, and if Jesus provided a way for a man to become rich, then it was proper and appropriate for that man to do so. After all, it was Jesus that had provided a way for his mother to have her operation. If Jerry Falwell and his family could become ridiculously rich, private jet rich, multimillionaire rich, off of the contributions of people that really could not afford the amounts they gave to his church, then Buford and his family could increase their financial position as a result of the contribution of a very, very wealthy man, whom, as an aside, had broken God's law regarding the sanctity of marriage. Buford was further convinced that anyone, if faced with his particular dilemma, would do exactly the same thing. After all, it was not illegal to be a tattletale. He was not giving up state secrets, just the secrets of some sorry schmucks that probably deserved it. Last, but not by any means least; Buford knew at that moment that there was no turning back. He had made a decision. He was not coming back; he was not changing his mind; he was locked onto a course of action. Without question, Buford was on his way to a new life.

He walked out of his bedroom and saw his wife. This made him smile. He felt tranquil and happy. He knew what he had to do.

Buford acquired a new hobby. Each day he would leave work with a different background check on a different person.

He was having some fun with this. He had radio talk show hosts, corporate heads, movie stars and sometimes, just plain rich people. Buford had made his final plans as to what he was going to do. He just wasn't sure as to whom it would be done. It was interesting to see the various secrets that people had. And, although there were many, he finally decided that his first choice was his best choice.

Buford walked into his home after work on a Wednesday, and kissed his lovely wife. He hugged his two wonderful children. He then announced that he was going to go down to Biloxi to visit his mother over the upcoming weekend. This had become somewhat commonplace since the operation. His family had become accustomed to these trips. Only Buford knew that this trip was to be different than any other. Buford had maintained the fees on the mailbox in New Orleans and he had plans to visit his box over the weekend on the way to his mother's house.

Buford made some excuse to go to the store. He asked if his wife needed anything while he was out. She asked if he would pick up some butter and paper towels. Buford agreed with a smile. "I'll be right back," he said as he left. Nothing could have been more mundane or nonchalant.

He drove first to the 7-11 at the corner. He purchased the butter and the paper towels. He did not want to forget them.

Then he made a beeline for the strip mall where he had first made his call to Mr. Dennis Van Wyck, and later to Mr. Washington. He felt confident and self-assured. Where he once lost his lunch doing exactly what he was planning to do right then, he felt no significant amount of nervousness or concern. This was old hat to Buford. He strode into the mall with a mission. He had reviewed Mr. Ned Khan's complete file and taken notes where necessary. He approached the same phone bank. Again, no one was around. He dialed Mr. Khan's cell phone number. That was always the best bet for success.

"Hello, Mr. Khan. I am glad I caught you all. Do you have a moment to talk, sir?" Buford could hear traffic in the background. This, he felt, was a good sign. Unless Mr. Khan had someone else in the car with him, he should be able to talk freely.

Ned Khan was a very important and wealthy man. He wondered who was calling him on his private cell phone. Ned was driving south on the Pacific Coast Hwy in his Bentley. The view outside his car was magnificent. The sun was shining as it always does and the Pacific Ocean was a glorious blue until it crashed onto the rocks below where it turned to a foamy white. He had just left the home of a colleague in Malibu, and was on his way home. He had no idea that this telephone call would forever change his life.

"May I ask who this is?" Ned said politely.

"My name is of no consequence, Mr. Khan. What is of consequence, sir, and I am sorry to have to say this so bluntly but there is no other way, what is of consequence is that I have knowledge that you have a second wife and a twelve year old son living in Teheran... Do I have your attention, sir?"

Ned nearly drove off the road. He thought of the years during which he had wondered if he would some day receive this call. He had been so very careful. He talked to his Iranian wife and son over, what he believed were, secure lines. He had shared this secret with no one. No one in the United States knew about it. No one. Few people outside of close family members in Iran knew. Only, those persons necessary to insure his son's status as an heir, and these were trusted associates who knew that they would die if they ever thought to divulge this information. How could this obvious stranger have come upon this knowledge? Ned looked at the display on his cell phone. He did not recognize the number or the area code. He finally said, "You do. You have my undivided attention."

"Mr. Khan...let me first apologize for what must have been a very startling moment just now, and assure you that I mean you or your family no harm whatsoever. No harm at all, sir. I am a Christian man and I am a man of my word. I know that you are not a Christian, but I also know that you understand the importance of that statement, having lived here all these years. I know that you all are a man of your word, as well, sir. I trust we can discuss this matter further, as gentlemen. Am I correct, sir?"

"You are." Ned pulled his car into the parking lot of a restaurant just off the highway. He did not want to say too much at this point. The tires of his big car crunched the gravel as dust rose from underneath them. He could not hear his cell phone for a minute until the crunching stopped and the dust cleared. He asked, "Did you say something else? I just pulled off the road."

"No, sir, I did not. However, if I may, I will explain the purpose of my call."

"Please do."

"Well, sir, as you might have guessed, I do want something from you, but I will begin by assuring you that I do not want to have you think that I plan to dog you for life, endlessly asking for more and more. I will not do that, sir. This is a one-time transaction. As I said, sir, I am a Christian man. I have come to believe that Jesus Christ has given me a unique opportunity to provide a better life for my family. I will not take advantage of this gift."

"Forgive me, but you really do not think that what you are saying is no more than one colossal rationalization to justify something that is not only illegal, but clearly is also contrary to the teachings of your Jesus Christ?"

"That, of course, is possible, sir. However, it is equally possible that my family and I have been given a gift. My Lord works in mysterious ways, as, I am sure, does yours. This is not a theological debate, however, is it, sir?"

"No, I am sure that it is not."

"The next subject that I wish to touch on, briefly, is the idea that a man of your means might think it would be easier just to hire someone to hurt me, or my family, or worse. Rest assured that, if that were to happen, your secret would be exposed. A complete recitation of the whole sordid situation is under lock and key, as you might have guessed. Further, if I were to be arrested...well...you know the rest. Don't you, sir?"

"Yes...yes, I suppose I do. Well, what is it that you want?"

"I want one million dollars, sir, no more, no less. Please put it into a box and wrap it in plain brown paper. It should look like business mail and it should be sent to...do you have a pen, sir?"

"Yes, I do."

"Mail that to: DJ, Inc., 141 Robert E. Lee Blvd., New Orleans, Louisiana 70116. I must receive that package by this Friday. No delays, sir. After that, you will never hear from me again. Do you all have any questions, sir?"

"No...no, I don't suppose that I do." Ned put the car in drive and carefully pulled back onto PCH as he heard his caller's last words.

"Do this, sir. You and I will never talk again if you do. If you do not comply, only enormous problems will result. " The statement was followed by the standard "click" that follows such a call. That was it.

Ned actually chuckled the kind of chuckle that comes out when you are thoroughly disgusted, or when life takes its inevitable turns for the worse. He shook his head sadly as he drove down the highway. "Fuck," he murmured to himself. He had some decisions to make. He had some very serious decisions to make.

36

NED KHAN TURNED HIS SLEEK, shiny expensive car onto Sunset Boulevard and traveled down the famous drive in an area of Los Angeles where sleek, shiny expensive cars were commonplace. He passed one multi-million-dollar home after another multi-million-dollar home and thought about how everyone strives to attain these things...and wondered why. Of course, he knew why.

He thought of his beautiful wife. He remembered their days back in southern Illinois and how fate had brought them together. He remembered how thoroughly smitten he was with her when they first met and how that infatuation had propelled him to do much of the things that had led him blindly to the very place he now found himself. He was not raised by his father and his uncles to be a romantic. Romance was a luxury that was supposed to be reserved for the common man, according to them. It clouded ones judgment, they had told him. Ned wondered...did it? Did love cloud sound judgment? Would his judgment be clouded today?

He remembered a thousand memories of their life together both prior to and after their wedding, all the places they had been and the wonderful experiences they had shared. He admitted that what had begun as an infatuation had grown into a warm, abiding, comfortable feeling of affection, partnership and love.

He then recalled the day that Anna came crying to him and announced through her tears that she had been informed by her doctors that she was unable to conceive children. She was barren. Did he love her any less at that moment? Of course he did not. He held her and comforted her and assured her that it did not matter. Was his judgment clouded then? He knew at that moment that this revelation was much more of a concern then he let on, much more. He was a prince. He was royalty. It was required of him to produce an heir, and in his culture it really did not matter how many women he had to be with to achieve that mandate. Should he have told his lovely American wife of his concerns? Did he use sound judgment when he decided at that time to create a secret separate parallel life, rather than risk that Anna would not understand. He was angry with himself. He knew the risks of such a course of action. He was a citizen of not only the United States, but of the State of California, easily the most famous "community property" state in the country. Was his sound judgment usurped by his romantic love for a woman? His father's and his uncle's words reverberated in his memory.

He thought about how much he had enjoyed and cherished his time spent in America. He had made his own fortune primarily here in the U.S. or through the alliances and partnerships he had cultivated here. He had increased his family's fortune accordingly. He then thought of the ever-widening divide that existed between the homeland of his birth and his adopted homeland. There could be a war...

"Ahmadinejad is such an asshole! Why can't he keep his mouth shut?" He said out loud to no one as he drove past the Beverly Hills Hotel and he returned from a period of intense introspection. "This is an unfortunate turn of events, isn't it?" Ned realized that he had no recollection of having driven all the way along Sunset. Perhaps an accident would have been better...or easier? "Not likely!" He exclaimed. There was clearly another solution. He would not let his judgment be clouded this time. If one person could unearth his little secret then another person could. He could not risk that. It was not the silly little million dollars that was the problem here. He could easily pay that, many times over. It was the prospect of a divorce that was the problem. He knew that. He had always known that. There was only one way to insure that a divorce was an absolute impossibility, only one way. A wife could not divorce him if he no longer had a wife. He thought again of his beautiful, wonderful loving woman that had been his partner for so many years and a single tear streaked slowly down his determined, resolute, saddened face.

When he arrived home, Ned walked into his office and den. He sat at his desk. He pulled his Rolodex over close to him. He flipped through it. When you reach the place in business that Ned had, you knew people, who knew people, who knew people. You also heard things and knew things about people. Ned was thinking of a story he had heard about an acquaintance of his. The guy had a wife that was talking about divorce. She had good reason. This guy not only cheated on her, he went regularly to Thailand, where he would pay for days and days of sex with two or three fourteen or fifteen year old girls at a time. He would smoke cocaine the entire time and drink whiskey. When the girls would get tired, he would order fresh ones. He would stay for a week or so. Then he would need a week to recuperate. Then he would return to the Wall Street clubs and to his office where he continued his role as a captain of industry.

He earned hundreds of millions of dollars per year. Only problem, he had done this so many times, it had become the only way he could enjoy sex, the only way he could get it up. His wife actually did not mind at first, but the guy hardly looked at her any more. It was becoming an obsession with him. Soon after she began talking about divorce, she had a tragic accident. She drowned in her own swimming pool. Very sad. It was said that she was stinking drunk at the time. She had been fighting alcoholism for some time, which was true, but most of her friends had sworn she was doing so well. It must have been a relapse. Very, very sad.

His acquaintance stood to lose approximately four hundred million in a divorce case, give or take, depending on the judge. He could not have that. His Thailand trips were expensive.

Ned had found the phone number he was looking for. He dialed the number.

"I need to enter into a contract like Michael did." He listened to the other person. He then said, "Immediately." He listened some more, then. "OK. You will let me know where to wire that?" Silence. Then Ned said, " Thank you." That was that. He hung up the phone. That was that.

37

BUFORD TUCKER ARRIVED IN NEW Orleans without incident on Friday in plenty of time to rent a car and drive to the Mailboxes Etc. on Robert E. Lee Blvd. He had rushed out of work and parked in short term parking, hoofed it through the terminal like an old O.J. commercial, and made it through security and to the gate with time to spare. His mood was fantastic. After all, he was on his way to pick up a lot of money.

You had to give him credit though; he actually wanted the money for his wife and children. He had not considered for even a second what *he* would do with the money. It was for his family. This was a truly Christian man with true Christian values, whom, sad to say, had actually convinced himself that Jesus wanted him to steal. This was a man that had lived his whole life in accordance with God's law, went to church on each and every Sunday, loved and protected his family, had been vetted by the FBI and the NSA and passed with flying colors and had been welcomed as one of their own. He was, for all intents and purposes, an ideal human being that should be emulated. Too bad he was in the middle of a plot to extort a million dollars from someone. How does this happen to an otherwise good person?

He was not nervous, as before. He was not frightened, as before. He was not feeling guilty, as before. He had Jesus on his side. As he arrived in the familiar neighborhood where the store was located, he did feel his senses become taut and he was internally excited, but nothing like before. He pulled into the parking lot where he had spent so much time on surveillance of the area during his last visit. He took a cursory look around for obvious signs of trouble, but he did not dally. He actually believed he was simply going to walk into the store and pick up a box with one million dollars in it and leave without incident. Funny, huh?

"Hello. I am here to pick up a package that would have been delivered to box #603. The package would be too large to fit into the box itself, so I thought you all might have it back in the back? Could you check on that?"

It was the same toothy clerk with the same frozen toothy smile. His little uniform jacket did not fit him well and it made him look like the quintessential nerd. He was smiling but he was shaking his head slowly. "No…ah… no, sir, we did not receive a package for box #603." He did not stop smiling.

Buford's heart sank. He actually could not believe his own ears. "What did this idiot know? Of course there was a package." Buford thought but did not say. "Would you all please check on that? I was led to believe that it would have arrived by now." Buford actually began to fidget ever so slightly. He looked around.

"I will be happy to do that, sir, however I am the manager. I would know if…" The clerk's words trailed off as he looked at Buford's face. He stepped backwards, then turned and opened the door to the back room. "Kelly…would ya'all check to see if a package came in for box #603. Check real good…OK? The customer thinks it should be there."

Buford could hear Kelly yelling from the back. "I'll check, but I know we didn't git one."

After a reasonable time had been spent "checking," Kelly appeared in the doorway. She smiled warmly at Buford. "I am sorry, sir, but there ain't no package for # 603. Sorry."

Buford was crestfallen when he probably should have been worried. He felt like he had just received coal in his stocking, when he should have been looking for the SWAT team. He was so sure that he and his family would be millionaires by the end of the day. He looked at the nerd, then at Kelly. He said "Thank you", and left the store. There was no point in arguing with them. They would know if a package came or if it did not.

When he got to his rental car he realized that he had not even considered this possibility. When he was making his plans, he had considered the possibility of getting caught, of Mr. Khan calling the police. However, he dismissed this scenario almost immediately. Mr. Khan could not afford to have this information come out. It would cost him over a half a billion dollars, for Christ's sake. He had heard him say that to his other wife. Plus, Buford knew this guy's net worth. He had read his file. "What the fuck." Buford allowed himself the curse word as he became angrier and angrier. "What was this guy thinking?"

Oddly enough, Buford didn't have a clue as to what he was going to do about this turn of events. He had not even considered it. Did he really want to expose this man and his secret? Could he do that without exposing himself and his own indiscretions? Did he want to devastate his poor innocent American wife? He had read about her. She was one of the truly benevolent philanthropists in the world. The background check on her husband included a great deal of information about her. Buford had grown to like her, or at least what he had read about her. Perhaps, this guy was relying on Buford's inability to actually follow through on his threats. This man was a billionaire for good reason. He was smart.

Buford drove east out of New Orleans toward his boyhood home on the Gulf Coast of Mississippi. He was, to say the least, dejected. He did not know what he was going to do. He would know that...soon enough.

38

THREE DAYS HAD PASSED since Ned made the telephone call that would prove to alter his life forever. He drove along the winding mountain road that led towards his palatial home in the Hollywood Hills, where he had lived with his wife for so many years. At one point, he could see the Hollywood Bowl and he remembered the many times that he and Anna had been to concerts and other functions there, most of them for charity. "She was a beautiful and kind woman," he thought. How could he go through with it? He shook off the thought. There were much larger considerations at stake, not the least of which was the small matter of over a half of a billion dollars. That was not the only concern, however. There were many others, his family in Iran was one, not just his wife and son, but the entire extended family. That money belonged to them, as well. They would not understand if he lost it to some American woman in an American court. They just would not be able to conceptualize such a loss. There were just too many concerns to count. The situation was untenable. He pressed the button on the gadget that opened the ornate iron gate that guarded his drive. It creaked open and he drove up his drive. He saw his wife's shiny new red Mercedes Benz roadster, her birthday present, parked in the huge circular part of the drive in front of the house. He opened one of the four doors to the garage with his garage door opener and pulled his car into the garage. He always parked his car in the huge four-car garage. She never did.

Ned walked into his huge home through the garage entrance and walked through the gourmet kitchen and into the house. It looked like photo shoot for Better Homes and Gardens. He was at a point where he could see the pool area. He could see the amazing view of the sprawling city below, then the endless Pacific Ocean. He would miss that view, he thought to himself. He checked the pool area for his wife. She was often out there tending to the tropical plants or sitting by the pool. She loved the sun.

"Sweetheart, I'm home."

"In here," Anna yelled from her home office.

Ned walked down the hallway and into to the office. He was impeccable, as usual. He filled the doorway. "How was your day?"

Anna jumped up and ran to hug her husband. She planted a big kiss on his tan, handsome face. He kissed her back. They still acted like newlyweds. People were jealous. Anna had gotten her hair cut earlier that day. She stepped back from her husband. Extended her hands out from her sides, did a kind of dip and said, "Well, what do you think?" Her smile was breathtaking. She was absolutely beautiful.

Ned stepped forward and put his arms around his wife. He held her close. His right hand slipped down to her perfectly formed rump, which seemed to be defying gravity. He pulled her closer, up tight against him. He whispered into her ear. "It looks spectacular. You look great. It is pretty wonderful. I did not have to remarry to get to have a trophy wife." He kissed her hard. "So, what's up?" They parted. She turned and walked towards her desk. He gently slapped her rear, as she went. "Let me show you."

"Show me what?"

"This is really cool."

"What?"

She handed him a letter. It was very official looking. He started to read it, but Anna could not wait. "I am going to be meeting Al Gore, among others. I am invited to a function that is to be hosted by Mr. Gore. It's a save the planet kind of thing. But, I am one of the guests of honor because of the work we have done on Climate Change here in the LA area. There are five of us that are going to be given a plaque or something. I don't really care.... but, I will be meeting Al Gore and maybe even Leonardo DiCaprio. Cool, huh?"

"Should I be worried? Are you going to run off with Leo?"

"If he asks me to, I might."

"Well… then I am not so sure I am happy about this."

"Sweetie, I don't think you should be threatened by Leonardo DiCaprio, I could *almost* be his mother."

"Right…when is this affair…do I have to go…how much will it cost?"

"Very funny… Next month… Only if you want to... It won't cost you a penny. However, we have contributed extensively to the cause. That could be part of the reason why they are having this shindig. You know me. I don't go in for awards or praise, but this is Al Gore. Honey. I am going."

"And I don't blame you. If I am in town, I will too. Congratulations, Sweetheart, You deserve it." He pulled her close again and kissed her. The letter got crushed in the process. Anna did not seem to mind.

"Thank you, Ned. Thank you for saying that, sweetie. It means a lot."

"OK, I have to make a telephone call. Are we having dinner together?"

"Yes. I have no other plans. Do you want to go out?"

"Good idea. Let's do just that."

"Where?"

"How about that new place on Hollywood, the place that the movie studio guy opened, Katsuya or something like that. It is supposed to have really good food. Plus, it is all the rage."

"OK. I'll get ready."

39

TOM GAZDIK HAD BEEN IN TOWN FOR two days. He planned to leave on the night of the third. His job would be completed. He had no particular plans after that. He had been busy, though. He had been very busy. He was a very smart man. When he saw that a cold front was predicted for Southern California, he decided he would employ, what he considered to be, an ingenious plan to complete the purpose of his employment, which required chilly weather. To that end, he was building an instrument, which he had used in the past. On two occasions the instrument had worked flawlessly. On one other occasion, he encountered a problem, but the part of the system designed for the stealth nature of the project, worked without a hitch. Therefore, he had decided to use it again.

His plan was simple and based on an old riddle. The riddle was as follows: A man is found hanging from a rope around his neck in the middle of a room. No apparent means or apparatus is left on the floor that he could have stood on to hang himself. Only a puddle of water remains below his hanging corpse. How did he hang himself?

Sometimes the more simple and obvious the plot, the harder it is for an investigator to discover. At least that was Tom's experience. Investigators are usually like everyone else. They take the path of least resistance. If they see a path that explains the answer to that which they are investigating, and if the answer produced is plausible and makes sense, they take it. People rarely take the stairs if there is an elevator. Tom always provided the "elevator" for investigators. It was not that his schemes were ever that complicated. He simply provided an alternative to the actual method, which was obvious and easier to find, very plausible, and inevitably, the path of least resistance. Thereby, obscuring the actual method. A known alcoholic, for example, might relapse and suffer an accidental drowning.

Tom got into his rented Buick Century and drove out of the building that he had leased. The garage had plenty of room for both the Buick and the Mercedes. Therefore he never had to park either car in the street or on the property somewhere. He liked being inconspicuous.

He drove towards downtown Los Angeles. He didn't like Los Angeles. He really did not have a reason for not liking LA. He just didn't. When he arrived in Hollywood, he drove up Laurel Canyon Dr. He was actually headed to Ned and Anna's neighborhood. He had a Google map of the entire area and several smaller more detailed versions of specific plots, including Ned and Anna's house. He stopped in a small local store that was half way up in the hills for lunch, just sandwiches and a coke. While waiting for his sandwiches to be made, he looked at the numerous pictures plastered all over the walls of the store. There were some very famous people pictured on those walls. This must be a very nice neighborhood, he thought. He accidentally stumbled onto a picture of many people from the neighborhood that included Anna and Ned. He immediately looked away. He never liked to know too much about his subjects.

He left the store and continued on to the vicinity of the house. He parked the car in an area that was provided as a scenic overlook. It was close enough to the house to walk, which he proceeded to do. He brought with him a camera and a note pad. He approached the house from the rear, taking care not to set off any security. He took pictures and notes. He knew what he needed. He had determined his access point. Tom returned to his car and leisurely drove back to his office.

There he checked on the items he had previously created. When Tom checked the Weather Channel and determined that the forecast for the LA area was unusually cold and rainy, his decision was made. He created a device, which would allow him to accomplish his task. It was a simple plan. After he took apart the heat ducts on the Mercedes that he had rented, he determined that he could slip a carefully crafted piece of ice into a section of the ductwork that was easily and quickly accessible. He fashioned molds out of melted paraffin. Once created and cooled, the molds allowed him to make perfectly sculpted ice vessels with hollow centers. He carefully drilled an access hole into the vessel. He filled the center with a "cocktail" of his own making. It included a combination of drugs, together with a delivery agent, which would cause the drugs to vaporize and immediately disperse into the small passenger compartment of the car. The primary drug used was a neuro muscular blocker named sevuronium. This drug was not available in the United States. It was specifically formulated to allow it to be inhaled rather than injected like most other neuro muscular blockers such as the commonly used vecuronium.

The effect of such a drug was complete paralysis of all normal body functions. One could not move their arms or legs or any other body part, even though the subject remained conscious. Drugs such as these are normally used in surgery to insure that the body does not twitch involuntarily. That would be disastrous during delicate surgery. These drugs have a very short half-life so the body quickly metabolizes them.

When the victim uses the heater due to the inclement weather, the ice melts thereby releasing the "cocktail." The drug is disbursed into the car. The ice continues to melt, turns to water, and then evaporates. The drug dissipates. No evidence remains. Particularly when you consider that the investigation is invariably of an accident scene.

Tom gathered together the tools of his ghastly trade, put the ice vessel back into the freezer, filled a cooler with dry ice, and went out to make a telephone call.

40

NED AND ANNA HAD A GLORIOUS dinner at Katsuya, a sushi restaurant on the Hollywood Boulevard of old. It was fast becoming the hottest new spot to see and be seen located right in the heart of the strip. It was opened as a result of a partnership between the head chef and a movie producer that loved sushi and wanted to be assured a table. It was a beautiful place, elegant but modern, with perfect seafood creations that were out of this world. After dinner, they returned home. It was about 9:00pm. Ned was in his office finishing up some work that he needed to complete. Ned's private business telephone line rang. It was a call he was expecting, and dreading. He took a deep breath, and answered the phone.

"This is a call regarding information that you require with reference to a contract that you have entered into. Are you prepared to discuss the matter at this time?"

Ned's heart was immediately in his throat. He had no idea that he would experience such an intense reaction to this call, but then, why wouldn't he? This was a call that would cause elements to be set in motion that were actually beyond his imagination. However, to his mind, these catastrophic measures were the only course of action left available to him. Life had turned and twisted, as it always does, and left him with the most difficult decision of his entire life. Unfortunately, Ned was unable to see past the overwhelming, all-encompassing notion, which was instilled in him since birth, seemingly stamped into his DNA, that the family fortune was a larger and more important concern than anything else, even a life, even the life of someone that he loved. It was a cold prospective on life.

Ned simply said, "I am."

"You must arrange to be out of town tomorrow. Can you do that?"

"Of course…if that is what you say is necessary."

"I will set up an evening appointment with your wife. I will be using the name: Jonathon F. Butcher. Vouch for this person if your wife asks about him. Tell her that you know him to be a wealthy man. You will leave town an hour or so prior to this appointment. Is any of that a problem?"

"No…no it is not."

"It is going to rain tomorrow. Before you leave for the airport, put your wife's car in the garage. Secure the hardtop in place. Leave the side door to the garage open. Turn off the security system. Will you be able to accomplish these things?"

"Yes. I can do all those things."

"When you have done this…go to the airport. Leave town."

Ned suddenly heard the dial tone. The caller was no longer on the line. Ned just sat there. He did not know how to feel. He could not stop thinking that it should not be that simple, but it was. It was just that simple. When you had money; you could buy anything. Anna, it seemed, would never meet Al Gore.

Ned shook his head in a very sad and deliberate manner. Evidently, that was it. He walked out of his office and down the hall. He saw the light on in his wife's home office. "Are you coming to bed?" he asked. He looked down the hall and listened for a response.

His wife appeared in the doorway to the office. She switched off the light and walked towards him. She had never looked more beautiful. She had changed into an oversized tee shirt and a pair of tight, very short, gym shorts, admittedly just knock around the house lounge clothes, but she would look beautiful in anything. Her legs were long and tan. The outlines of her breasts were not at all hidden by the flimsy tee shirt. Her nipples protruded clearly through the white of the shirt. Her long blonde hair was tousled slightly. She ran her fingers through that hair as she approached him. She flashed him a huge gorgeous smile. "What did you have in mind?" She was walking towards him, smiling, and removing the gym shorts as she walked. They fell down her legs and she stepped out of them, and kicked them off and to the side. The tee shirt barely covered her. Ned could not control or diminish his immediate response. He could not stop himself... even now. He never could, not as long as he had known her. They walked into their bedroom arm and arm. Anna flicked off the light as they passed it.

In the morning, Anna and Ned lingered in bed a little longer than usual. From their king size bed they could see the sprawling city and the ocean. The day was promising to be one of the dreary chilly, rainy days that were so rare in Los Angeles. It was not conducive to jumping out of bed to face the morning. Plus, they had been up late the night before and had experienced pleasures that made them both feel young and reminded them of their college days. Anna snuggled close to Ned and whispered that she was still tingling. Ned smiled warmly and held his wife close.

The whole experience, the night and the morning after, was becoming surreal to him. He could hear the weather prediction from last night's caller reverberating in his ears. He looked outside. It was just what the doctor ordered, exactly as predicted. He reviewed the list of tasks that were expected of him. He suddenly felt a chill run throughout his body. He was not sure he could go through with it all, but he again was reminded that, in his mind, he really had no choice.

"Honey, I received a call last night and, as it turns out, I am going to have to run down to Houston today. There are some concerns regarding the Park Tower Project." Ned was making a lame, but plausible, excuse.

"That's too bad...I would have liked some more of the same... tonight." Anna was being playful and teasing him. Ned was struck with the realization that he would never "be with" his beautiful wife again. "Why had life turned out this way?" he thought to himself. He felt sick.

"It's OK...I guess if you think a stupid skyscraper is more fun..." She was not letting up.

"You know I have no choice..."

Anna interrupted. "Sweetheart, stop. You don't have to say anything...I understand...I understand... really. Just make sure you get your butt back here as soon as possible. When will that be, anyway? Is this going to be a long trip?"

"No, Darling, it is not going to be a long trip... honestly."

"OK, then. No big deal. I am used to it."

"Now…I am going to make you breakfast…myself…" He looked at his watch. "Brunch, actually."

One hour later, they were sitting in the breakfast nook, having ham and eggs with hash browns and fresh squeezed orange juice. Unfortunately, they could not have their cozy meal out by the pool. The weather was not cooperating. The rain had begun in earnest. It was not pouring, just a steady rain, and cold, at least for California. The quiet, secluded breakfast was, however, just what Anna needed. The breakfast nook was surrounded by an expansive bay window. What she still really loved was spending time with her husband. They were able to do this all too rarely, considering each of their busy schedules. She did not mind the rain as long as they were together.

"I want you to be with me at this function with Al Gore." She flashed her cutest smile. "Promise me you will."

"I do not want to make that promise because I have no idea what next month will bring. However, I will say this… I will be there… unless there is a compelling reason that I cannot do it." Ned felt like a snake.

"OK, I can live with that."

Anna's personal telephone rang. She looked at Ned. He said, "Take it…it's your business line. Are you crazy?" She laughed and took the call. Ned heard one side of the conversation.

"Yes…yes, this is she…

Tonight is a bit short notice, isn't it?

Hold on a minute, will you?"

She turned to Ned and asked if he had ever heard of a person named, Jonathon F. Butcher from Sherman Oaks. Ned looked up as if he was thinking. He then said, "Of course… I know of him…that guy is loaded. Meet with him, Honey. Your causes will make a bundle. I will be out of town, anyway. You would just be home alone. Go sign the guy up. Turn on your charm. Save the environment. Why not?" Anna turned back to the telephone. She was nodding.

"I can do tonight…what time?

OK…and where?

Of course, I know it. I have been there before. It is a landmark…

OK…OK. I will see you there. No…no problem. Tonight will be fine. That will be fine. See you then."

Anna looked at Ned and smiled. "You are not the only busy person in this family."

"Where are you guys meeting?" Ned did not really need to know this but he wanted to sound interested.

"We will be dining at the 'Pig n' Whistle'...one of Hollywood's oldest and finest hot spots."

"That is a bit of an overstatement. Wouldn't you say?"

"Well...it is old...and it actually does have good food. Maybe it is not a 'hot spot'. Nonetheless, I will be there with bells on... while you are off in Texas."

They had finished their brunch.

"Well... I have some work to do. What about you?"

"I actually do have a bunch of calls to make. Shall we retire to our respective offices?"

"As much as I would rather not, I suppose we should, Sweetheart. Don't you think?"

"Yes...I know that is what we must do... but, let me just say that today has been a really great day. We should do this more often. Its nice."

"I agree...I agree wholeheartedly. We will, too. Today was wondrous. It wasn't just great. It was wondrous, Sweetheart...really. I love you." Ned was beginning to feel ill. He could not continue this charade.

"I love you too, Ned… See ya." Anna smiled back at her husband as she left the room and walked off to her home office. Ned left the dishes on the table. It is nice to have money. He went to his office. He actually did have work to do, billionaires always do.

So, Ned went to his office, but he could not work. He kept getting off track. He continued to attempt to focus on work issues, and then invariably found himself thinking of his wife. He knew he would miss her terribly. They had been together for so long. He could not stop thinking that when he told Anna that their day had been "wondrous," he was not lying. He was speaking the truth straight from his heart. He did love her, no question. If that were true, why was he about to do this terrible thing, which was looming as the inevitable? Why? He knew why. He was not proud of his realization. The simple answer was this: If forced to choose between his wife, or the money, a number in excess of six hundred million dollars…the money always wins…period. Plus, now that his young son was getting older, he did have to dedicate more time to him. He had responsibilities that were larger than the life of one person. Like a world leader that has to send men into battle, he did not have the luxury of letting love or personal feelings, cloud his judgment. He actually believed this tripe.

Ned stood up from his desk. He walked out of his office and looked down the hall. He listened intently. He heard Anna on the telephone in her office. She was in the middle of some kind of charitable conversation. Charities. Actually he was going to be glad to be done with those once and for all. He walked down the hall and through the house. He grabbed Anna's keys off of a table near the front door. He opened the front door.

He made it to Anna's car in just a few steps. Anna had put the top up but it was not secured. He started the car and pulled it up to the garage. He picked up Anna's garage door opener and pointed it towards the door. It opened and he drove the shiny new Mercedes into the garage. He then secured the convertible top in place. He got out and walked to the side garage door. He unlocked it.

He walked into the house and hung the keys to the car on a hook in the kitchen marked KEYS. He had bought and installed it because Anna could never find her keys. He had purchased the gaudy thing at a J.C. Penny store. He then went and disabled the alarm. She would never check it; he knew that. Hell, the damn alarm would never be used if he didn't live there. He walked through the house and back down the hall. He heard his wife gabbing away. He walked through his bedroom and into the huge bath. He took off his clothes and got into the shower. He tried to wash away the guilt and the pain, but it was too late.

He appeared in the doorway of his wife's office. He was impeccable, as usual. He smiled at Anna for, what he knew would be, the last time. She was on the phone. She was stunning. He kissed her goodbye. "I will call you from the airport before I take off." He was whispering so as not to disturb her call. She smiled and nodded. She waved and then she turned back to her call. He walked out of the house and into the garage, got into his Bentley, and drove away. That was that.

By the time Anna had gotten out of the shower, she was late. She was always late. Why hadn't she cut that last call a little shorter? She pulled on some jeans and got into a very comfortable black cotton sweater. She ran a brush through her hair and walked out of her room. Anna was mumbling to herself. "Now…where the heck did I put my keys…"

41

"**WHAT HAVE I DONE?**" Buford cried out again. His face was buried in his hands. He still could not believe he was sobbing so uncontrollably. Then it began to come clear to him. He had caused the death of another human being, plain and simple, no getting around it. It was as if he had held a gun to that woman's head and pulled the trigger. And why? Why? Money. That's why. No worse sin existed.

It seemed to Buford that he had never seen the room that surrounded him. It was his bedroom, the one he and his wife had slept in for years, but it seemed foreign. Everything did.

He stood up slowly and began to pick up the pages of the Washington Post that he had attempted to throw. He saw the heading on one of those pages. Obituaries. The guilt poured into his very heart again. He was wiping snot and tears from his face and shuddering. Reality gripped him. He had killed that woman, as sure as if he had done it himself. He had set in motion the events that caused her death. He knew that in his soul. It was *his* fault.

Buford heard his wife's voice coming from outside the house. He looked out the window. "Honey...I am taking the kids with me to the store. Are you hearing me?" Buford went to the window and waved. He was waving at the people that he loved most in the world. "Do ya'all need anything?" Buford shook his head. "No, nothing for me," he said without letting on to his true feelings.

"We will be back in an hour or so." His wife was waving to him and smiling, completely unaware that she was waving at a murderer. He watched them drive away. It was as if he was in a dream from which he could not wake. He looked around the room. On one wall was a picture of his loving family. On another wall…a crucifix. He stared at the image of Jesus. He suddenly knew he had committed an unforgivable sin, absolutely unforgivable. He had caused the death of an innocent human being… *for money*. This was surly a sin for which there was no forgiveness. No amount of repentance would be sufficient.

Buford walked over to the small desk in their bedroom. He scribbled a few words on a paper, then knelt down and lifted his head to the heavens. He began to pray. "Dear Lord, please forgive me. I was misled. I was tempted by the trappings of Satan. I am so very sorry for having offended you, my Lord…" His prayers sounded so hollow to say. He knew he had no chance at being saved. He was going to Hell. He knew that. His life would never be the same. How would he ever be able to look his wife or children in the eye? How would he ever be able to look anyone in the eye ever again? How could he be a parent, a husband, a team leader? How could he possibly go on?

Buford walked to the closet and pulled a mahogany box from the top shelf. He was shaking both inside and out. Tears streaked his face. His heart was pounding like never before in his life. He opened the box and pulled out a 45 caliper automatic. He immediately put the barrel of the gun into his mouth. He did not want to hesitate. He knew he would not go through with it if he did. He pointed the barrel tip up, scratching the roof of his mouth. Blood dripped down the barrel of the gun. Tears streamed down his face. He thought of his beautiful kids... his wife. He screamed an unholy, guttural scream, getting louder and louder, which culminated in the shrieking words, *"I am sorry."* He pulled the trigger.

42

DETECTIVE MARK ROTH WAS SITTING in his office when the phone rang. This, of course, was nothing new. However, this was not a typical call.

"Detective Roth, my name is Bergquist, Lieutenant Vern Bergquist. I am with the Ft. Meade, Maryland Police Department. How are you today?"

"Oh, you know how it is Lieutenant, some days are bad… some days are worse in this business, right? What can I do for you, sir?"

Detective Bergquist chuckled knowingly. "Yeah, I know what you mean. I know exactly what you mean. Let me get right to the point. I understand you had an accidental death out there recently; it was a woman… an Anna Khan. Is that your case?"

Roth sat up straight in his chair. The Lieutenant had his undivided attention. He picked up a pen and pulled a pad of paper closer. "Why on earth was some cop from Maryland asking him this question? He thought. Then he said, "Yes, that is mine. As a matter of fact, I have just been discussing that case with some people here. Why…do you have something on that?"

"Well, quite frankly, I think I just may have something for you. We are investigating a suicide death here. Some guy blew his brains all over the ceiling of his bedroom. Sad case really, this guy was, from all accounts, an incredibly straight shooter, oops, bad pun. He was a Desert Storm veteran, Christian, husband, father. He was, at the time of his death, working for the NSA, the National Security Agency, very top-secret shit, high clearance. It is baffling to me why a guy like this does himself in, but, I have been doing this shit for a long time...nothing surprises me anymore."

"Tell me about it." Mark Roth was taking notes.

"The guy's name was Buford Tucker. What a name, huh? Not a name you forget right away. Anyway...the reason I called you is this. We recovered a note...actually it is not what would be considered a suicide note, or letter. It is simply the disjointed scribblings of a man who was contemplating suicide. However, it will probably be of great interest to you."

"Yeah, yeah, tell me more. I am intrigued."

"The guy writes 'I am sorry' over and over again. He has 'It's my fault' a couple of times. Now, the interesting part, he writes 'I caused a death', 'I caused her death', then... 'I killed Anna Khan.' Of course, he did not kill Anna Khan. There is no evidence that he has been to California in years. There is evidence, however, that he was here in town on the date and at the time of this woman's death. I checked. There is something here, though, because the newspaper...he had the Washington Post, opened to the obituaries, strewn around the room. Some of the pages were on the floor. Some were on a table in his room. We hypothesize that he read the obit, freaked out, and did himself. At least that is what it looks like to me...to us. Now, can you fill in any of the blanks?"

Detective Roth took a slow, deep breath. He was still scribbling the last of his notes. He was a beat behind his compatriot. It seemed that an otherwise mundane day was turning out to be much less mundane. He suddenly blurted out, "See, now, this is the reason I do this shit. This, right here, is the reason, days like this. Don't you agree?"

"You said it all right there, man." The two men had an immediate connection that only they, and all other cops, could understand. "It's all about catching the bad guys."

"Let me begin by saying that this case was a closed file. I mean it was over. Two days after the incident... this file was collecting dust. Actually, there was no case. It was a traffic accident, nothing more. Oh, we may have looked at it a little harder because the lady was rich. Whenever there is a lot of money involved it gives you reason to pause. But, there was nothing. I mean nothing at all, no hint that this was anything more than a tragic accident. Then, a couple of days ago, these guys show up in my office, guys I respect, I might add, and give up a reason to think that it might not be an accident after all, and now...this."

"What did these guys say?"

"Well...let's see..." The detective was collecting his thoughts. "Ms. Khan's brother does not believe that this was an accident. Now, if I had a dollar for every relative that did not believe...yadda, yadda, yadda. You know the rest. So, usually, unless there is clear and convincing evidence to change my mind, I do not pay a great deal of attention to these claims by relatives that foul play *must* have existed. I don't go looking for something that the evidence does not support."

"Me either. I don't think you can be criticized for taking that position. I believe you have aptly stated the position of most good cops."

"Right. Unfortunately, in this case, these guys have turned up some of that aforementioned clear and convincing, mind changing, evidence, which makes you wonder... That aside, what they discovered was that the rich as fuck husband has been consolidating his financial interests for, what looks like, an attempt to liquidate and run. I have checked this out. It is true that the guy is secretly consolidating his interests, no question. Now, could Mr. Khan have other reasons that are motivating his activities? Of course he could. If we all understood why billionaires do what they do…then we would probably all be billionaires, right? However, these guys also uprooted a lie, a lie that, to me, has no alternative explanation."

"You keep saying 'these guys'. Whom are you talking about?"

"Arthur Buckingham, the brother, brought in a couple of old friends. One of these guys is an old friend of mine, whom I trust and respect. That is how I became privy to this new information. The other guy is an ex-lawyer that I had heard of before. He helps people out. I trust him too. Their names are Willie Brennen and Jigs Donahue. I have known Willie for years. He used to be an investigative reporter… Anyway, Arthur, the brother, had access to Ms. Khan's telephone messages. They each heard the husband make a statement in a phone message that was one hundred and eighty degrees, flat opposite, from a statement that he had made to one of our investigating officers. I don't know about you, but I hate lies and liars, especially when they are lying to cops."

"We think alike. Plus, when taken together, I can see why this information would pique your interest. Was there anything else?"

"At the present time I am still investigating. There are some small matters that do not add up. The husband does not seem to be grieving to the degree that you might expect, but anything could explain that. Hell, maybe he just didn't like his wife. However, this bit of info that you have laid on me here is frigging amazing. I have to find a connection between Mr. Khan and Mr. Tucker. Can you fax me a copy of that 'note', plus anything else you may come across?"

"That was my plan."

"I'll tell you what, you can call me anytime, Lieutenant Bergquist. That was one of those very much-appreciated kind of calls. I will let you know if this goes anywhere."

"I would love to hear what happens. Maybe you just got lucky. I will fax that right out to you. You will have it in minutes."

"Thanks again. Not everyone would have gone that extra mile.

"My pleasure. Let me know…"

———————————

"Ten minutes later, Mark Roth was holding a copy of a police report which included the particulars of a gruesome suicide, the names and addresses of all interested parties, and, on a separate paper, the mad scribblings of a man whom was clearly losing touch with all reality. Reading it was like being in the shadows and watching a man go far enough insane to take his own life. If you closed your eyes, you could watch the whole tape play. Roth shuddered. Then, he picked up the phone and dialed Willie Brennen's number.

"Willie, we just got what looks like an humongous break on this case that you guys dumped in my lap. Gather together your little buddies over there and get your butts down here."

"Mark, man, you seem excited. Calm down. What are you talking about?"

"Come down to my office. I just got a call from a Lieutenant on the Ft. Meade, Maryland Police Department. Some guy that worked for the National Security Agency offed himself and left a note. I have a copy of said note in my fat little hand. It says that he was responsible for the death of Anna Khan. Now, get the fuck down here so we can figure out what it means, OK?"

Detective Roth did not have to say another word. However, Willie, always the smart ass, asked, " This person wasn't a mechanic that worked on her car and forgot to tighten down a bolt or something, was he?"

"Very funny, now, if you are quite done, get down here. I think you will all be glad you did."

Willie was suddenly all business. "We are on our way. See you shortly."

When Jigs, Willie and Arthur arrived at the Police Department they first encountered the cop with the hairy ears. "Detective Roth, please?" Jigs was smiling at the rotund man. "We actually know the way."

"Then what are you bothering me for?" The sergeant was acting busy.

They all walked down the hall to Roth's office. When Jigs peeked his head into the office, the Detective looked up from his desk and his paperwork and said, "Jigs, come in...come in. Isn't Cheryl out there?"

"No...nobody named Cheryl out here."

"Well you guys come on in...come in," Roth said out loud as he stood up from his desk to welcome his visitors. Then under his breath he said, "Fucking civil service workers."

As the three men walked in and found chairs, Jigs was saying, "So, Willie tells me that you solved the case. Funny, I was beginning to believe that Ned Khan had something to do with this whole thing, but I guess, I was wrong. It was all accomplished by some guy in Ft. Meade, Maryland, huh, all the way from the east coast, no less?"

"You like to joke around, don't you, Jigs?"

"You got a problem with that?"

"Not at all. Makes life interesting. OK, let me tell you. I am sitting in my office, minding my own business, and this nice Lieutenant calls me up and really changes my mood. He introduces himself and proceeds to explain that he is working on a suicide matter in his jurisdiction, and he stumbles on a scribbled note that seems to indicate that his dead guy killed someone. He is naturally curious about this, being a cop, so he checks to see if somebody died by the name of Anna Khan. He finds that our Anna Khan has, in fact, died recently, and he immediately calls me. Here is a faxed copy of the note." Roth laid the piece of paper on the desk in front of him.

"Now," Roth continued, "if I was investigating a murder case, I would probably have already sent one of my guys out to Maryland to check this out. However, I am not investigating a murder case. I am looking into a case that has already been determined to be an accident on behalf of, and at the request of, an old friend. I don't think I can justify sending one or two of my guys out to Maryland to investigate a traffic accident. I don't think I could get authorization for that. Are you guys getting my drift, here?"

"Right," Jigs said, "we will go there. We would want to go there anyway. Willie and I will go out there and see why a suicide victim would write such a note." Jigs picked up the paper and examined it. "It sure does say that he killed her." He began reading out loud. "It's my fault. I caused a death. I'm sorry. I killed Anna Khan." He looked up at the others in the room. "We have to go out there…and fast."

"What about me?" Arthur was looking like a kid that did not get picked for the team.

"Arthur, you should stay here and be in touch with your broker friend and Tim Keefhaugher and Mark here. There is not enough evidence for Mark to make any significant moves, on behalf of the department. The department still sees this as an accident. You might have to tackle Ned on his way to the airport, figuratively speaking. However, I have a sneaky feeling that there will be more evidence by the time we get back. Does this plan sound good to you, Mark?"

"You read my mind. There is only so much money I can spend, on behalf of the citizens of Los Angeles, on a case, which is presently classified as a traffic accident."

"Well I can spend as much as I want to spend on it because…I'm rich." Arthur said with a laugh. Everyone else chuckled too. "Although, I am pretty sure that the citizens of Los Angeles are also somewhat well healed as well, I guess I can pony up. What are you guys waiting for? Get going."

"We get to fly first class, right?" Willie was being Willie.

43

JIGS AND WILLIE ARRIVED AT Reagan National Airport and proceeded immediately to the Avis Car Rental area. They rented a car and drove to Ft. Meade, Maryland. They got adjoining rooms at a local Ramada Inn. It was Friday afternoon. Willie called Mrs. Tucker, expressed his heartfelt condolences, and explained that they were checking on some facts that had arisen as a result of her husband's untimely demise. Mrs. Tucker was aware of the "note" that was found in her husband's room when he was discovered. He asked if he and his associate could meet with her at her home later that afternoon to discuss these matters. She agreed to the meeting.

They arrived at the Tucker household and walked up the walk. It was a "Pleasant Valley Sunday" kind of home, very cheery. Needless to say, the mood inside the home did not match the delightful, flowered exterior. Mrs. Tucker was a beautiful southern belle whom had clearly been in a state of continuous stress and fully consumed with grief since her husband's death. It was obvious she had not had true sleep in days. Her face was drawn and there were bags under what were, under normal circumstances, very pretty brown eyes.

She invited the two men in and asked if they wanted coffee. They each said that they would love some. Jigs watched her go into the kitchen to get the coffee. There were ducks all over the walls, in pale blues and yellows, a "country kitchen". Everything about this place screamed "happy healthy home". Something very much out of the norm had invaded this home and caused the head of this household to do what he did. This wasn't the home of some old drunk that had just "had enough". This was where a happy, healthy, successful, Christian man had lived and loved his family. "What in the world had happened here?" Jigs asked himself, as he turned to this nice lady and began his questions.

"Mrs. Tucker, I cannot express how sorry we both are for your loss." She nodded her acceptance of their offering of condolence. "Ma'am, my name is Jigs Donahue, this is Willie Brennen, and we work for the surviving family of a woman that died in California. The cause of her death was, by all accounts, an accident. Her brother does not agree with this assessment. He hired us. As I am sure you know, Mrs. Tucker, the police recovered a piece of paper with some writings on it, in your husband's own hand, that mentioned this woman's name. I believe you know in what context her name was mentioned. Do you know the context, Ma'am?"

"Yes...yes I was told by the police about the note. I don't have it. The police have it. I certainly cannot explain the content of the note. It makes absolutely no sense to me. However, I do know the context in which the woman's name was mentioned. The police told me about it. I have no idea what it means, none whatsoever."

"Well, Ma'am, that is one of the reasons that we asked to meet with you. Perhaps, we can be of some assistance in explaining the content of the note, and thereby bring some closure to the issue. That might be better than leaving the rather large questions that are posed by that note...unanswered. Do you agree with that premise, Ma'am?"

"I suppose I do. I am certainly baffled by what is written in that note. My husband would never do such a thing...and further, my husband has not been to California..."

"Ma'am," Willie interrupted. "Please rest assured that no one, least of all us, but no person that we are aware of, actually suspects that your husband did anything to physically cause the death of anyone. There is no evidence of that. None. We simply wonder why he wrote what he wrote. We also believe that if we can determine the answer to that question; we may be infinitely closer to finding the true culprit, if, in fact, there is one. Does that make sense to you?"

"Yes...I suppose it does. Although, I cannot explain it, my husband must have written those words for a reason, but I certainly do not know what that reason was."

"Well," Jigs began, "in a former life, I was an attorney, and Willie here, was an investigative reporter. We have both left our former professions and joined forces to help others solve just this kind of issue. Without blowing our own respective horns, I can report to you that we have had some significant success in this area. What I would like to ask you to do right now is to help us know your husband better. To that end, I would like to ask you some questions that may not have been asked of you by the police, and which may, at first, seem surprising to you. I do not want to make you feel uncomfortable, Ma'am, but I do want to solve this dilemma. Perhaps, tough questions are necessary. I realize you have been through a lot in recent days…can you handle some of those questions at this time, considering that this may help you the have answers to some of your own unanswered questions?"

"Mr. Donahue, I may look to be a fragile sort, particularly in light of what has happened, but I assure you that I'm a tough old bird. I grew up in Mississippi, sir, on the Gulf Coast. We knew tough times. You won't offend me if you ask questions that will help me to understand what drove my husband to take his own life, and to write what he wrote in that letter or note or whatever you ya'all want to call it. Don't you worry about me."

Jigs immediately liked this shattered woman sitting in front of him. He was, all at once, put at ease by her, and he felt confident that this would be a productive meeting. "Well, Ma'am you are a woman after my own heart. That is exactly what I had hoped you would say, and you said it perfectly."

Mrs. Tucker simply nodded stoically.

"First, did it seem to you that your husband had recently changed his routine? Was he doing anything at all differently in the weeks or months prior to this incident? Second, did your husband have any habits that he kept from others? For example, did he drink? Did he see other women? Did he gamble?"

"Ya'all don't beat around the bush do you, Mr. Donahue?"

"I think I promised that I wouldn't, didn't I? You would not respect me if I did, would you?"

"I spose not...Let me see...my husband was a model man, the kind that all the girls wished they had snagged. I knew that. He was popular in High School. That's where we met. He was the quarterback of the football team, and real smart, as well. You know how some of the football players were not smart. They were popular, but not smart. Well, Buford wasn't like that. But, Buford was real religious, real Christian, like me, like I am, so I believe that I can safely say that he never once cheated on me. Now, no woman, or man for that matter, knows that for positive sure, but I would put money on it." She had the somewhat smug look of a woman that knew, without a doubt, that she had satisfied her man to the point where he did not have to stray. Mrs. Tucker continued.

"He and his buddies joined the 308th right out of high school. That was his Coast Guard unit. He was in the Reserves, but when Desert Storm came, he volunteered to go active; and he went to Iraq. He got medals and commendations from that war. When he came back, gambling had come to the Gulf Coast of Mississippi, so he got a job at the casino, like everyone else did. Those casinos saved the Gulf Coast of Mississippi. We needed the jobs."

"Did he gamble?" Jigs was fishing.

"No he didn't. That is why he was moved into the management of the Grand Casino. I'm tellin' you. If ya'all are looking for an interesting story, here, you had better go to the movies, cuz you aint getting one from me. My husband was boring...not boring...but...predictable and solid and a straight arrow, the kind of man that you want to marry, if you are a girl. Maybe the girls want to date the wild excitin' guys, but they want to get married to a man just like my husband." She looked away and bit her bottom lip. She took a deep breath, and continued.

"Anyways, you don't need the whole history, but I wanted to give ya'all some perspective... before I say what I am about to say, in answer to your question…to be honest with you… my husband did regularly bet on football games. He didn't think I knew that, but I did. I knew it, and I never once said a word about it. You want to know why? Well, it was because he even did that well. He never got into trouble with his bettin'. I don't think he even considered it bettin', because he won most of the time. Maybe he considered it bettin', but not gambling. It's funny to think of now…one day I get this mail from a bank that we did not even bank at. I open it and it is not an advertisement; it's a statement. So, I went into the bank. I smiled, and played dumb, and got this young guy at the bank to tell me all about the account. That was so many years ago. I just never told him I knew about it…the account, but I did, and I kept my eye on it. He never got into any trouble, so, I never said anything about it."

Jigs and Willie smiled at this. The statement was more than a wife confessing that she had secretly known about one of her husband's quiet habits. The statement was a miniature expose' of how wives everywhere secretly control their husbands without confrontation.

It seemed to Jigs that this conversation was, in a strange way, working to ease some of the pain that this woman was experiencing. Sometimes, a trip down memory lane, after a death of a loved one, produces such warm feelings and remembrances that it creates a cathartic effect, rather than more pain.

"What about changes in his daily routine?" Willie asked tentatively.

"Well now…Buford's mother got real sick right before all this happened, so he was runnin' down to Biloxi a lot more than he usually would have, but I just chalked that up to her being sick. Now, could he have been doing something else during those trips? Yes he could have. However, if he was, I didn't know about it."

"Did your husband have any unusual expenditures during this time?"

"I will say this, his mama needed a very expensive operation, and they were fighting with the Medicare people, he and his brother and sister and dad were fightin' with them, well… lets say negotiating, then one day there was no more talk about that fight. I was not sure what happened about that and he did not tell me. One day it was just fixed."

Jigs and Willie continued to ask questions and Mrs. Tucker continued to answer them. They all drank coffee and spoke about a deceased man that obviously had a secret. None of the questions seemed to be exposing the secret, however, and the boys were running out of questions. Then Jigs suddenly had a bit of a brainstorm. He felt that the relationship between the three of them was going in the right direction. So, he took a chance.

"Mrs. Tucker, have you looked at the most recent bank statements from your husband's 'secret' bank account?"

"No, I have not seen any statements for a while."

"Is that bank far from here?"

"No, it's not far at all, why?" Mrs. Tucker knew perfectly well why Jigs had asked that question, but she did not let on.

"When do you children come home from school, Ma'am?"

"They will not be home for a couple of hours..." She paused for a long moment. "Are you suggesting that we go over to the bank?"

"You are going to have to go there eventually, right?" Jigs looked at Willie as if to say... "It's worth a try". "I am a lawyer, ma'am. I may be able to help you with the paperwork that is going to exist with reference to that account, if he did not put your name on the account."

"Well, Mr. Donahue, my name is on the account. You forget, I have been keeping an eye on that account." At that point, both Jigs and Willie believed that any chance of seeing the account or anything else regarding the man's private documents had gone poof. However, Mrs. Tucker was not done talking.

"The problem is though, my name is on the account with an 'and', not an 'or', you get what I am sayin'? My husband and I both would have to sign on a check, and I am quite sure my husband has been signing my name, all along, when he did business there. So, I may need a lawyer to straighten out the discrepancy between his version of my signature and my actual signature." She had a mischievous smile on her face, and Jigs and Willie both realized that this woman had already decided to go on this little fact finding mission with them, and that she was just giving them a hard time.

Jigs smiled back at her. You can never figure women out, if you live to be one hundred, he thought. "Well, ma'am, it would be my pleasure to volunteer my help in this regard…free of charge, of course. Do you have a copy of the death certificate?"

"Of course." Mrs. Tucker was already standing. "We will have to hurry. My kids will be home before too long."

They arrived at the bank in less than a half an hour. They all approached one of the vice-presidents and absolutely overwhelmed the poor guy. Almost immediately, they were all given access to the accounts, and, it turned out, a safety deposit box.

"We are going to have to have the key to the box if we want to look in there, no matter how persuasive we think we are, we cannot get around that little fact." Willie was stating the obvious.

Mrs. Tucker had the same mischievous smile on her face. She reached into her purse and pulled out a small gold key. "You mean this key?"

Jigs fell head over heals in love with this woman. He just said, "Yeah, that one." He was beaming at her. She seemed to understand how important this fishing expedition might turn out to be. Everyone handles grief differently. Perhaps she was curious about what caused her husband to make the choice he did. Maybe she wanted to know if she was destitute or rich. Perhaps she just wanted to help these two nice strangers who had temporarily walked into her life. Whatever her motivation, she had surely joined the team, so to speak.

Jigs said, "Let's check out the box before we do anything else." Mrs. Tucker was nodding her assent. They all walked past customers waiting in line on a Friday afternoon, payday. The bank was busy. The safety deposit boxes were towards the rear of the bank in a special room.

After going through the process of identification, they entered the safety deposit box area. On the key that Mrs. Tucker was holding was the number 3927. They saw the box. It was a large box, the largest of the various types available for rent. They had been accompanied by an over weight young girl. She had mentioned that she was new to the job, but she was well trained. The girl and Mrs. Tucker both inserted their respective keys in the slots and turned. After they had gained entry, the new girl left the room. Willie helped Mrs. Tucker lift the box onto a table that was provided for the viewing process. Mrs. Buford opened the box.

What they all saw in the safety deposit box would not leave their respective memories for the rest of their lives. The obvious thing that was immediately apparent was a pile of cash. It was thousands of dollars. They did not count it right then. Neither of the men believed that it was any of their business. Plus, knowing how much money was there was not going to help them figure out who killed Anna Khan, or, more succinctly, prove that Ned did it. What they saw next was what they would never forget.

There were files, lots of them, lots of manila files full of lots of names. Many of the files were about people that they all knew, famous people. Some of the files were about rich people, very rich people. In each case, the files were organized and neat and they each delineated a particular secret, which the person had. They were all about something that these people had done, or didn't do, that they would clearly not want anyone else to find out about. There were many files where the subject of the file had cheated on their spouse. There was a file about a very famous conservative radio personality that had gotten a penile implant. Lots of facelifts and other plastic surgeries had been performed. One guy was an "in the closet" gay. Sometimes, the person had been arrested and had been successful in hiding the arrest from the press and all others, but somehow Buford knew. Not only did he know about the respective secret that each person was concealing, there was a complete background check, compiled by the FBI, on each person. It was becoming clear to them all, as they read file after file that Buford knew a lot of secrets about a lot of people, and that each of the secrets was worth millions of dollars. The people named in those files would pay anything to maintain the secret nature of the information contained in those files. Finally, buried near the bottom, there it was, a file with the name neatly written in the upper right hand corner. Ned Khan.

As the three of them perused the Ned Khan file, it became immediately apparent to them all why Buford might have been drawn to this file. Mr. Khan had, hands down, the most money. He also had a secret that was immense. *He had another wife and a child in Iran.* That was a secret. As secrets go, that was a doozy!

Jigs looked at Mrs. Tucker and he was slightly surprised by what he saw. She was crying. After all that this woman had been through, this was the moment that caused her to silently sob. Jigs wondered... "Why now?" He put his hand on her shoulder and asked, "Are you alright, ma'am?"

She shook her head and wiped her eyes with back of her hands. "Oh, don't mind me... I just can see what he was trying to do. What he did... he did for me. He did this for his wife and for his children. Don't you see? My husband was not an extravagant man. He did not have fancy cars or fancy clothes, nor did he want them. He was a simple Christian man. To me, it is just so perfectly clear. He was doing what men have been doing for all time. He was doing what a man is supposed to do. He was providing for his family. He saw an opportunity where he could give to his family a better life, without seriously hurting any other person. This man could certainly afford it. He would not miss some money. What would seem like a lot of money to our family... would mean nothing to this man, this Mr. Khan. I know my husband, ya'all. That was his plan. I just know it!"

Her face contorted, and tears flowed silently down her cheeks. No matter how convoluted the logic, this woman was obviously filled with love and forgiveness for her departed spouse.

"Look at this," said Willie. These two files here..." Willie paused, looking at Mrs. Tucker. He contemplated not continuing, but he decided to go on. "It looks like he successfully received $200,000.00 from these two files, a businessman and a football player. He was very organized. There are notes here on everything. There is an address of a Mailboxes

Etc. in New Orleans. This is incredible. Evidently, these guys just paid the money."

"I guess that explains his mama's operation." Mrs. Tucker was done crying and was looking at the files along with the other two men.

"Let's take all this shit, oops, stuff, out of here. It is getting late. Your kids… right?"

"Oh my God… yes. We have to go."

They stopped by the desk of the vice-president whom they spoke with on the way into the bank. They asked if he would see to it that copies of statements encompassing the past six months were sent to Mrs. Tucker. He agreed. They arrived back at the Tucker home with time to spare. Willie had put together a stack of papers that he believed would help them back in Los Angeles. Mrs. Tucker said that they could take the items with them. They thanked her, and promised to return everything to her at a later date. Mrs. Tucker agreed that she would cooperate with any future activity or investigation regarding the matter. They seemed to have found an ally in her, and why not, if one were to use the most sideways logic possible, Ned Khan had contributed to her husband's death. If he had simply paid the money…

44

JIGS AND WILLIE HAD RETURNED TO their hotel and were reviewing the items that Willie had brought with them. He had all the files regarding Ned, of course, and he had kept all the files and notes that Buford had created regarding the two individuals from whom he had successfully received money.

"This is fucking amazing," Willie said as he looked through the materials. "It looks like old Buford asked for $100,000.00 from each of these two jamokes about three or four days before they coughed it up. Evidently, he just called them up and said 'send me money' and they just sent him money, just like that. I want that job. How do I get a job at the NSA? Do you simply fill out an application form and send it in? Then, I guess they just call you up and give you an interview, right? They probably pay for your flight and all expenses on your way to the interview too. Maybe I will apply. What do you think?"

"I think you are too fucking old, you old fart, but I bet those guys would absolutely love your stupid political ideals. I'm guessing most of those guys are Republican, just a wild guess."

"They sure as hell wouldn't take you, hippy. You can just forget about getting a job at the NSA with me. When I get my letter from those guys saying they would love to have me working for them, I'll be saying goodbye to you, tree hugger. That will be that..."

"You joke. But, if you look at this fucked up mess in its totality, you will notice that the goddamn Bush administration has created a monster here."

"Oh please, hipster, do not start with your liberal, George Bush hating drivel."

"This is not drivel, Willie. Look at what we are seeing here!" Jigs seemed to be getting worked up over this issue.

"What are you saying? Are you suggesting that we should not conduct surveillance against our enemies?" Willie's veins were starting to show at his temples.

"Of course I am not saying that. Of course we have to spy on our enemies. No question about it. No one would ever suggest otherwise. But, we have specific procedures in place to do that, don't we? Why do you conservatives feel that it is appropriate to go outside the bounds of the Constitution of the United States of America to do that, which is perfectly possible to do within the bounds of the damn Constitution? Why? You guys are always the ones screaming about activist judges... Look at these files, Willie. Which one of the people in these files do you consider an enemy of the State? These people are just

citizens. Simply people that were going about their business...
doing their perfectly legal daily activities... and some asshole
from the National Security Agency was listening to every word
they spoke over the telephone. Now, why don't you tell me how
that process has protected this country from attack, or how
opposing such a practice makes me somehow unpatriotic?"

"You can't use this as an example. Old Buford was on a
bit of a frolic of his own, wasn't he? He was not authorized to
spy on these people. He took it upon himself to do that. He was
way out of the scope of his employment, and, I dare say, way
outside the scope of the law."

"The law? The law? The law in effect at this moment
specifically provides that if old Buford, as you say, or any other
employee of the NSA for that matter, wanted to listen in on a
telephone conversation, he, or she, was required to obtain a
warrant from a judge. What is so hard to understand about that?"

"Oh sure, that is what all you liberals say. Take the
matter in front of a damn liberal judge. See what he has to say
about it. What in the world does some damn judge know about
surveillance, about covert activity, about keeping this country
safe? Why do you believe that a judge knows better than an
agent, who is in the trenches, trained to do the very covert
operation that he is trying to conduct? What qualifies a fucking

judge to decide what surveillance is appropriate and what surveillance is inappropriate? Please... tell me."

"That is the problem with you weirdo conservatives. You all seem to think that judges are specifically put in place to foil all of your paranoid plans and schemes. No one is suggesting that a judge knows more about spying than a goddamn NSA agent. No one is suggesting that a judge is smarter than an agent of the NSA. The reason that the law, and the Constitution I might add, requires a warrant before proceeding with surveillances activities has nothing to do with judges being smarter or being better suited to make decisions of this nature. It has do with insuring that there is probable cause to conduct the activities, and insuring that we create a record of the whole damn thing, and maybe that we create some restraints and restrictions as to how the spying may be conducted. Without a record, there are no guidelines or rules. That is exactly how we wound up with this pile of files that we are looking at right here." Jigs picked up the files that were right in front of him. He symbolically shook them in Willie's face.

"You don't know what you are talking about," Willie said.

"Look, Wil, something gave Buford Tucker the idea that he could get information on anyone he wanted. He could order background checks on anyone. Will you please look at what I am holding here? He has a damn file on people who have done absolutely nothing wrong, famous people. He chose these people because they were rich. That is the only reason. His plan, as we know, was to make money."

"You cannot predict or prevent a person from committing a crime in advance, Jigs."

"Ah… but you are wrong, my conservative friend. When the Bush administration instituted the warantless wiretap program, and made it so friggin' secret that even Congress didn't know about it, it was like putting a bag of money in front of the poor saps who had to actually implement it."

"Now you really are talking out of your ass."

"No… I am talking from out of my mouth. Can't you see my mouth moving when I talk? Bear with me a moment... Let's say you work for the National Security Agency. You are told that from now on you no longer have to go to the FISA Court to get a warrant before you conduct surveillance. So, essentially you no longer have any kind of body overseeing your activities. Plus, you are now data mining. Therefore, you have increased the scope of your reach, while decreasing the oversight. That is like putting a big bag of cash in a room with a person and saying to them… 'we don't know how much money is in the bag, and we will not know if you take any out of it, but… don't take any.' It is a little much to ask of anybody, don't you think?"

Just then Jig's cell phone rang, he looked at the display of the caller ID, "Its Arthur," he said.

"Hi, Arthur. Willie is going to go to work for the NSA. What do you think of that?"

"What?"

"Based on what we can tell, if you work for the NSA, you get to receive free money from people with secrets. Willie thinks that is cool, so the old conservative fart is going to go work for them."

"What the fuck are you talking about?"

"I'm sorry, Arthur. We have unearthed some information on a former NSA employee...never mind. It is a long story. I'm kidding you."

"Well, I am afraid that it is time for you two guys to get serious. You guys have to get back here."

"Why, what's up?" Jigs immediately became stone faced and motioned to Willie to pay attention, as if he could hear Arthur on the phone.

"Labuda called me. He says that this being Friday, the buzz on Wall Street is that the rumors of the impending sale of Ned Khan's holdings are going to be confirmed on Monday. The official announcement would be Monday morning. He says that if what he is hearing is true, which he says he will know for certain within the next ten to twenty hours, Ned is free to leave at any time. In other words, if the buzz is true…the deal is done. He could leave this weekend. This fucking weekend… So…I hope you guys have something… Do you?"

"Hold on a second, Arthur." Jigs held the phone away from his mouth and pointed at the files strewn on the hotel room bed. He looked at Willie. "Wil, would you please pull everything that incriminates, or in any way pertains to, Ned Khan and go downstairs to the hotel fax machine and fax it all to Detective Roth. Ask him to get warrants. Warrants to search…and, if he feels he has enough, a warrant for the arrest of Mr. Ned Khan. Tell him time is of the essence. No…tell him to fucking hurry. Also, get us on the next flight back to Los Angeles. After I am done talking to Arthur, I will call Mrs. Tucker and explain that we are going to have to cut our stay short. We gotta go man…It's on."

Willie's face lit up with a huge smirky smile. He started to laugh. "Ha…this is the trip…this is the best part of the trip." He immediately began going through all the documents on the bed, pulling out that which he needed. Moments later, he was gone.

Jigs turned back to the phone. "Don't worry, Arthur. We are on our way. By the way, we got it all. Are you sitting down?"

He began to tell Arthur of the salient points of the afternoon, which now seemed to have lasted an eternity. He explained about the meeting with Mrs. Tucker and how she had turned out to be a pretty tough cookie, and an incredible help to their cause. He told of how she allowed them to go to the bank and how they found the files on all the famous people. He mentioned how they had finally gotten to the file on Ned Khan. Then he asked again, " Are you sitting down?"

Arthur said that he was.

"Well, Arthur… it seems that your brother-in-law has another wife…and a twelve year old son back in Iran."

"What?"

"I am sorry, man. This guy is bad news. The reason that your sister was killed is clear now. Buford Tucker worked for the National Security Agency. He had access to information. That is what the NSA has as its stock in trade. Buford must have overheard a telephone conversation during which he learned about this other family of Ned's. He was using this information to extort money from Ned. Ned made a different choice. Again, I'm so sorry."

Arthur wasn't talking. He mumbled something obscene. Jigs continued.

"The only possible semblance to a silver lining in all this is that we have the evidence, the motive, against Ned. As we speak, Willie is faxing the information that we have found to Detective Mark Roth. Roth should have no problem getting a search warrant for Ned's home and for all records, such as telephone records and business records on him, together with a possible arrest warrant for the asshole, himself. It's small consolation, Arthur, but..."

"We have to get this guy, Jigs. We have to. We are going to get this guy, right? I want to see this guy in cuffs."

"You will, Arthur...you will. Willie and I will be back there in a matter of hours, and we will get this guy together, OK?"

"Hurry." That was all Arthur could say, then he had hung up. Jigs stood there looking at the phone before he slapped it shut. What would it be like to know that someone killed your only sister? What if that person was your sister's husband? Jigs could not imagine.

There was a knock on the door. Jigs opened it. It was Willie.

"I didn't have a key. Let's pack. We have to get to the airport. Our plane leaves in two hours."

"That's cutting it kind of close, isn't it?"

"No. We'll make it. I take it that Mr. Khan is on the move?"

"Yep. It looks like this consolidation deal of his is going down. There are rumors that the announcement is scheduled for Monday. That means he could be leaving at any time. Let's get to the airport. I will call Mrs. Tucker on the way."

They threw all their clothes into bags and gathered the files together. They jumped into the rental car and hightailed it towards Regan National.

"What did Roth say? Did he say he had enough to get warrants?"

"I didn't wait around to find out. I wasn't going to wait for him to review the files, ya goofy fucking hippy, I would still be down there.

The Washington, DC area traffic reminded the two transplanted island dwellers of Southern California traffic. They dodged in and out of lanes, stopped and started, and in general got frustrated and swore a lot, but they made Regan National in fifty minutes. During the drive, Willie repacked the suitcases and found a way to put all the files into the cases as well. Jigs called Arthur while he drove and gave him their ETA and flight number. He then called Mrs. Tucker, and thanked her for her help. He assured her that they would return all the items that had borrowed. Mrs. Tucker said that that was nice but she really did not care. She was more concerned that they catch the billionaire who, in her mind, helped to drive her deceased husband to take his own life. After he hung up, Jigs laughed with Willie about this rather convoluted position of hers.

"I guess when someone commits suicide, the survivors will look in any direction to blame it on anyone but the dead guy, at least that seems to be the case here." Willie was only guessing, but it sounded good to him.

"I don't care why she feels that way. I am just glad she does feel that way. She saved our respective asses, you know."

"Yes she did."

They bullied their way through the airport, negotiated the security lines, and made their flight. They both tried to get some sleep while on the plane. It did not work that well, but they got a few winks, which helped a little. When they arrived at the Long Beach Airport, Arthur was there to meet them. He filled them in as they all quickly walked to Arthur's car. The airport was quiet at this late hour, in stark contrast to the daytime. The SUV was parked in one of the first spots.

"I talked to Roth. He said he would be able to get a warrant to search Ned's home and to get some records, phone records and the like, but he is not sure about an arrest warrant yet. He says he has to see what judge he gets on the weekend. He might just go straight to the home of a Judge Amirante. His Honor owes him a favor or some shit. I don't know anything about all that legal crap, but he is excited. That guy really gets off on getting the bad guy."

Willie laughed. "No way you want to be a criminal with that guy on your tail."

Arthur continued. "I haven't heard anything from Labuda yet. I suppose that is a good thing. If he had called by now, we would probably miss the motherfucker. I just hope that prick isn't planning to skulk away in the middle of the night."

"This *is* the middle of the night…look around." Jigs was getting excited too. He was talking fast. "If he had any plans to actually get on his plane and fly away, we would hear from Tim Keefhaugher. We can call him first thing tomorrow morning, in a couple of hours, to see if anything is up on his part in this. Unless this guy plans to walk out of town and then out of the country, we have him pretty well covered. He isn't going anywhere without us knowing about it."

They arrived at Arthur's home in a matter of minutes. Driving around the Los Angeles suburbs wasn't that bad in the wee hours of the morning. No traffic. They all got out of Arthur's car and went into the house.

Willie said, "I need a beer…who else?"

This brought some chuckles from the other two. Then Jigs said, "I'll have one, Willie, what the fuck." That brought more smiles. It actually calmed the mood. Arthur was next. "Give me one too, Willie. What can it hurt? Let's get drunk."

"I've never been drunk in my life." Willie was behind the bar getting the beers. He popped up with a smile. I don't get drunk. I just drink."

Jigs gently lifted one of the suitcases onto the pool table. He opened it and pulled out all the files that they had. He spread the files out on the pool table.

"What the fuck are you doing?" Willie asked.

"I am looking through our files. I am putting things in order here. I am trying to see…if I were a judge, would I give us a warrant for the arrest of Ned Khan?" Jigs began to peruse the papers in front of him.

Willie's cell phone rang, which somewhat startled everyone. It was the wee hours after all. Willie picked up the phone, opened it, and said hello.

"Willie…hi, it's Mark Roth. I take it you and Jigs are back in town?"

"Yeah, we are over here at Arthur's home…waiting to hear from you. How are things coming?"

"I have called in a few favors and I am about to have a couple of warrants signed by my friend the honorable Judge James P. Amirante. He says I have enough for a search and an arrest warrant. After I procure said warrants, I intend to go straight to his home and pick up the motherfucker and charge him with conspiracy to commit murder. There are plain clothed officers on their way over to Mr. Khan's house as we speak, just to sit on him till I get there. They will not bother him, unless he tries to go somewhere."

"Arthur will be very pleased to hear that, as are Jigs and I. Thank you for your help on this thing. You have really gone the extra mile on this."

"Hey, the fuckhead lied to one of my guys. I don't like that…OK…I can see the honorable judge's house from here. I will call you guys when we have him in custody. Sit tight."

"Thanks again, Mark. Talk to you soon."

Willie closed the phone and looked at the other two men. He was smiling, so that was a good sign, but he didn't say anything. There was a very pregnant pause.

Finally, Arthur said, "OK, OK…out with it, already. What did he say?"

"They are going over to arrest Mr. Khan."

"Well…I…ah…guess that's a good thing."

Jigs looked at Arthur as if he was wearing a dress. " I thought that is what we were all doing here. You sure don't sound very happy. Did you hear what he said?"

"Yes, of course I did. And, of course I am happy. However, Ned is still the person that was my brother-in-law for the past twenty or so years and…"

Willie's phone was ringing again. Arthur was glad. He did not know if he could explain his mixed emotions. Arthur was also realizing that Ned being arrested was not going to bring Anna back.

Willie picked up his phone, opened it, and said, "Doesn't anyone sleep at night anymore?"

"I figured this was important enough to risk waking you." It was Tim Keefhaugher. Willie made a sign to the others to be quiet.

"No…no…I wasn't…we aren't sleeping. We are all wide-awake at Arthur's house. In fact, a detective friend of mine is on his way over to Mr. Ned Khan's house to arrest Mr. Ned Khan. We are all sitting around waiting on word...Tim...I am guessing you called for a reason. What was it?"

"Well, I doubt if Mr. Ned Khan is at home."

"What would make you say such a thing? We were all in such a good mood over here."

"If I had to guess, I would say that the fine Mr. Khan is probably on his way here...here, meaning the airport. I say that because his pilot is fueling up his aircraft and has filed a flight plan to Dubai. I figured you guys would want to know that so I called..."

"You can't let that plane leave, man, there is a Detective from the Los Angeles Police Department procuring an arrest warrant as we speak...can you stop him from leaving?"

"The gentleman that we are discussing is ever so slightly important. What you are asking me to do is to delay a billionaire from taking off, without a reason. I think that that is exactly the reason that he bought the big, rather expensive jet airplane in the first place... so he would not have to wait to take off. We make passenger planes wait for him... Don't tell anyone that. You did not hear that from me."

"We will be there in twelve minutes...*don't let him leave.*"

Willie turned to the others. "We have to leave, right now! The motherfucker is trying to make a run for it. He has got a flight plan filed and his pilot is fueling up the goddamn plane." They all jumped up and began to collect the things each felt they would need.

"We have to call Roth."

"Call him from the car. We have to hurry."

They all scurried out the door. Arthur ran up to his big SUV. He had his hand on the door handle when Willie ran past him and said while pointing, "Arthur, the limo."

Arthur said, "Good idea." They all ran up to the limo. Willie went to the driver's door. Arthur threw him the keys. Seconds later they were pealing rubber, sending little stones into the air behind them. Willie was taking corners wide because of the stretch nature of the limo. The crystal glasses in the cupboards clinked and the utensils on top of the cupboard flew around the top, but somehow did not fall off. With each wide turn there would be a low groaning screech, unlike the sound made by a normal length car, but the limo hugged the road better that one might expect. Each time they hit a low spot or dip in the road, the car would slightly bottom out and minor sparks would flash from beneath the gleaming black Lincoln.

It was barely daybreak, plus, it was Saturday; so there was very little traffic. At times, Willie reached speeds of eighty miles per hour before he would have to slow for an intersection. He never fully stopped for stop signs. He got lucky with the few stoplights that existed between Huntington Beach and Long Beach. Arthur was shouting out directions well in advance and Willie was following them to a tee. It was quite a sight to see. Jigs was screaming into his cell phone. "Get here...*now.*"

"Don't worry, I got a warrant, Roth yelled back over the sound of the shrieking sirens of his own police vehicle. "I will be there in a few minutes."

As they approached an intersection that was guarded only by a stop sign, Willie saw an older model Mercury about to pull away from the sign, crossing their path. The car had made a full stop and it was actually its turn to go. An elderly woman, probably on her way to church...on a Saturday, that could just barely see over the steering wheel, was driving the car. One thing was sure; she was not expecting a big black stretch limo to be barreling along, approaching the intersection. Either she didn't see them or she was the feisty type that was going to assert herself, they never stopped to find out. Either way, in spite of the fact that it was clear that the limo was not going to stop, she did not even tap the brakes. The Mercury slowly began to fill the intersection in front of the limo.

Willie hit the brakes and yanked the steering wheel to the right. This time everything that was on top of the cupboard went flying. Jigs and Arthur tumbled onto each other in the back. The limo hit the curb and bounced over it. Jigs and Arthur both hit the ceiling. The stop sign was next. The front bumper hit it. The sign seemed to fill the entire windshield for one second. Then it flew over the top of the car, bouncing off the roof and landing in a lawn twenty-five feet from the side of the road.

It seemed that the long car was going to break in half. Willie yanked the steering wheel to the left. They traveled back onto the roadway and swerved back and forth a bit before Willie straightened out and continued on. Willie actually floored it at this point because they had come to a long straight stretch. He seemed unaffected by their little confrontation with the Mercury.

"Good one, Wil." Jigs yelled from the back. They were all snickering.

"Yeah, that was a good one, alright," Arthur said. "But, lets not do that again."

Willie continued at break-neck speed. He was actually wishing that a cop would see them, so they could effectively pick up an escort, but, as everyone knows, there is never a cop around when you need one.

As they approached the front of the airport, Willie slowed slightly. They went past the main, civilian entrance to the airport and traveled to the entrance for Signature Flight Services. He pulled in as if he was just another limo dropping off just another rich person. Willie stopped in front of the main entrance to the small terminal. "Go in. I will park or wait, I don't know, call me on the phone."

Willie and Arthur jumped out of the limo and quickstepped to the doorway. Jigs pulled out his wallet. In it he had a Florida State Bar I.D., which identified him as a lawyer and a member of the Florida Bar. He also had a State of Florida Private Investigator's License, which was soon to expire. He walked up to the one person that could be considered security. She was at least fifty-five years old and obese. There was no other description for her girth. She was obese. Jigs tried to explain their plight in a couple of sentences. It did not work.

"I am a lawyer and a P.I. and I am working on a case with a Detective from the L.A. Police Department. He is on his way here. There is a man that is attempting to leave the country. He cannot be allowed to leave..." That is as far as he got.

"Sir, you must move away from this station if you are not a passenger on a plane that is flying out of this terminal."

"But, ma'am you don't seem to understand..."

"Sir, if you do not move away from this station I will call Homeland Security. You are not a policeman or a prosecuting attorney. You do not have proper Identification…" She was still talking; but Jigs could not hear her. He was backing away from the station and looking out the huge windows, from which one could see the many parked private planes lined up outside. *He could plainly see Ned Khan boarding his private plane.* Jigs took out his phone and pressed the button that was Willie's speed dial.

"The colossal prick is getting on his fucking plane."

Willie said, "I know, I can see him. I just talked to Tim. He is trying to delay him, but he says that he can only do so much, under the circumstances."

———————

Tim Keefhaugher was standing in front of his screen. He was listening to the pilot of the Gulfstream V, which was registered to Khan Industries, request clearance to taxi onto the runway. He could see the plane from the tower. He was totally surrounded by other controllers, all talking at once, each in front of his or her personal screen. It was a scene of pure chaos. One wonders how they do the job they do. "Khan Gulfstream, this is Long Beach Tower, I have you. You are not clear at this time. You will be clear presently. Hold your position." Tim turned to his cell phone. "This pilot is requesting clearance right now,

Willie, you have to give me something I can use to delay this guy. This guy is so rich it is like I am trying to delay then damn President of the United States."

Mark Roth was on the 405 traveling at approximately ninety miles per hour, flying by the few cars that were out at that time of the morning on a Saturday. He was driving a black Ford Crown Victoria, which was unmarked, but it had all the flashing lights, normally hidden behind grills and disguised as back-up lights and turn signals, flashing their warning to other motorists. The siren was screaming. He was on his cell phone barking orders at a poor sergeant back at the precinct, trying to get through to the proper channels to have them deny clearance to a certain plane. He thought it odd that he could easily have a passenger plane stopped, but he was encountering resistance trying to stop a private plane from leaving the airport.

"Patch me through to that person," he was saying, "I want to talk to him directly."

The nervous sergeant successfully connected the two calls. Roth yelled into the phone.

"I guess I fail to understand the problem. I am telling you that there is a suspected murderer on that Gulfstream V, so it has to be detained. Why is that a problem?"

"I understand your frustration, sir, but there are procedures for this, and you are not..." Detective Roth heard his call waiting beep. At that point, he stopped hearing the nice man at the airport. He looked at the display on his phone. It was Willie. He pressed the "send" button.

"Mark, I can see Khan's plane from where I am sitting, and he is on the plane. How long until you arrive?"

"I am minutes away. I have been talking to one of Homeland Security's finest bureaucrats... I am not getting anywhere with him."

At that moment, Willie saw the tail of the large private aircraft begin to move slowly past the other planes parked in a row on the tarmac.

"The plane is pulling out...*right now*! The son-of-a-bitch is leaving."

Jigs could see the same thing from his vantage point in the terminal. The plane with a big red "K", written in script on its tail, was slowly lumbering away from its parking spot and beginning to taxi down the access lane to the runway.

"Tim...the fuckstick is pulling away. He is leaving."

Tim could see the plane from the tower. He spoke into his microphone in a very measured and calm manner. "Khan Gulfstream, this is Long Beach tower. You are not yet clear to taxi. Hold your position... I say again... hold your position." The pilot on the Gulfstream V answered.

"Tower, I am simply getting into position for clearance. My passenger is pressed for time. Please advise at your earliest convenience when clearance is secured."

"Roger, Khan Gulfstream. You do not have clearance at this time. Hold at runway."

On the Gulfstream V, the pilot was muttering to himself, and to his co-pilot. He was shaking his head. "What the heck is the goddamn problem out there? It's dawn, for Christ's sake. It is not like there are hundreds of planes out there waiting in line. Look around." His co-pilot nodded his agreement.

Back in the cabin of the plane, Ned Khan was sipping coffee. He was looking out over the runways and taxiways. He could not see an obvious reason for the delay. He was beginning to come to the conclusion that something was up. He motioned to the cabin hostess. She immediately hurried towards him.

"Would you please go and ask the captain why we have not taken off."

"Certainly, sir. I will be right back."

Ned continued to search the runways and the surrounding access taxiways, together with the roads and areas around the confines of the airport. He was craning his neck a bit to see all aspects. He was actually starting to look for other signs of trouble, such as a police car. He knew that not only were Arthur and his friends from Florida nosing around, but there had also been cursory police questions being asked. He knew the clock had been ticking for some time. He did not know, at that moment, that he had, literally, minutes left of freedom if he did not make a rather drastic move. He was beginning to suspect it, though.

The hostess approached with a frozen smile on her face. "Sir, the captain is waiting for clearance to taxi. He believes it will be forthcoming at any moment."

"What is the delay, Sheilah?"

"He really does not know, sir, but he expects that we will have clearance momentarily. Would you like more coffee, or anything else, sir?"

"No…no thank you, Sheilah."

Ned looked around the airfield again. He was becoming more and more convinced that something ominous was afoot. He suddenly stood up and walked towards the cockpit.

———————

Tim Keefhaugher's supervisor walked up behind him. "What is the problem, Tim? Why haven't you cleared the Gulfstream yet?"

Tim looked up at him. He looked at his cell phone in his hand. "I have information that there is a suspected murderer on that plane, but I do not have anything official yet."

"Tim, we only care about that which is official...you know that. Do you know who that is? Give him clearance."

———————

Jigs and Arthur watched helplessly as the jet plane continued to move towards the runway. Then the plane stopped. It was not moving out onto the taxiway. "Tim," Jigs thought. He immediately called the controller from the list on his phone.

"Hey Tim, this is Jigs Donahue. Do we have you to thank for that plane sitting still out there?"

"I have been talking to Willie. I have been delaying that plane for as long as I possibly could. Unfortunately, I have just been told by my supervisor to give clearance to the son-of-a-bitch. Without some kind of warrant or official word from somebody more important than the prick onboard that plane, which is pretty hard to find, I have to let him go."

"OK, I'm going to hang up now. We have a Detective with a warrant on his way here. I am going to check on his progress. Then, I will call Willie. He or I will get right back to you."

"OK, I'll talk to you."

Jigs called Detective Roth. Roth was actually exiting at the Long Beach Airport exit.

"This is Jigs, man, where the fuck are you?"

"I am right outside the airport, hippy, where are you?

"Stop dallying. We don't have all day, you know. They need that warrant you have."

"Very funny. I will be pulling up in a minute or so. See you then."

"OK, see ya." Jigs motioned to Arthur. "Let's get out and see what is up with Willie." They both started to walk towards the exit. Then, Arthur stopped. "Fuck me…they are moving again," he said. They both saw the big tail on the plane begin to move forward. Then worse, they watched as it began to make the turn onto the taxiway and begin to pick up speed as it taxied towards the runway.

"Jesus Christ...come on...let's get out to Willie and Roth!" Jigs was scrambling to the exit of the terminal."

Ned appeared in the door of the cockpit. He walked in and closed the door behind him. He locked the door.

"Gentlemen, why haven't we taken off? I have urgent business...very urgent. We must go now."

"I am very sorry, sir, but we have not received final clearance yet. I cannot imagine what the holdup is..." As the pilot was speaking, he grabbed the microphone. He spoke into it. "Tower, this is Khan Gulfstream V requesting immediate clearance to taxi. My passenger has urgent business. What is the holdup?"

There was no response. They waited a beat, then. "Tower, this is..."

"Never mind that," Ned interrupted. "Let's just go."

"Sir, I am sorry...but I can't just take off without clearance."

"How would you two guys like to receive the sum of ten million dollars for your fee on this flight? Ten million each, and five million for your little cutie pie back there. I guess you are underestimating the importance of the business to which I must attend. Now, you know I am a man of my word. That is the deal, twenty-five million total. Get this plane in the air."

The pilot and co-pilot looked at each other in astonishment. They each had their own momentary fantasy about how they would spend ten million dollars. Then they both realized that something was amiss. They both realized that the delay that they were experiencing was not arbitrary. It had been calculated. They spoke to each other with their eyes. They each had another momentary fantasy. This time it was about a prison term. The pilot turned to Ned and voiced their combined opinion.

"Sir, I am sure we will get clearance in just a moment. It is a generous offer…but…"

That was all Ned had to hear. He reached inside his sport jacket and pulled out a 38-caliber revolver. It was small. But, it was big enough. "I am sorry that you boys did not accept my first offer. My second offer will not be as lucrative. Now, *get this plane in the air!*

Both men looked at Ned. They could see that he was desperate at this point. They did not want to test him. The pilot moved his hand onto the throttle and pushed it forward. The big jet engine whined loudly and the plane began to creep forward. "I have to tell the tower something. If we don't, we might be taxiing right into another plane." The pilot was looking forward at where he was going. He was talking to Ned.

"Be careful what you say." Ned had adopted a very calm demeanor, but he kept the gun pointed at the pilot's head.

"Tower… this is Khan Gulfstream, we lost that last transmission. We are beginning our taxi approach to runway 1-4. Please acknowledge." The plane continued down the taxiway at a normal rate of speed. They would be required to make what amounted to a very wide U-turn when they reached the end of the runway. Then they would be in position to take off. They were almost to that point.

The radio squelched. "Khan Gulfstream V this is Long Beach tower. We acknowledge your position." That was it. No clearance, but they did not deny clearance. "What was that about?" The pilot thought to himself. He did not let on that it was at all unusual. He simply continued to his position on runway 1-4. He did not want to die. "They can see me, " he thought. "They are not going to let me run into another plane."

Willie was watching the Gulfstream V make its slow turn onto the runway 1-4. It was obvious to him that the plane was about to begin its final take off procedures. He looked around the interior of the car. On the floor of the front seat passenger side, he noticed the regular driver's chauffeur's hat. It was a black little beanie affair, with a tight small brim. He reached down and picked it up. He put it on. He smiled at himself in the rear view mirror. He put the car in drive and began to pull up to the gate where other limos would go to drop off their highest profile passengers. These were passengers that did not have to board through the terminal. They were brought directly to their plane. There was just one security guard at the gate. The guard could see Willie approaching slowly towards him.

There was a chain link fence surrounding and separating the area where the planes parked from the outside parking lot and the outer access to the terminal. It was approximately eight feet tall with a barbed wire top. The opening into the tarmac area where the rich and famous boarded their planes was perhaps fifteen feet wide. There was a small booth in which the single guard sat with a clipboard. The guard was smiling at Willie and Willie was smiling back. Willie waved at the elderly man as he approached and motioned or half pointed in the general direction of the line of expensive planes, which were parked in a neat row on the other side of the fence. Willie was nodding and smiling and pointing. The guard was motioning to him to pull up. He was smiling. He leaned out of his little booth holding his clipboard.

Willie was about a car length away from being even with the guard shack. He was smiling. He was pointing to the back seat with his thumb, like a hitchhiker, and then he would point with his forefinger at the line of planes, all the while smiling away. As he pulled up even with the guard shack, he began to lean out of the driver's side window as if he was going to order food from the guard in the booth. The front end of the limo was through the fence. Willie was motioning with his hitchhiker move. He leaned out further and began to say to the guard, "Good morning...I have Mr.... *fuck it!* Willie floored the big limo. He shot through the opening and out past the parked planes, spitting pebbles and dust at the poor old man in the booth. The man dropped his clipboard as he quickly leaned back inside his little booth. His official guard hat, which looked like a policeman's hat, was cocked all sideways and falling off the man's head. The guard had a policeman's walkie-talkie radio clipped to his belt with a microphone secured to his shoulder, just like a real cop. That was the last time Willie saw the guard. He could see him in his rear view mirror frantically screaming into that shoulder microphone with his hat falling off his head.

From the tower, Tim Keefhaugher could see a big black sleek limousine bounding out across the many access roads and across the grass that separated the roads. The limo was bouncing up and down as it cut across the airfield at a right angle to the single private jet which was in position for take off at the start markings on the runway marked 1-4.

On that plane, no further word had come from the tower with reference to clearance to proceed to take off; however, the runway was, in fact, clear as far as the eye could see. Ned Khan had no options left. He said again, "Get this plane in the air." He added. "Now!" He also used the gun to punctuate his command. At this point, the pilot realized that he, also, had no other options, if he wanted to remain among the living. He could see how desperate Ned actually was. He pushed the throttle forward to its take off position. The jet engines whined loudly, once again, and the sleek plane began to shoot down the runway, picking up speed with each passing second. That is when all on board the plane noticed the incredible sight before them. A shiny black Lincoln Continental stretch limousine was bounding across the airfield at a right angle to the plane.

As the plane picked up more and more speed, one could easily calculate with ones own eyes that the limousine was going to reach the point of impact before the plane would reach the speed required for take off. It was simply one of those things you could just tell.

"If we hit that car at this speed, it will rip open this fuselage. They will not find a recognizable piece of any one of us. When it's over, it will look like a John Woo movie!" The pilot was screaming at the top of his lungs. He and Ned made a decision at the same moment. As Ned began to lower the pistol he was pointing, resigned and defeated, the pilot pulled back on the throttle and the plane immediately lost its foreword thrust and began to slow. He then reversed the engines and the slowing became dramatic.

Willie and his classy battering ram were barreling towards a point on the runway that would position him in front of the oncoming plane. Unfortunately, directly between him and that point, was one of the many red and green lights that line the runway. It looked a great deal larger from that vantage point, on the ground, approaching at a ridiculous speed, than they did when one is flying over them on a standard approach and landing. Willie braced himself. He hit the fixture full on with the center of the front bumper of the limo. The light, the fixture, the housing all exploded into a thousand pieces, glittering like confetti in the dawn sunlight, then tinkling on the pavement in the wake of the speeding limo. Willie then slammed on the brakes and the big car screeched to a stop, sliding slightly sideways, but fully blocking the path of the oncoming jet plane.

Watching a huge jet airplane bearing down on his position at high speed was a new experience for Willie. It was a bit disconcerting. Any plane would look large and menacing from that vantage point. This plan looked immense. The plane was obviously slowing rapidly, but Willie jumped out of the car just in case. He watched the plane approach. It came closer and closer, but it was traveling slower and slower. Finally, is too skidded to a stop, as the front wheel of mammoth vehicle dropped off the pavement of the runway and sunk slightly into the softer turf along its side. Willie stopped holding his breath, looked around, and realized that he didn't have anything else to do at the exact moment but wait for the legions of screaming, blinking emergency units which seemed to be approaching at high speeds from every direction. Willie thought for a split second… then he knew what he wanted.

Mark Roth's unmarked squad car screeched and bounced up the drive, siren blaring, as it turned in directly in front of the entrance of the diminutive terminal for the rich. The bumper of the car dipped low and the tires slid on the pavement as the car came to a complete stop. Roth snapped off the siren and jumped out of his car. Jigs and Arthur were just coming out of the doors to the terminal. "The motherfucker is about to fly away," Jigs yelled as they both ran towards Roth. Suddenly, Jigs stopped dead in his tracks. He looked around. "Where the fuck is Willie?" He asked as he and the others heard the first of many sirens begin to wail at all corners of the airfield.

They all ran to the fence near the guard shack where Willie had been just moments before. They could see two bright yellow fire trucks speeding towards the runways from the far southeastern corner of the airfield. Both trucks had their emergency lights lit and oscillating, and both had their sirens wailing. Then, from the west side of the field a big black, oddly shaped "urban assault vehicle", (to coin a phrase from the movie *Stripes*) also with lights blinking and siren blaring, appeared and motored towards the center of the airfield. That probably belonged to Homeland Security. In seconds, it seemed that there were emergency vehicles coming from every crevasse and corner of the field, some were trucks, some were cars, all with lights and sirens. It looked like roaches heading for a dropped crumb of bread.

They all looked at each other again. Jigs started giggling. "Where the fuck is Willie?" He whispered with mischief in his eyes. They all looked back to the airfield. They could all clearly see that the cause for the commotion was out in the middle of the field, but they could not quite make out what it was.

"Come on," said Detective Roth. "I can go anywhere I want in that thing." He pointed at his squad car. They all ran over to the car and piled in. Roth flicked on his lights and siren and joined the legions of emergency vehicles on the airfield at that time. As it turned out, they were the closest to the actual commotion, which was coming into view. They could see a private jet stopped in the middle of a runway. It looked oddly cocked to one side. They were going to be first to arrive on site, because the others were coming from the far reaches of the field. The fire trucks were also fast approaching from their left.

As they came closer and closer the scene became clearer and clearer. They could all see the black limo parked and cocked slightly cattycorner across the runway. It effectively blocked the runway. They saw the big Gulfstream V, partially on and partially off the runway, also slanted sideways, with the front wheel off the pavement and sinking in the turf of to the side. They traveled closer. Then... they all saw Willie.

Willie was sitting on the hood of the limo with his legs crossed at the ankles, leaning back on the windshield like he was laying on a chase lounge. He had three fingers of bourbon in a cut crystal glass in his left hand...and a big black cigar in his right hand. He was still wearing the stupid chauffeur's cap, but he had it tilted foreword on his head just so. He had an ear-to-ear Cheshire cat grin on his face and he was slowly blowing a huge cloud of blue smoke into the air.

Jigs, Arthur and Detective Roth got out of the squad car chuckling and shaking their heads. They all walked up to Willie. He was saying as they approached... "Arthur...man, why didn't you tell me you had Montiechristos in that car of yours. They fell out of the glove box when I was bouncing that car across the airfield. Where were you guys anyway? What took you so long?"

The sirens were getting louder as the first of the emergency vehicles began to arrive. Uniformed men were jumping out of cars and trucks, brandishing weapons of every stripe, screaming out orders at each other and at the motley crew that had arrived there first. Roth already had his Police ID out, which he was holding high in the air. The rest of the armada was put slightly at ease by the fact that the men first on the scene had arrived in a police vehicle, but they still had weapons drawn.

"My name is Detective Mark Roth of the Los Angeles Police Department." He held his ID higher into the air. He was taking charge of the scene. "These men are licensed Private Investigators and their operative." He reached into his pocket very slowly. He pulled out another piece of paper. "This is a warrant for the arrest of one Mr. Ned Khan. Mr. Khan is one of the occupants of that plane right there." He pointed at the plane. As if on cue, the hydraulic door on the Gulfstream V began to whine and opened. The door became the stairs as it opened and touched the ground. The occupants started to deplane, first the girl, then both pilots, then, last but not least, Ned. He did not look impeccable as usual. He looked disheveled and pale.

"That is my suspect." Roth was pointing and walking towards the plane. All of the other weapons on the field turned and pointed towards Ned. Ned raised his hands in the air. He could not believe what he was seeing. There were at least twenty-five weapons pointing at him, maybe more. He knew he was beaten. He had no options. None. All of his money could not help him at this moment.

Roth approached him. He took one hand at a time and placed them behind his back. He clicked each one into a handcuff. He began to walk him towards his squad. He said out loud, for everyone to hear, "Nadir 'Ned' Khan, you are a citizen of the United States of America. Therefore, you have the right to remain silent. Anything you say can and will be used against you in a court of law. You have the right to have an attorney represent you during questioning. If you cannot afford an attorney..." At that point there was muffled laughter from the crowd, as some looked at the huge private plane casting a shadow on them all. "I think you know the rest." Detective Roth put his hand on Ned's head and guided his head away from bumping on the roof of the squad car. Ned was in custody. He looked at Arthur through the window glass from inside the squad. They held each other's gaze for a moment. Then, Ned looked away, in shame.

Arthur was not sure how to feel. Anna was still dead. Revenge, it seems, was not as sweet as he might have hoped. Now that the search was over, he would have to live without his sister for the rest of his life. However, he was sure that he felt better now than he would have if he had watched Ned fly away. Perhaps justice, not revenge, was the consolation prize.

Roth looked away from his prisoner. He yelled out to the other men and women standing around, "Who would be in charge here if I wasn't here?"

That brought some laughter and mumblings from the crowd. At least one guy said under his breath, "Who the fuck said you were in charge?" Then a tall man in black gear with a bulletproof vest that matched his other rather impressive uniform components stepped foreword. "I am in charge of the Homeland Security operation here."

"Well I am sure you will want a copy of my report. What is your name and information?" Roth had a pen in his hand.

"Wait, you don't think that you guys are going to just walk... or drive... away from this scene, do you? You all caused the whole damn airport to shut down."

"Well, we tried to do this through channels. It seems there was a flaw in the system, because it was a private plane. I'm sure you guys will want to look into that. I will fax you a complete copy of my report first thing in the morning. I promise." He looked at Jigs, Willie and Arthur and said, "Let's go."

Roth then looked back at the guy dressed in his Homeland Security gear. "I will be sending a crew out here. They will work in conjunction with Long Beach and the Airport Authority and your people. Everything will be done by the book. I will take complete responsibility. In the meantime, this whole area must be treated as a crime scene, my crime scene."

Willie and Jigs got a ride to the front of the terminal from another black uniformed operative, in a mysterious black vehicle. They thanked the humorless driver. Arthur rode with Detective Roth. The detective had some questions for Arthur, so he drove Arthur to his house. During the drive Ned and Arthur did not speak. Jigs and Willie took a cab. They all met up at Arthur's at the same time. Arthur got out of Detective Roth's squad car. As he did, he took one last look at Ned. Ned was unable to look up from the dirty squad car floor. He was in the cage that is the back seat compartment of a police vehicle. He realized that he would likely be in a cage of one type or another for a long time to come.

"I will be in touch," Roth said as he drove off.

45

BACK AT ARTHUR'S HOME, the three compadres sat with a cold beer each and tried to dissect the rather tumultuous events of the morning.

"That was a wild ride," Arthur said with a sigh. "I suppose I should be ecstatic. However, I have to admit that the feeling that I have is somewhat more hollow than I might have predicted."

"That simply means that you are human," Jigs said. "No matter what happens to Ned, it will not bring Anna back, right? That is the hard part here, because now that our efforts at trying to see to it that he is brought to justice seem to be over, all that is left is the loss that you feel."

Willie stood up and headed for his room. "I'm hitting the hay," he said. "I have to check some things out on the computer, first. Then it is time for a nap." Willie walked off. Arthur turned back to Jigs.

"Yeah… that makes sense. So, what will happen to Ned, anyway? I know you cannot predict the future, but if you had to guess, what do you think is going to happen?"

Jigs looked at Arthur for a long moment. He slowly shook his head. "Well, Arthur, I am not going to pretend that this is going to be an easy case to prosecute. It is not. Let's face it... Ned did not actually kill anyone. He was over a thousand miles away when Anna died... or at least on his way there... and he can prove it. However, lest we forget, this is the state that convicted Charles Manson, and he didn't actually kill anyone either, that we know of. So, that is a good thing, but Ned will gather together the best lawyers in the country, sort of O.J. style, and they will fight tooth and nail to get him off."

"I knew you were going to say that," Arthur said... rather discouraged.

"Don't get all down in the dumps on me. Let's just review what we know...   First, we have your gut. Don't discount that. Sometimes that is all you have at the beginning of an investigation. That is what started this whole thing off, right? It sounds, when you say it, like you are relying on sheer intuition or guess. That is not what it is at all. Often, when a person has a guilty mind, it is perceptible by others, especially people that are known to the person who is guilty. You saw Ned immediately after he arrived here from Houston. You saw something then that made you suspicious. That does not mean you were crazy... it means that Ned may have been telegraphing his guilt. By the way... you can testify to that. You can give an opinion in court

that sets forth your perception of his actions. You can testify as
to how he was acting."

Arthur smiled. "I like the way you think. I just thought I
was losing my mind. Funny, it does not seem that way now.
Now we know, based on the events of the morning, that I
thought what I thought for a reason."

"No, it sure doesn't seem that way now. I began to
become convinced when we discovered the George Castanza
guy. It is actually more of a stretch to believe that, in all of LA,
there was one restaurant where Anna had an appointment with a
person, and a totally different person had an appointment at the
same restaurant, at the same time, and that person did not show
either. Do you know what I mean? Especially when you figure in
the other factors, like the rental car, and the fact that there
actually is no Jonathon F. Butcher living in Sherman Oaks.
Unfortunately, your gut feeling and this business about George
Castanza are a bit circumstantial in nature. It is hard to translate
this type of thing into actual evidence. The prosecutor will have
to build on that."

"Yeah, even I know that. You don't have to have a law
degree to figure that out." Arthur had an unsure look on his face.
Jigs could see it; so he went on.

"The other evidence will show that Ned had a colossal
motive and being able to show and prove motive is one of the

keys to a successful prosecution in a murder case. Plus, lets face it, the guy tried to run away. That shows what prosecutors like to call, 'consciousness of guilt.' It is used very successfully in all kinds of prosecutions. Whenever anyone attempts to hide or obscure his or her crime, or tries to 'make a get-a-way,' so to speak, that is evidence of consciousness of guilt. So, don't worry Arthur, this guy will end up paying for what he did. He will pay dearly. Also, don't forget, Roth and his boys are looking for more evidence as we speak. It is likely they will find plenty."

"Well, whatever happens, you guys have turned out to be a godsend. None of this would have taken place without the help of you and Willie... Thank you Jigs... thank you from the bottom of my heart."

"Don't start with that mushy shit. We all worked together on this."

"Well, you may say that... but..."

"OK, save it... I need to get some sleep. When was the last time we slept, anyway?"

"You have a point there."

By the time they all met back out at Arthur's poolside area it was early evening. Therefore, the breakfast nook/ bar was no longer a breakfast nook/ bar... it was officially... just a bar. Of course, Willie was already sitting by the pool with a beer in hand. He was fully showered and dressed. His hair was combed and he looked like a well-dressed island dweller.

"What? Do you have a date, old man?" Jigs could not help himself.

Actually, everyone looked refreshed and rested. Arthur walked behind the bar and turned towards the other two men.

"Who wants a beer? Willie... another one for you?" He was already bending down and pulling out cold beers from the small refrigerator behind the bar.

"Yeah... make my beer a whiskey on the rocks," Willie said. "Jameson's... if there is any left." Everyone started laughing. Willie threw his empty beer bottle into a large trashcan.

"Your liver must be screaming uncle, Willie. Do you ever give it a break?" Arthur was chuckling and pouring at the same time.

"I have an Irish liver. Scientists have studied this... through years of evolution; the Irish have come to have a special liver, unlike the normal livers of mere mortals...dare I say, a super liver. You can look it up. It is in scientific journals."

"Yeah, right. I let my subscription to *Scientific American* laps. I'll have to renew…" Arthur passed the glass to Willie by way of Jigs. As Jigs was handing the glass to Willie, he said something that caused them all to groan.

"If you guys think that is a fucked up theory, wait until you hear mine… George Bush killed Anna."

The others began laughing and groaning and shaking their heads.

"Arthur, call the paramedics. Jigs here, is having a mental break. He needs help… fast." Willie was oozing faux concern for his friend. He patted him on the head. "Everything will be OK, Jigs. You just need some rest."

"Wait. Hear me out. I am half serious here."

"I don't think it is a mental break. Arthur, check his room. He is on some kind of very powerful drug or, perhaps, combination of drugs. You know, Arthur, these hippies… it's so sad… they always revert back to their drug addled, acid flashback induced psychosis. Poor creatures. It really is sad."

"Anna's death was an unintended consequence of a misguided, unconstitutional and, therefore, illegal program, which was created by a pack of paranoid, opportunistic dolts, whose thirst for power is unquenchable and dangerous, which was disguised as patriotism and the need to keep us safe."

"Come on, Jigs. We were all in such a good mood here... Ned is in jail. Do we have to...really?"

"Look, Willie, information is power. If you don't believe that, just ask anyone that knew J. Edgar Hoover. Check the history books. But, instead of seeing Hoover as a megalomaniacal, power hungry queen that obtained and maintained power throughout his lifetime, while watching president after president and administration after administration come and go, through the use of information, which he acquired by having his minions sneak around and tap phones and dig for dirt on anyone and everyone over which he wanted to have power, instead of seeing that, this crowd sees him as a mentor."

"What on earth are you talking about?"

"I'll tell you what I am talking about. Buford Tucker was one of hundreds of men and women that are employed by our government to listen in on our telephone calls and read our emails. Right now, they are still out there. They are having dinner with their families or driving home from work, or driving to work because they are working the late shift. Some are hard at work at their job. Their job is to keep us safe. They do this by listening for subversives. Right?"

"Right... what is wrong with that?"

"The problem is that this is being done without the prior restraint of having to first procure a warrant to do so. There are not the normal rules and regulations and safeguards. There are no records being kept. That is how we got Buford Tucker in the first place, metaphorically speaking. He was born as a result of this silly misguided program. If he had been required to procure a warrant prior to listening in on Ned's telephone conversations, together with the conversations of many others, he would not have been tempted to pull this scam of his. He would not have been able to do it." Jigs was on a roll. He continued.

"Giving a person the power to listen in on a citizen's telephone conversation is like giving them the power to be *invisible*. Now, when you ask *anyone,* and I mean anyone, what they would do if they were suddenly, actually, *really* able to be invisible, they all answer in the exact same way. So, lets try it. *What would you do if you were suddenly, actually given the power to be invisible? **Be honest.**"

Both men blushed slightly. They hemmed and hawed, while various visions of naked girls passed through their minds. They both saw some variation on a theme of being in the locker room at the Miss America contest or being in Brittany Spears' bedroom. Everyone has his or her own personal fantasy. However, one thing is universally true. Once they were through thinking about their own original silly sexual fantasies, once that passed and they got serious about the question, and this was true for both of these men but would also be true for *anyone, man or woman, young or old...everyone says the same thing.* What they said, what anyone would say, is this:

"I would get rich."

"The answer is universal. Ask anyone. *Ask anyone.* Everyone says the same thing. This does not mean that everyone asked is a potential criminal, because, if you were invisible, you could get rich legally, or semi-legally. One would simply have to sit in on the right board meeting, and then hightail it over to your favorite stock broker's office or just call him on the phone." Jigs was very serious about this issue and the others were starting to listen to him.

"So, what this means is that Buford Tucker is not dead. There are hundreds more Buford Tuckers listening to hundreds of thousands of our telephone conversations and reading hundreds of thousands of our emails and learning secret after secret right now. How long do you think it will take for another sad story like this one to come to light? Plus, we don't even have to discuss this in terms of hypotheticals or metaphors. Suppose that one of our 'Bufords' happen to overhear, in the early stages, plans by Bank of America to buy Countrywide or plans by Microsoft to purchase Yahoo. Can you imagine the repercussions?"

"I don't know, Jigs," Willie said as he took a long drink of his whiskey. "But, I am glad that it is not our problem. Aren't you?"

"How can you be so blasé' about this, Willie?"

"Because I am hungry… Lets go eat."

"Wait… you are not concerned about this problem? You don't care that there are men and women busily crouched over keyboards with head phones on their heads listening in on the telephone conversations of American citizens, learning our secrets, all in the name of stopping terrorism?"

"Its not our job. Lets go get something to eat."

"Willie…"

"Look, I would rather a few housewives get overheard while they talk about how they fucked the pool boy than have another successful attack against our great nation, but I don't want to talk about that right now because I am hungry. Plus, I talked to Roth while you guys slept, and I was in contact with Detective Biancafiore in Italy by email. Now, if you two would kindly finish those beers, we can go get some food and have a nice discussion over a nice dinner where we can talk about any fucking thing you want…after I eat."

"You talked to Roth," Arthur was at once very interested. "What did he say?"

"Am I not speaking English?"

"OK, OK, let's go eat," Jigs said. But, we are not done with this issue."

The Florida contingent acquiesced to their host regarding their choice of restaurant. Arthur assured the others that they would thoroughly enjoy his selection. He was correct.

On the way to the restaurant, Willie said, "Jigs, I realize that you are just chomping at the bit to get into it over this stupid leftie theory of yours, but we are going to discuss facts first, if you don't mind. Arthur, I am sure, is very interested in what Detective Roth had to say so just hold your tongue, OK?"

There were chuckles all around. Willie was sounding a little like a school marm. Jigs did not talk.

"The good news is," Willie began, "that the search warrants, which Roth was able to get, have been productive. The most interesting thing that they found was in Ned's phone records. They traced all of Ned's incoming and outgoing calls to their source. All of them checked out as calls he would be expected to make or receive, business associates, his bank, his club, all familiar and expected calls... except one. Ned received a call from a disposable cell phone on the night before Anna died. That phone only made one call. In other words, it was purchased. It was activated. A call was made to Ned from that phone. No other calls were ever made from that phone again, pretty clandestine, huh? The phone was purchased at a Walgreen's Drugs Store in Los Angeles. Now, the fun part... they found the fucking phone. Evidently, it had a GPS chip. They found it in a dumpster about a half a block from where it was purchased. I will tell you what... this is not the day and age to be a criminal. The shit they can do is uncanny, isn't it?"

"Willie, stay focused. What about prints? Were they able to identify the guy that purchased the phone?"

"Cool your jets, lib, I am getting to that." He paused for dramatic effect. "Unfortunately, there were no prints on the phone." He paused again.

"Alright old man, cut the drama."

"There were no prints but they did get a picture of the guy from a security camera. It is not a good shot. It is from a high angle and a bit behind, but he is described as being short, stocky and bald. They are going to take it to our $50.00 hostess at the Pig n' Whistle. Maybe we will get lucky. Of course, I would bet a thousand dollars right now, today, that it is the same guy that we refer to as George Castanza. The problem is... that doesn't tell us much. We still won't know who he is. Nor, will we ever know who he is, if you want my guess. That guy was a pro… no one is going to find that guy.

"What do you mean? That guy, the person that actually killed my sister, is never going to be caught?" Arthur did not know how to feel about that.

"Arthur, Ned killed your sister, Anna, and Ned is presently behind bars. If he had used a gun, and he threw the gun into the ocean, and it was never found, that would not bother you. The George Castanza guy was the instrument that was used, nothing more. Maybe he gets caught eventually, but I doubt it. However, maybe that will be a future project that Jigs and I can work on someday. That might be fun."

They arrived at Captain Jack's. It was a nice place, casual but swanky with great food. It was the best-kept secret in Huntington Beach, only locals new about the place. It was regionally famous. Three guys ordered three steaks with all the trimmings. That wasn't hard. After they ordered, Arthur took the floor.

"Jigs…Willie, this is my opportunity to formally thank you both. You guys have been great. I cannot tell you how much I appreciate all your efforts. Without you guys, I would have gotten no where fast." As he said those words, the maître d' walked up with an envelope. He handed it to Arthur.

"Thank you, Harry," Arthur said as the man half bowed and backed away. "I eat here a lot. They know me here."

"I guess," said Jigs.

Inside the large envelope were two smaller envelopes. Arthur took them out and he handed one each to his friends.

"It is one thing to say thank you. This is my attempt to express how truly thankful I am." Arthur was saying this as he handed one envelope to each man.

Jigs and Willie smiled sheepishly. "What is this, Arthur, Valentine's Day?" Willie was surprised at this unusual display.

Jigs was opening his envelope. "And the winner is…" He was joking. When Jigs saw what was in the envelope his jaw dropped. He looked back up at Arthur. It was a check made payable to him in the amount of five hundred thousand dollars. Willie got one too.

"Arthur… I can't except this…" Jigs was speechless.

"I will not even hear about it. I will be eternally grateful to the two of you."

"Well, that's all well and good but this is too much…"

"Do you guys have any idea how much money I have? That is the least I could do. Now, I do not want to hear anything more about it. Put those checks away. Don't spend them all in one place." He took a drink of wine. He smiled. Then he said, "Jigs I was fascinated by what you were saying earlier, all that business about being invisible." Arthur was trying to change the subject. He was succeeding. It was clear to all that Arthur was not going to accept any resistance to his little show of appreciation.

"Well, I am not going to argue with you." Willie was already putting the check into his pocket. Actually, he already had most of it spent in his mind.

"How did you... How is it possible that we are sitting here and a man walks up with that kind of money?" Jigs asked.

"I made a telephone call," Arthur said with a sly smile. "You really don't know how much money I have, do you? My grandfather was a very shrewd businessman. That tradition has been carried on."

"Well then, maybe this amount is not enough," Willie said jokingly. That got a laugh and lightened the mood. The steaks came, which allowed everyone to move past the subject of money.

"The Italians have taken a second look at their case as a result of my visit there." Willie was well past the subject of money. "They think they know how this John Doe 'the Great' makes a person drive off of a cliff, without leaving any evidence of how it was done. It is a pretty ingenious process, if they are right. We have to get access to Anna's car. Has that been returned to you, Arthur, or did it go to Ned?"

"Really, how do they say it was done?" This was particularly of interest to Arthur. He was the first to doubt that his sister would drive off of a cliff without some kind of foul play. He never accepted the accident theory.

"When Biancafieore was faced with the reality that there were two seemingly identical accidents in two different countries, both involving women that were among the super rich, he felt it was necessary to take a whole new look at the automobile that was involved in his case. They poured over every inch of that car. They noticed that parts of the heating duct system had at least once been disassembled, after it was manufactured. This is a trip... They knew this because they noticed that minute amounts of paint had been scratched off of the screws that held the ductwork together... Now, get this... They checked the maintenance records of the car and determined that no work had ever been done on the heating system. So, they tore it apart. They found that one section of the ductwork was once subjected to intense cold. It was ever so slightly warped in one place. It never ceases to amaze me how investigators can find the methods of even the most meticulous of criminals. So, they then hypothesize that the heating system of the car was used as the delivery system for a drug that would cause the driver to pass out or to be incapacitated in some way, and that the drug was incased in ice until the heating system caused the ice to melt, thereby releasing the drug into the passenger compartment of the car. Isn't that in-fucking-credible?"

"Holly shit," Arthur said over his plate of food, with a mouth full of medium rare filet. "You think that is what happened to Anna?"

"We have to check out the car, but at least we know where to look. That was the beauty of this guy's plan. What investigator would ever even consider looking at the heating duct when investigating what he already believed to be an accident? It really is a sweet concept. You have to give the guy credit. Frankly, Arthur, that is why I really don't think that anyone is ever going to find that guy.

"I am beginning to accept that," Arthur reluctantly admitted. "The 'gun in the ocean' analogy worked, I guess."

"Well, tomorrow I will fill Roth in about this theory and put him in touch with the Italians. So, stay tuned.

The steaks were perfect. The wine was old and mellow. The ambiance was warm and the three old friends sat and discussed the final aspects of the long journey that had brought them there. They had shared a lot in the few short days of their collaboration. Ned was behind bars and all the pieces of the investigation were falling into place. They all agreed that they would not let so many years pass between that dinner and next time they all got together, but they knew it was time for Jigs and Willie to head back to the Sunshine State.

46

THREE WEEKS HAD PASSED since Jigs and Willie returned from their trip to the left coast but the work on the case had continued in earnest by all parties concerned. At 5:00am the two old friends were on Jigs' boat preparing to head out to do some fishing. It was a toss up between golf and fishing and fishing won out.

"So, what did Roth say?" Jigs was dropping a cooler and packing gear onto the boat. When he finished, he bounded up the ladder to the bridge. He fired up the big diesel engine while Willie pulled in the lines. The huge, sleek craft slowly backed out of its slip, then inched away from the dock as they idled towards the main channel. It was still dark so the running lights were on. They joined other boats of various sizes all heading out towards the open sea. As Willie came up the ladder, he was giving the latest information from out west. Roth was becoming more optimistic with reference to the case that was building against Ned Khan. Willie was relaying to Jigs the particulars of his last conversation with the detective.

"He thinks they have him. He thinks Ned will be convicted. He never stops qualifying his statements with the words… 'Anything can happen in a courtroom', but I know he is just hedging his bets. He is confident that they have him cold. Ned is never going to see the light of a free day again. He is on a no bail hold, so…"

Jigs had a familiar look on his face as he almost involuntarily mumbled, "I never get tired of this. Are we two lucky sons of bitches to be able to do this anytime we want?" The breathtaking view ahead of them, the smells, the sounds of the puttering motor and the gulls screeching overhead as the boat slid silently, slowly toward open waters were overwhelming.

"You said it."

"I'm sorry. You were saying?"

"Yeah, Roth is confident."

"What is the latest?"

"Well… let's run it down. They theorize the following: Ned received a call from old Buford setting forth the terms of his attempt to extort money. They have no idea how much Buford was trying to get, but they do know Ned got a call from a pay phone in a mall in Ft. Meade, Maryland a few days before Anna died."

"Today's technology freaks me out."

"No shit. It may still be possible to commit a crime, now a day, without getting caught, but if they do find out about you... you will be convicted. They can find out anything."

Jigs simply nodded his agreement.

"So, the theory is that... earlier in the day of Anna's death, Ned gets his instructions from his accomplice during the telephone call from the disposable cell phone, which they unearthed. You do remember that, right?"

"Yeah, Wil, my brain is not pickled in alcohol."

"Speaking of alcohol... Do you want a beer? I'm going to have one." Willie jumped up and scurried down to a big cooler on the deck below. Jigs was not interested. He was drinking coffee... like normal people. When he returned, Willie continued.

"They then hypothesize that Ned moved Anna's car into the garage. There will be testimony from all of the domestic help that she never kept her car in the garage, not even when it rained. Plus, and this is pretty cool, they have a great big Ned thumb print on Anna's garage door opener. Some expert will testify that the last person to use the garage door opener left that print. That would be Ned. They say that Ned then secured the convertible top in place and opened the side door to the garage. Ned's prints are all over the roof of the car, which were left on the said roof after the car was brought in out of the rain. I guess they can tell that, too."

"If I am a juror and I hear all this together with the facts related to his attempt at fleeing the country, this guy is toast." Jigs was actually laughing at this point. "Ned... don't drop the soap."

"Yeah, you got that right." Both of them chuckled.

"Now we can put this thing to bed," Willie said. "Anna's killer is caught."

The eastern sky had a burnt orange hue beginning to become visible at the horizon. It was reflected off the cool blue water and contrasted against the velvet cloudless expanse above. A sliver of moon still shone but was fading.

Willie looked at Jigs. "I say again, Anna's killer is caught."

"Yeah, so..." Jigs was unsure what Willie meant.

"So, I guess President Bush can go on about the business of running the country, of prosecuting the war, you know, things like that?"

"What the fuck are you talking about?"

"Well, I believe you have a theory that President Bush killed Anna."

"Oh that, well, now that you mention it… that is true."

"I cannot believe the shit that goes on in that liberal fucking head of yours. Do you know how fucking crazy you sound saying things like that? How do you even come up with shit like that?"

"It was Bush administration policies that began the warantless wiretapping of our own citizens…"

At that moment the sound that all anglers long for began. It was a sweet sound. ZZZZZZZZZZZZZZZZZZZZZZZZZZZ.

Something had taken Jigs' line… something big.

Both men's feet hit the deck at the same time. They both sprang into action. Jigs grabbed his pole while Willie took the ladder to the bridge two rungs at a time. He sat at the helm and spun the wheel so as to maneuver the boat in such a way that the line from Jigs' pole stayed off the stern of the boat.

Jigs was holding his pole high as the reel sang and the animal on the line attempted to head out to sea. ZZZZZZZZZZZZZZZZZZZZZZZZZZZZZZZZZZZZZZZZZZZ ZZZZZZZZZZ.

The line was leaving the reel at about fifty feet per second and Jigs was allowing the fish to run. He was holding his pole high in the air and finding his way to the fighting chair.

"Set the hook, you fucking tree hugger. What is your problem?"

"Oh, pipe down you old fart."

"Set it, hippie. Don't you know how to fish?

"Don't tell me how to fish, righty." Jigs was just about to sit in the chair and begin his fight with what was clearly a big fish.

"You are going to loose him…you silly lib…"

The boat bobbed on the waves, alone on the water, not another vessel could be seen in any direction. The sun was peeking over the horizon, turning the morning sky deep blue. The voices of the two old friends echoed across the water and then out to sea.

THE END

ACKNOWLEDGEMENTS

I am writing this on June 25, 2008, my oldest son's 18th birthday. Happy birthday Jack. This is your present. You and Patrick are the reasons that this book exists. I have a lot of nerve writing this before the fact. Anyone that knows me knows that, on this date, the book is in draft form and only about eighty people have read it. However, I already have countless people to thank. Without each and every one of you, this book would never have been written, let alone read by anyone else in the world. I don't know how to adequately thank all of you except to say that no one does anything alone. Every person mentioned here helped to write this book and fulfill a dream for my two sons and me. Each of you knows what you did, or did not do, and how you played a part in the success of this project. I offer my heartfelt thanks to each and every one of you. Dreams really do come true if you believe in yourself, don't give up, and have the help and support of others.

Kelly Calderon, Vern Bergquist, Jim Labuda, Bill McGrath, Bob Broderick, John Baumgartner, John Butcher, John Schwab, Vanessa Trobec, John and Teresa Namy, Gary and Diane Hanson, Dennis Van Wyck and Sue Van Ewyk, Mark, Greg and Katie Van Ewyk, Tim Kiefer, Larry and Nancy Rozzano, Terri and Bridget Rozzano, Michael Broderick, (Jimmy and Geri Broderick), Bob and Patty Lewis, Mike and Peggy Calebrese, Tom and Mary Gazdik, Dave and (Margaret) Lombardi, Mark Roth, Joe Klest, Sam Amirante, Jim Etchingham, Ned Khan, Cheryl and Ken Fox, Katie O'Connor Buckingham, Willie Norris, Tom Eggert, Brian Murphy, Pinky Soriano, J. Craig Williams, Imebel Chavez, Ellen Pitt, June Norris, Kathy Kroening Palmer,(Hershel "Harry" Heater), Aldo Moreno, Kelly Sutton, Jim Belushi, Samandhi, Phil Cowen, Paul Nordlund, Dennis DonDero, Steve Wild, Kenny Klein, Arun Gopinath, Steve Day, the angel known as Roberta Williams and her husband, Dave, Jeff Anderson, David Maguire, Wendy Strachan and everyone at Booksurge, Leslie Gist and the team at GoDaddy, Bob Diforio, Daryl and Kathy Holly, Tony Venezia, James M. Nickell, James Micelli, Beth, Tommy and Jim Malouf, and everyone at the College of DuPage, Sarah Thomison and the folks at Digital Color Graphics, with special thanks to my son Patrick Broderick, who was there every single day, a very special thanks to Tom and Roxanne Broderick, you guys made it all possible, and to my dear, sweet, Irish Mother, Jacqueline Broderick, thanks mom.

ABOUT THE AUTHOR

DANNY BRODERICK is a graduate of The John Marshall Law School and Southern Illinois University. He was a practicing criminal defense attorney for twenty years. He is the proud father of two sons, Jack and Patrick. He resides in Chicago, Illinois. *When Money Talks* is his first novel.